The Last Banquet

Lee Duigon

STOREHOUSE PRESS

VALLECITO, CALIFORNIA

Published by Storehouse Press
P.O. Box 158, Vallecito, CA 95251

Storehouse Press is the registered trademark of Chalcedon, Inc.

Copyright © 2012 by Lee Duigon

This book is a work of fiction. Names, characters, businesses, organizations, places, events, and incidents either are the product of the author's imagination or used fictitiously. Any resemblance to actual persons, living or dead, events, or locales is entirely coincidental.

All rights reserved, including the right of reproduction in whole or in part in any form.

Book design by Kirk DouPonce (www.DogEaredDesign.com)

Printed in the United States of America

First Edition

Library of Congress Catalog Card Number: 2011933788

ISBN-13: 978-1-891375-58-3

ISBN-10: 1-891375-58-X

CHAPTER I

The Castaway

"I think I'll go fishing," Gurun said.

"You should be getting ready for your wedding," her father answered.

Gurun was sixteen; this day was her birthday. Tomorrow she would be married to a man named Lokk. He was her father's friend, and his farm lay next to theirs. To combine the two properties would greatly enhance both families' political position. The facts that Lokk was twenty years older than Gurun and had a large, unsightly wart on his cheek were unimportant.

"I'm as ready as I'll ever be," she said. Her father nodded. He knew his daughter didn't love Lokk, but also knew that she would do what was best for her family. Bertig, son of Flosa, had many troubles that would go away if he had more votes in the District Meeting; and every tenant on the land had a vote. If Lokk's tenants voted with him all the time, Bertig's enemies would have their claws clipped.

He made a noise in his beard. "Go ahead, go fishing," he said. "I don't think you will throw yourself into the sea."

"Don't give me ideas," she said; and he laughed at that.

Gurun stepped outside. Like all the homes on Fogo Island, her family's house resembled a low, sprawling hill of sod. Bertig was a wealthy man with a wife, four children, his old mother, and a crew of servants living with him. But there was no better way to build on Fogo Island; no other kind of house would survive the winter winds. Besides, lumber was always hard to come by. Long ago, when people from the south first settled the islands of the northern sea, they quickly learned to fear the winter. Those who survived the first winter only did so by taking shelter in barrows. These had been built to hold the bones of the dead: there was no one living on the islands when the settlers came there. What had become of the natives, no one knew. Only their tombs survived. And so the new arrivals patterned their homes on the houses of the dead.

But this was a fine and sunny summer morning. You might have thought it brisk and chilly, but to Gurun it seemed a perfect day for fishing.

Like most of the islanders she was tall and fair, pale-skinned, blue-eyed. She wore a one-piece woolen dress, cinched at the waist with a sealskin belt, and sealskin moccasins. That was all she needed.

She launched her little skiff into the cove and paddled out to sea. The day was still, without a breeze: no point in raising the sail. When the water was as still as this, it often meant a storm was coming. But the sky was clear of clouds, and it was not quite the season for storms, and Gurun was good with boats. Lokk had promised to take her along when he went whaling.

All over the horizon rose the peaks of snow-clad mountains. Every island had at least one. No one ever sailed out of sight of the mountains. These northern seas were prone to fog, and you had to be careful not to sail too far from land. In each settlement there were men who blew horns to guide boats overtaken by the fog.

Gurun baited her hook and let out her line. Inside of ten minutes she had two fine codfish. The waters this year teemed with fish. That was a good thing, for you had to catch more than enough to live on during the summer, and sun-dry the surplus to keep you through the winter. It did not strike Gurun's people as a hard life. It was the only life they'd known for centuries, and they were happy in it.

Suddenly the line went taut and the boat lurched forward. Gurun hung on with both hands, bracing her feet against the gunwales.

"Praise God, it's a big one!" she cried. A halibut, maybe. She mustn't lose it. She prayed the Lord to bless her line so it wouldn't break. When the fish tired of towing the boat, she could begin to haul it in.

So intent was she on fighting the fish that she didn't notice the sky darkening overhead and black clouds sweeping in from the north. She didn't notice anything until the wind began to blow her hair into her eyes. All she could do was shake her head. She didn't dare let go of the line with either hand.

"I won't let go!" she thought. "I won't lose this one!"

The fish towed the boat farther out to sea. The wind blew. The clouds piled up, blotting out the sun. Then it began to rain, and Gurun realized she'd been caught by a storm. But still she would not let go.

When the line finally broke, the storm had Gurun's boat in its teeth. Between the driving rain and the darkness, she could hardly see.

She knew better than to try to fight the storm. All she could do was to wrap herself in the sail and try to stay alive. The boat rushed up the waves and plummeted back down again—up and down, up and down, endlessly. Gurun was used to that: she'd spent much of her life on boats, and she knew this boat would ride the waves. She also knew the rain and the waves were filling the skiff with water, but she was too cold to bail. She knew it would be a miracle if she survived. Her teeth chattered so badly that she couldn't pray aloud. But her father had built this boat with his own hands, and it would stand much more punishment than other boats.

"It's all in God's hands," she thought. "There's nothing I can do."

For how long, or how far, the storm carried her, Gurun had no way to tell. She couldn't even tell night from day. She huddled in the leather sail and munched on biscuits that she'd brought along. When she was hungry again, she ate raw cod. She might have even slept, although that could have been an illusion.

At some time in the immeasurable future, the rain stopped; the wind died down from a frantic howl to a muted, steady roar; and the darkness lightened. Gurun peeked out from under the sail.

The boat was full of water, a floating island in a sea of fog. With both hands she began to slosh the chilly water overboard.

"Behold, the Lord is with me: I shall not fear the tempests of the earth," she said, reciting Scripture: one of the songs of King Ozias, from the ancient days. It was a verse dear to the islanders, who knew more about storms and tempests than most people. "Though I be plunged into the depths of the sea, my God shall bring me up again."

She rested, and finished what was left of the second codfish. It seemed to her that for all the water she'd bailed out of the boat, there was still more in it than there ought to be. That could only mean the boat was leaking faster than she could bail it out. The storm had strained its joints and fastenings more than they could stand.

"At least I won't have to marry Lokk," she said to herself. "Although aside from his wart and his boring way of talking, he might not have made such a bad husband after all."

Yes, this was the end. The boat was riding lower and lower in the water. She now admitted to herself that she should have cut the line when first the wind blew up, and paddled furiously to the nearest island. Under the circumstances, even her father's worst enemies would have taken care of her: for the storm was the enemy to all.

"Live and learn," she thought.

In a few minutes the boat would go under. But what was that? She heard something, just ahead of her.

It was the sound of waves lapping. The fog wouldn't let her see what they were lapping against, but it certainly sounded like a shore. Land! It must be land.

Shedding the sail, Gurun stood up and dove out of the sinking boat. She was already chilled. The water, when it closed over her body, was warmer than the air.

Gurun swam, pausing every few strokes to listen for what she could not see. She was a strong swimmer. In a few minutes her feet touched sand. A few more strokes and she could wade. A few weary strokes brought her to a sandy beach littered with clam shells. She fell to her hands and knees and gasped a prayer of thanks.

Where under heaven was she? Every fiber of her body begged for sleep. But this land looked like tidal flats, and if the tide came in while she was sleeping, she would drown. She had to find higher ground, if there was any. But all around her lay the fog.

She struggled back to her feet. One of her moccasins was missing; she must have kicked it off while swimming. Deciding that one shoe was worse than none, she got rid of the other. The soft sand felt good to her bare feet.

"Hello!" she called; but there was no answer.

For all Gurun knew, she was on a tiny island that would be entirely underwater when the tide came in. She couldn't stay where she was. Shivering, she turned away from the water and began to walk.

And then, as if by God's command, a breeze came up and the fog began to lift.

Gurun stood waiting as the fog thinned and melted away. Before long, she saw a dark mass in the distance. A little longer, and the mass resolved itself into stands of shrubbery and low, wind-beaten trees, all perched on rolling dunes.

The sun came out. The foliage turned from grey to green. Beyond the dunes rose hills, and on the hills—

She caught her breath. What were those things up there? Gigantic boxes, cubes, straight lines; they rose above the trees. What were they? You would have recognized them instantly as buildings, but Gurun had never seen an ordinary, above-ground building.

Her mind raced. It churned up verses of Scripture that

had to do with houses, palaces, and castles: things from ancient times and far away. Words that had no meaning for the people of the islands, who lived in barrows heaped with turf—what could they know of palaces or castles?

But what else could these enormous objects be but palaces or castles? And where were the people? Inside, perhaps?

Gurun marched toward them to see for herself.

CHAPTER 2

Gurun Explores the Ruins

Up the dunes and up she climbed. Now the fog was all gone and the sun high up in the sky. All the chill left Gurun's body. She soon realized she was hungry and thirsty.

"Where am I?" she wondered. "What country is this? What kind of people live here?"

She went from being warm to being hot. Was she sick, or could it really be this hot?

Gurun's people knew, of course, that there were other countries, other peoples. There must be. They themselves had come from a distant country in the south, ages ago. Occasionally they visited the mainland, although sometimes men who did so never came back. That was the only way they could get real lumber. The shores they visited were as cold as the islands themselves, and uninhabited. There was no sign that anyone had ever lived there.

Bertig's cousin, Zill, was a reciter—one of the sages who copied and memorized the Scriptures. Books among the islanders were few and far between, so reciters served as living books. The custom had been established a thousand years ago to ensure that the people would never lose their knowledge of the Scriptures.

"A thousand years we've been living on these islands," Zill used to say. "We came here fleeing wickedness, and God hid us away, up here in the North, where we could be safe.

"All those places mentioned in the Scriptures—seats of kings, the sites of famous battles, great rivers, forests, famous cities—they have all passed away. No man will see them anymore. There's no going back to where we came from."

The sand gave way to soil; real trees rose up here and there; and Gurun found a path leading uphill to an enormous structure made of stone. Others stood around it and beyond it.

Gurun's people kept their sheep and cattle underground, bringing them out each day to graze. The deeper they dug into the earth, and the lower they built on top of it, the better. You could dig in the ground and line the hole with rocks, panel the rocks with timber if you could afford it, and insulate with armloads of dried moss. You would need timber to roof it over, and pile turf onto the roof until all the chinks were filled and you were safe from the winter.

Such was the only kind of building Gurun knew. These stone structures, with their straight lines and right angles, which towered over the land like trees—these astounded her.

"Hello!" she called. No human being answered her, only the cries and whistles of some gulls.

The footpath led straight up to a yawning rectangular hole in the expanse of tightly fitted stones. Higher up were several smaller openings, squares of darkness. Had people built this monument—or trolls? What if there were trolls inside, waiting for her in the dark?

"Trolls!" Zill used to say, with a snort. "Who has ever seen one?" But that didn't stop most islanders from believing in them.

Trolls or no trolls, Gurun had to find some drinking water soon, and food, and something to use as a weapon—she'd lost her fisherman's knife when the boat sank. She knew she wasn't going to find any water on top of a hill, so she looked for a way down.

Cautiously she trod among the silent buildings. You might have thought most of them no bigger than ordinary houses, but to Gurun they seemed immense, unnatural, and threatening. There should have been people; it unnerved her that there weren't any.

Beyond the cluster of buildings, on the other side of the hill, down at the bottom, she found a pool of water nestled in high, luxuriant grass. Around it, frogs croaked. When she approached, a few of them jumped into the pool. Gurun shied away. She'd never seen frogs before, and she didn't know what they were.

But frogs or no frogs, she was thirsty. She stretched herself on the ground and dipped her face in the water, rubbing away the salt. The water seemed deliciously cool. She drank. It was barely drinkable, with a brackish taint to it, but it would do. She drank slowly, savoring it. She washed her arms and soaked her hair, then lay back, resting. The pool lay in the shadow of the hill, but Gurun was still warm enough to enjoy it.

Not meaning to, she fell asleep. Luckily, something woke her before nightfall.

She climbed back up the hill. Not for a hearty bowl of chowder would she care to spend the night inside one of those buildings! Still, she ought to take a look inside one while there was still some light. It would be cowardly not to. Her three brothers would have laughed at her—little worms.

She found a good-sized stick and adopted it as a weapon. One of the less gigantic buildings stood close at hand. She supposed that black hole was an entrance.

Gurun was afraid—of darkness, of trolls, of not knowing what to expect. But she got a got grip on her stick and went inside.

She had to wait while her eyes adjusted to the murk. Now low in the western sky, the sun was well-placed to trickle light into the interior.

And as it turned out, there was nothing much to see—just some shapeless heaps of rubbish and a thick coat of dust on the hard stone floor.

"Is anybody here?"

Her words echoed briefly, died away. There was no one, living or dead.

"Great was God's wrath upon this place," she thought: for the reciters taught that God destroyed the wicked nations of the South, sparing only the dwellers in the islands. Perhaps the dust that lay everywhere was all that remained of the people. Her bare feet might be treading on the dust of kings and queens.

"So," Gurun said to herself, "the storm has blown me to a country of the dead. Better find some food soon, or my dust will be mingling with theirs."

CHAPTER 3

The Trapper

Gurun slept outside that night, in a hollow between two dunes. The night wind made queer noises, rushing among the empty buildings.

She woke up hungry in the early morning. Gulls serenaded her. Having been taught that the people of the South had perished in God's wrath, she supposed there wouldn't be anyone around to give her food. Well, there would be clams to dig up from the sand, and it might be possible to kill a seabird with a stone. Gurun was good at throwing stones. There might be fruits growing wild that she could eat.

Somehow she would have to get back home. But how? Build a boat, or walk? But she had no idea how far the storm had blown her, nor had she any tools with which to build a boat. Meanwhile, remaining in the neighborhood of all these empty buildings held no attraction for her. She was a castaway in a strange and empty land. She didn't know if she were on the mainland or an island.

So she set about exploring, looking for food, looking for knowledge. Inland from the buildings rose some higher hills, green with grass and shrubs and trees. "There are more things growing on those few hills in front of me," she thought, "than in all the islands put together. There must be something I can eat up there; and the higher I go, the more I'll be able to see."

She had never done so much walking in all her life. By the time she reached the top of the nearest high hill, her legs were weary and the sun had climbed up to the top of the sky. Along the way she'd found nothing to eat. Small animals rustled among the underbrush, but she couldn't see them, let alone catch any.

Atop the hill she stood, panting, while the sea breeze cooled the sweat off her brow. To the west lay the sea, boundless and blue. She turned slowly to survey the land.

To the north and to the east the country spread out forever, matching the sea in vastness, dotted with woodlands and ponds, hills and dales. "I must be on the mainland," she thought. But when she turned to the south, she saw two things that took her breath away.

The first was a river, a great and mighty river that flowed into the sea from the east, as far as eye could see. No islander had looked on such a river in countless generations. It shone like silver. Where it met the sea, it widened into a bay sprinkled with low islets of green and yellow sedge. Flocks of gulls flew over it. If the Scriptures had not preserved the memory of rivers, Gurun would not have known what to call it. It lay a mile away, perhaps. It must be full of tasty fish. Her mouth watered.

But then she saw something even more amazing.

Smoke! Someone down there had a fire going, somewhere behind that clump of trees. And where there was a campfire, there would be people—and food.

Gurun hastened down the hill as fast as she could without falling on her face. It never entered her mind that the maker or makers of the fire might be a danger to her. Among the islanders, any castaway was to be fed and sheltered. That was the way she'd been brought up. To persecute a castaway was to incur a doom of outlawry and perpetual banishment. It was a crime worse than manslaughter, and the District Meeting treated it as such. So Gurun had been raised to have no fear of strangers, and she acted without considering any alternative.

"Hello! Hello, there!" she cried, as she galloped down the hill, flailing her arms for balance. She wanted them to hear her coming and not be alarmed. "My boat sank, and I need food!"

Out from the trees in front of her stepped a living man.

He wore strange clothes—a buckskin jacket and leggings, with decorative fringes on the jacket. No one in the islands had anything like that.

To Gurun, his skin looked unnaturally swarthy, because all her people were very pale. He had dark eyes, too, which were unusual among the islanders, albeit not unknown. He held no weapons in his hands, although a big knife in a leather sheath hung from his beaded belt. His hair and beard were light brown, shot with grey—again unusual but not unknown. But he was shorter than most men Gurun knew.

He looked surprised to see her. He held up his hands and said, "Whoa, young lady! Hold up, before you break your neck!" Gurun didn't understand the words, but she understood the gesture. She pulled up to a walk and sighed with relief. There were people, after all. Everything would be all right.

"Sir, I hope I didn't startle you," she said, "My boat

sank, I'm lost, and I'm hungry. My name is Gurun, Bertig's daughter."

"Sorry, lass—can't understand a word you say. What kind of funny talk is that? But burn me, it almost sounds like I ought to understand it."

She stopped in front of him and paid him the compliment of a Fogo Island curtsey.

"Who are you," he said, "and what are you doing here? This is no place for a girl all alone. You're lucky I didn't turn out to be an outlaw."

He spoke a strange language, and yet not so strange. A thousand years ago, before Gurun's ancestors fled into the North, she and this man would have spoken the same language. The centuries had split their languages—but not so far apart as to dispel a haunting similarity.

He put a hand on his chest and said, "My name's Tim. Tim!" He thumped his chest for emphasis, and Gurun understood. "Tim," she repeated, and he smiled.

"That's right, little lady. Tim—Trapper Tim, they call me. Because that's just what I am, a trapper." He pointed at her. "And what's your name?" She pointed to herself and said "Gurun," and he understood.

"Are you hungry?" he asked. He patted his belly and made chewing motions. "Yes, yes! Hungry!" Gurun tried to say the word the way he'd said it. He grinned at her and said, "Come on, then—let's eat."

Yes, she thought. It was going to be all right.

He cooked her some delicious kind of meat she'd never had before—it was rabbit—and while she ate, he talked. She didn't understand his talk, but she would learn.

"I don't know where you came from, lass. But over yonder lies the River Winter, and north of that, the Winterlands. Everything south is part of Obann. I come up here every spring to trap, but I live in a nice little town called Pokee, about a hundred miles to the south.

"Your language tells me you're a stranger here. Where you're from, I can't imagine. But you've picked a fine time to turn up in this country! Maybe you already know, and maybe you don't: but there's a war on, and a big one. Barbarians from the East, more than any man can count, have come across the mountains. Heaven help us if they get this far! I hear the people in the big cities, down by the Imperial River, are nigh out of their minds with fear—and there's all kinds of crazy business going on. Prophets crying in the streets, just like in ancient times. People saying that they've seen queer beasts, the like of which nobody's seen before. Maybe I've seen a thing or two myself."

He went on and on while Gurun ate. One word of his stuck out—the word "Obann." That troubled her. Obann was the country in the Scripture stories: the country of Ozias and all the other kings. Had she come by the breath of God to the country of the Scriptures? Was this where all those wicked people lived, the ones whom God destroyed? But this man Tim was not wicked, and God had not destroyed him. Maybe the country was inhabited by new people, who'd come from somewhere else.

And maybe, just maybe, this man could help her get back home, she thought. Maybe he could provide her with a boat.

She offered a silent prayer of thanks.

CHAPTER 4

Another Journey

Tim camped near the great river and set his traps in creeks and marshes, taking furry animals that he called muskrats, coons, and otters. The country was full of birds, and flowers in every color you could imagine, and amazing creatures, as colorful as flowers, that fluttered from bloom to bloom. These were called butterflies, Tim said. Gurun understood his language better every day.

"You've never seen a butterfly?" he marveled.

"No! Nothing at all like them," she answered, doing her best to speak as he spoke. "No butterflies where I live, and only little flowers. Mostly stone and moss and heather and seaweed. Not like this country."

For all that her people's tradition said a curse lay on it, Obann made Gurun feel as if she'd been blind all her life and only now could see. There was almost too much to be taken in; she wished she had four eyes. Maybe the curse had passed away. How could so much life and beauty lie under a curse?

Sometimes she went with Tim when he visited his traps. Sometimes she just wandered, dazzled by the things she saw. Such trees! The few trees on Fogo Island were little more than shrubs, but Obann's trees reached for the heavens. And the land was full of animals—deer, rabbits, squirrels, crows, red and blue and yellow birds—whose like was not to be found on any of the islands.

But she shunned the hilltop with the empty buildings on it. Tim said they weren't important, "Just left over from old times," but Gurun didn't like them.

One morning, sunny and warm as it was almost never sunny and warm at home, she was standing near the edge of a little dark pond, looking at some odd little creatures basking on a floating log, when someone spoke to her. She looked up and saw a man standing on the opposite side of the pool.

"Gurun," he said, "you mustn't stay here too much longer."

She startled, for he spoke as one born and bred on Fogo. Indeed, he looked every inch an islander—tall, pale, blue-eyed, clad in a woolen tunic and sealskin boots. What could he be doing here?

"Who are you," she said, "and how do you know my name?"

"I have come to tell you to go to Obann the city and see the king. Tim will guide you there. Leave soon; it's a long journey."

There was a splash as the turtles all dove into the water. It distracted her for a moment. But when she looked again, the man was gone.

When Tim came back to camp with a few more rats to skin, Gurun told him all about the stranger. Halfway through her tale, she noticed he was staring at her, openmouthed.

"What's the matter?" she said.

"Oh, nothing! Only there ain't another living soul for fifty miles all around, and all of a sudden you can talk as well as I can!"

She understood every word of that without the slightest difficulty. "Say more," she said.

"More? Listen, girl, if there were anybody else around here, I'd know it! The jays would squawk at him; he'd leave tracks in the mud; and I would smell his campfire and see the smoke. I knew you were coming before you sang out to me; I could feel it in my bones. It's just the kind of thing a trapper gets to know after twenty or thirty years of being alone in the wilderness. But what I don't know is how you learned all of a sudden to speak my language!"

It was true: she did understand.

"I don't know, either," Gurun said. "Maybe it's because of the man by the pond. Maybe he was not a man at all. He must have been a filgya."

"What's that?"

There was no word for it in Tim's language. Gurun tried to explain: "My people believe that sometimes, when it's necessary for you to know something that you can't find out in any ordinary way, you might see someone who isn't really there, and he will tell you. My father says that one night his grandfather went out to the privy and came back in looking grim and weary. 'I have seen my filgya,' he said, 'and so I know that tomorrow Ostic the Black will kill me.' And it happened just as he said."

Tim shook his head and whistled softly. "So it's bad luck, then!"

"No—no, I don't think so. This man told me I must go to the city of Obann and see the king."

Tim laughed. "Well, now, that'll take some doing—seeing as how there hasn't been a king in Obann for hundreds and hundreds of years! But I guess this filger of yours didn't know that."

"He said you would guide me to the city and that it would be a long journey."

"Oh, he did, did he?" Tim shook his head. "Just pack up my traps and pelts and traipse all the way down to Obann, where there ain't no king of any kind. Did he happen to say why I'd do a silly thing like that?"

"No. But a filgya never lies."

In the end Tim did agree to take her to Obann. "I can't help it: the whole thing makes me more curious than I can stand," he said.

He had two donkeys to carry his pelts and his gear, and he and Gurun went on foot. From the River Winter to the city of Obann was a long, long way to walk. Gurun found it hard to imagine such distances on land.

"Anyone we meet," Tim said, "we'll tell them you're my sister's daughter."

"Why?"

"Because there's already too much going on these days to make people uneasy, without me telling them you're a girl who got blown down here from a country no one knew existed. In a boat, no less! Nobody in his right mind would take a boat out on the sea."

"What are these things that are making people uneasy?" Gurun asked.

"Funny things! For instance, they're still talking about

the bell—the bell that rang in places where there ain't no bell for miles and miles around. Prophets said it was God's bell, ringing in the end of the world."

"What's a bell?"

He had to explain. He'd been to Obann once, where there were many bells, and he'd enjoyed listening to them. The chamber house in his own little town was too poor to have even one bell.

"So that's what it was!" Gurun said. "We heard it, too. Everybody heard it, on all the different islands, all at the same time. Nobody knew what it was—only that, for a little while, it made the whole world seem fresh and new. And since that morning the fishing has been better than anybody can remember."

It wasn't the kind of thing you would forget. Winter still had the islands in its clutches that morning. And then, from out of some unknown corner of the heavens, or from out of nowhere at all, sweet music rang, waking the people in their beds and the livestock in their stalls. From that moment on, winter yielded to an early spring and the waters teemed with fish.

Nobody knew what it was. There were no chamber houses in the islands, nor presters to preach in them. Reciters studied the Scriptures and went from dwelling to dwelling to teach and recite Scripture at district meetings, weddings, name-days, and funerals. There wasn't a bell to be found in all the islands. Some said the music was produced by angels. Others thought that maybe some spirit of the sea itself had decided to sing. A few said it was mermaids.

"Well, the whole world's going funny, and people are scared," Tim said. "Up north there are giant shaggy monsters that no one's ever seen before—they wrecked a town. Ain't seen one myself, but that don't mean that everybody's lying.

"Still, I've got to say the trapping was more than fine this season. I've taken more pelts in a few short weeks than I ever took before in a whole summer. Whatever it is that's happening, it can't be all bad."

It took them a week to hike to Pokee, where they had to stop while Tim sold his pelts to an agent who would resell them up and down the Imperial River. The trapper didn't get the kind of prices he'd hoped for.

"Sorry," said the agent, "but you know there's a war on, and it's going badly. I can't sell furs to people who've been burned out of their homes by the barbarians. It's one Heathen army after another coming over the mountains, all heading down the river to Obann itself. They mean to take the city."

"They're fools," said Tim. "Ever seen Obann's walls? Ain't no army can take that city!" But the agent wasn't so sure of that.

Tim found reasons to tarry in Pokee for longer than Gurun liked. Yes, it was interesting to see people farming, raising crops like corn and grapes and melons, which had never been grown in her country. It was interesting to see so many people living in wooden houses built on the ground instead of under it. But she was eager to reach the city and see the king, even though Tim said Obann had no king.

What with one thing and another, summer was almost over by the time they headed south again, and they still had more than half the journey yet to go. They stopped again in another town, this one with a high log fence around it—

more timber than was found in all of Fogo Island. Kantreff, it was called. There they heard bad news.

"You can't get into the city anymore," a townsman said, "and no one can get out. Haven't you heard yet? The Heathen are all around it in a siege—miles and miles of countryside depopulated, people running away in all directions. It's the end, I say."

They found a place to stay, an inn with little stuffy rooms. They had supper in the common room with other travelers. These all had the same tale to tell.

"The prophets were right, but no one listened to them," said a merchant from a place called Cardigal. "My city's been destroyed. Good thing I was traveling when it happened! But around Obann the barbarians are as thick as flies on a carcass. If you killed a hundred of them every day, they wouldn't even notice. The prophets warned us, but the presters just said they were crazy and to pay them no mind. Now it's too late!"

When they were alone again, just before going to their separate rooms to sleep, Tim said, "It's just no use, lassie. We might as well turn around and go home. We can't go to Obann now."

"You can go home," Gurun said, "but I shall go to Obann. I want to see the king."

"Burn it all, girl, there ain't no king! By the time we could get there, there might not be an Obann, either. Don't you listen to what people have been telling us?"

Gurun shrugged. "A filgya never lies," she said, "and it's useless to go one way when the filgya bids you go another. If my father's grandfather had tried to avoid the man who killed him, he would only have met him in a place where he didn't expect him."

"That is a heathenish superstition," Tim said.

Nevertheless, after they'd been in Kantreff several days, Tim set out with her for Obann.

"I don't know why I do it," he grumbled, when they were clear of the town. "Maybe it's because you remind me of my big sister. She caught a fever and died when I was just a little boy. But she sure did love me; and I loved her."

"You've been as an elder brother to me," said Gurun, "and God will bless you for it."

CHAPTER 5

An Interrupted Journey

Summer gave way to fall. The farther south they fared, the worse the news. Even so, they still had far to go: they were only halfway to Obann.

The towns they visited were full of refugees. There were no rooms to be had in any of the inns; but camping under the stars was no hardship for a trapper. Tim knew how to build a fire that wouldn't go out, how to put up simple shelters that kept out the wind and the rain, and how to live off the land. They never went hungry. Gurun learned from him everything she could.

"A hundred miles left to go, give or take a few," he told her one day. Because of rain, they'd gotten off to a late start. "Can't say I'm looking forward to getting there! This country hereabouts should be full of people, but we haven't seen anyone for two whole days. They've all cleared out. I wonder if the city's fallen."

They were in a land of grassy plains interspersed with woodlands and abandoned farms. Tim had been keeping clear of towns because they were jammed with refugees and conditions weren't pleasant. People were getting short-tempered, and there was violence. Besides, anybody traveling south would be suspected of insanity, he said.

"Perhaps the city has a king by now," said Gurun.

"That's foolishness. Obann is ruled by oligarchs—has been for, oh, a hundred years, at least."

"What are oligarchs?"

"Never you mind. They ain't kings."

It began to drizzle. They put hoods over their heads and tightened their cloaks, for it was getting cold. The grass around them had begun to turn yellow, and few of the trees were still green. Their masses of red and gold leaves struck Gurun as gloriously beautiful. But already a few trees had shed their leaves and were bare.

The cold and drizzle stopped their talk, and they plodded on in silence, making for a wide gap between two stands of trees. They were halfway through it when, with outlandish whoops and howlings, a band of men ran out and suddenly surrounded them.

Gurun didn't know if they were men or trolls. Darker than Tim or any of his countrymen, short and squat with crow-black hair, they menaced the two travelers with short spears and gabbled at them like a flock of ravens.

"What are these?" Gurun asked.

"Heathen—and they've got us!" Tim squeezed her hand, hard. "God help us now."

There were two dozen of them. They wore leather jerkins and trousers bright with colored checks, red and blue and green. They made a terrible noise, all gabbling at once. After several minutes of this, one of them jammed his spear into the ground and harangued the others, shouting them down.

Gurun didn't understand their language—if it even

was a language. If they were trolls, it would be fatal to show fear. But it seemed that one of them ran out of patience with the speaker and cocked back his arm to hurl his spear.

It was aimed right at Tim's chest; and without thinking, Gurun stepped in front of him.

"Stop this jabbering!" she cried, holding up her hand against them. "What have we ever done to you that you should harm us?"

The first speaker knocked the spear out of his comrade's hand and pushed him to the ground. He turned to the rest and broke out in a loud tirade. Gurun didn't know what he was saying, but it was this:

"Idiots! Fools! Have you learned nothing? Do you all want to die in this miserable country?

"Look at her! Any fool can see she's different. Is she not exactly what we've been looking for? Look at her eyes, her hair, her skin! And she stood between her servant and your spear, Bolok. Would an ordinary maiden do that? Can there be any hope for us without her?"

The men all looked ashamed. One of them muttered, "You're right, Shingis. See if you can speak with her."

"If she's not the one, we'll know soon enough," added another.

The man turned to Gurun and made an odd kind of half-bow, half-crouch to her, with his hands balled at his hips. He spoke to her in a fractured Obannese, which both she and Tim could understand.

"Be no angry with us, maiden. I sorry we scare you. My name Shingis; I chief to this band. We are all Blays. We come here from country far-far away. Thunder King send us to fight Obann.

"We fight hard, but we lose. Army all broken now, chased away from city. Boy riding great beast, he scatter us like dust. All Blays died but us."

He paused to see if she understood. She nodded.

"My name is Gurun," she answered, speaking slowly. "I come from far away, from the North. Over the sea. This is my friend, Tim. We were going to Obann."

"No go there now—stay away!" He looked scared; they all did. "Obann god very angry. He sent great beast to trample us. Thunder King be angry with us, too. He take away our gods, so we think he is a god. But Obann god kill-kill his army.

"Please, maiden—you stay with us. Be queen. We take good care for you. You pray for us, maybe find gods to take care for us."

Tim looked like he wanted very badly to say something, but didn't dare. But Gurun could see for herself that it would have been dangerous to decline the invitation.

"If I am to be your queen," she said, "then you must obey my commands. A queen should be obeyed, or she is no queen. Then I will stay with you, and pray for you." Why they would need someone to do their praying, she couldn't imagine; but now was not the time to ask.

Shingis turned to his fellows and translated her words. There was some discussion about it.

"You'd better accept her," he said. "We can't survive without gods to protect us. We're all alone in the country of our enemies. This maiden is our only chance—and I say the gods sent her to us: whatever gods there be that the Thunder King has not destroyed. Or would you rather wait for his spells to find us out and kill us one by one?"

"We shall see how well she prays, Shingis," answered one of the men. "But it's true that in the beginning the Old Gods came out of the North." The others murmured their agreement.

"If she came over the sea, the gods must have sent her," said another man.

"Maiden, we agree," Shingis said to Gurun. "You be queen for us, and we obey you. Then we live, and not die."

He bowed again, and Gurun curtseyed. And so Gurun the castaway became queen of a strange people in a strange land.

Maybe these men would help her get to Obann and see the king. For the time being, she would have to make the best of things.

CHAPTER 6

The King and His Council

Jim was wrong about there being no king in Obann. There was indeed a king, now. The old oligarchy, what was left of it, had ceded its power to him.

Two of the city's gates were broken. They would be repaired. But in the heart of the city was a ruin that could not be repaired.

The Temple, the great Temple that had been erected centuries ago, lay in ruins, destroyed by fire, collapsed under its own weight. Not one stone of it remained upon another. It was all a heap, a mountain of rubble. The First Prester, Lord Reesh, lay dead somewhere beneath it—or so men believed.

Nevertheless, the Heathen host was scattered, the siege lifted, the danger past. And Obann had a king.

The king didn't even know how old he was, but he couldn't be much older than ten. A boy king, born into slavery in Heathen lands beyond the mountains; who could neither read nor write; whose closest advisers were a clique of Heathen chiefs, a hermit, and a wild man from Lintum Forest; who by the power of God rode a great beast to the rescue of a city that he'd never seen before—this was Ryons, King of Obann.

On the same day Gurun met the Blays, King Ryons

sat in audience in a great black tent pitched before the city, on a throne that had belonged to the late governor-general of Obann, slain when the Heathen broke into the city. The throne was too big for Ryons, and he would have dearly loved to be elsewhere.

Around him in a semicircle, on their ivory stools of office, sat his councilors in all their finery, Heathen chiefs who now believed in God. Tall, bearded Wallekki; little Attakotts; tattooed, shaven-headed Abnaks; men in furs and feathers, men with painted faces; men as black as buffaloes; men from all the countries of the East—they were Ryons' chieftains.

Behind him stood twenty men of his bodyguard—swarthy, bowlegged horsemen with almond-shaped eyes: Ghols, who had adopted King Ryons as their father.

Off to one side, leaning on a staff, stood a big man dressed in patched-together rags of many colors, his head crowned with a wild mane of straw-like hair. You wouldn't have been surprised to find mice nesting in it. This was Helki the woodsman, Giant-killer, Ryons' general, whom men called the Flail of the Lord, but who called himself Helki, son of nobody in particular.

Before the king stood his teacher, and the teacher of all his formerly Heathen army, Obst, the hermit: Obst, who had climbed Bell Mountain and descended with the gift of tongues. He understood everything that was said to him in any language, and whatever he said, the hearer understood it in his own language. He was an old man, tall and lean and straight, with iron-grey hair and beard. It was Obst who was speaking now.

"The Heathen armies have been driven from the city—

but now they're on the loose, all over the country. There must be hundreds of bands of marauders spreading out in all directions, thousands of men! And yet the thousands who were killed here are still waiting to be buried or burned. It had better be done soon, or we'll have a pestilence.

"Somehow, someone must clear away the ruins of the Temple. More importantly, a better temple must take its place—built not of stone, but of the word and spirit of God. A temple not built by human hands cannot be torn down by human hands.

"And still there is one more thing that may seem to some of you a small thing, but which must not be overlooked. We do not know what has become of Jack and Ellayne, God's servants, and Martis, their protector. They were left behind in a walled town for their own safety, but the children ran after the army—and never found their way to us. Martis followed them and has not been heard of since. All three have vanished.

"It must be remembered that these three went all the way to the summit of Bell Mountain, where Jack and Ellayne rang King Ozias' bell so that the whole world heard it. And it was these three who recovered for us the lost books of Scripture, written by Ozias in his own hand. But for those three, none of us would be here today. I would have died a hermit in the forest; you, my chieftains, would all be Heathen; and Obann would not have her king. We must find them!"

The wild man, Helki, sighed loudly, drawing attention to himself.

"Say the word," he said, "and I'll go out and find them. I reckon if anyone can do it, I can. But the longer we wait, the harder a job it'll be."

"But then who will command the king's armies?" Obst said. "There's much to do! Those remnants of the Thunder King's armies must be rounded up and either brought to God or expelled from the country."

Helki laughed. "Hah! This tent is full of men who know more about managing a war than I'll ever be able to learn. Twelve of them are sitting right in front of you. But I don't think any of them can match me for tracking. What do you think, Your Majesty?"

Ryons wasn't ready for a question. Why had Helki asked him? He stammered, hunting for words.

He'd met Jack and Ellayne, but he didn't know them well. He knew Obst set great store by them and that they'd done great things, although they were only children like him. From what he'd heard of them, they were heroes.

Of course, Ryons himself was special, too. They'd made him their king, hadn't they? And the great beast that was like a mountain walking had plucked him off the ground and set him on its back and chased the Heathen from the city. All the chieftains said he deserved to be king and that they would have no other.

"I don't know how to decide, my lords," he said at last. "You'll have to decide on what's the wisest thing to do. We've done all right so far! But, Helki, do you really think you can find them?"

The woodsman shrugged. "It won't be easy. But we can't send the whole army out looking for them, that's for sure. As it is, we'll need a bigger army to do all that needs doing around here. It might as well be me who goes hunting for them."

Zekelesh, chieftain of the Fazzan, who wore wolves' heads as helmets, spoke up. His tribe-talk had improved. Obst didn't have to translate for him anymore.

"How will you hunt them, Helki? One man, with a whole country to search! Will you talk to the birds? Will they tell you where to look?"

"Birds can tell a hunter many things," said Helki. "You just have to learn how to listen."

Captain Hennen from Caryllick, whose mail-clad spearmen had saved Ryons' army once, then joined it, spoke: "If ever those Heathen recover from their fright and get back together again, they might be strong enough to seize the country. Obann's general, Lord Gwyll, is dead. Most of the oligarchs are dead. We must raise and train an army to take the field as soon as possible—no later than the springtime. The army we have here can only be a cadre. Where are we to find a general?"

"We can start by making you a general," Helki said.

"If there are any Abnaks on the loose, they'll join us," added old Chief Spider, who spoke for his people. "That is, unless they just decide to go back home. I'm sure they've had their fill of fighting for the Thunder King."

"Many of the Wallekki will join us, too," Chief Shaffur said. He commanded Ryons' cavalry and spoke for the Wallekki in the army. "With enemies scattered all over the country, a thousand horsemen will do us more good than ten thousand men on foot."

Hennen nodded to him. "Very true, Chieftain! But do any of you truly believe the Thunder King is finished with us? Having sworn to do it, do you think he'll ever rest until he sacks Obann? I tell you he cannot! To give up would destroy his slaves' belief in him. Come spring, there will be Heathen hordes moving west again—depend upon it. We'll need those ten thousand infantry, my lords. And fifty thousand would be better!"

Around and around went the discussion. Ryons listened intently and did his best to understand. Someday he would grow up, and then he really would have to make decisions. He was not looking forward to it.

In the end, they decided to let Helki go and see what he could do, provided he returned before the spring if he couldn't pick up the missing children's trail. In the meantime, the chieftains would cooperate with Obann's surviving officials and army officers to reorganize the defenses of the country and put the new king on a solid footing.

Just as the audience was about to be dismissed, a young Abnak begged leave to speak—Hlah, the son of Spider.

"One more thing, my lords!" he said. "I hope nobody thinks that any army can get across the mountains without the cooperation of the Abnak tribes. A big enough army might force its way across, but it would have to pay a heavy price in blood. We hold all the best passes leading into Obann.

"We Abnaks joined the Thunder King because he tempted us with the glory of sacking the city and the great plunder we would take. He could not make good on that!

"I ask leave to go back home, before the winter comes, and make sure all the tribes know what happened here. More—my people must be told the truth, that Obann's God is the God of all peoples, everywhere. Our God has saved us many times, as He has saved this city. Each one of us knows that for the truth! I won't rest until I make this known to all our people back home. It is a shame to us, to serve the Thunder King!"

"Don't try to keep him here—he'll just sneak away," put in the scarred old subchief, Uduqu. "I'd go with him, only I'm not so sure my legs would carry me that far."

"He has my blessing," added Spider. "Hlah is a warrior, and he knows his own mind. He has taken enemy scalps; he can speak for himself."

"Then go with the Lord God's blessing, too, young man," said Obst. "May you be the first of many missionaries."

CHAPTER 7

What Can a Blind Man See?

Jack and Ellayne, with Martis, had been captured by a band of one hundred Griffs somewhere between Obann and a town called Gilmy. Now they were some little distance up the Chariot River—the three of them and the captain of the Griffs, who had been struck blind in his sleep. Terrified by the omen, the Griff warriors had all run away and left them.

Chillith was more than just the captain of a band. He was a mardar, too—one of the Thunder King's medicine men. These performed sacrifices in the Thunder King's name and served as his eyes and ears among his captive nations. But now Chillith was blind, and his men had deserted him.

"Why don't you just kill me and go on your way?" he asked. "You're a killer, Martis. I marvel that you've let me live this long. Am I not your enemy?"

"He can't kill you now," Jack said. "It was God who made you blind. If He wanted you dead, you'd be dead already." He left off the "your honor" demanded by Griff etiquette.

"Jack's right," Martis said. For most of his life he'd been an assassin in the service of the Temple, until he'd been unable to stop the children from ringing the bell atop Bell Mountain. Now he was their guardian, and God had turned his brown beard white to remind him. He didn't look like an assassin. That was one of the things that had made him such a deadly one. He looked like a clerk. "God has laid His hand on you, Chillith, even as He's laid it on the three of us. We'd be fools to remain enemies."

"And this is not a curse put on me by your little hairy one?"

"Wytt can't do things like that," Ellayne said. "He's our friend, and he protects us. He's probably scouting for food right now, or danger. He won't hurt you."

It had been Chillith's plan to take them all the way into the East and present them to the Thunder King at his castle at Kara Karram on the far side of the Great Lakes. They'd consented to go, provided no one tried to harm them on the way.

"I suppose you'll be taking me back to Obann now," he said. "Yesterday you were my prisoners. Today I'm yours."

"We must decide what to do," Martis said. "It's a long way back to Obann."

"But not so long to Ninneburky!" Ellayne said. Ninneburky was her hometown, and Jack's. "Let's go there! My father will know what to do." Her father, Roshay Bault, was chief councilor in Ninneburky. Ellayne longed to see him.

"How would he know?" Jack said. "How would anybody know?"

"Whatever we decide, we must decide carefully. We have to take our time," Martis said.

"Well, we certainly don't want to go to the Thunder King!" Ellayne said. "I say we turn around right now—"

Martis held up his hand. "Peace, Ellayne! It's time to think, not talk. Chillith, what do you see?"

"Do you mock me?" said the mardar. "What can a blind man see? Nothing!"

"No—no, I'm not mocking you, your honor," Martis said. "But I don't mean, 'What can you see with your eyes?' It may be that God has taken away the sight of your eyes so you can really see! You were a shaman before you were a mardar. I think you understand me."

Chillith fell silent, thinking. Jack wondered what Martis could mean. How could a blind man see anything at all?

"I do understand," Chillith said. "But there is only darkness. The gods of my people used to speak to me and show me visions. Now when I seek them, they aren't there. But the Obann God is silent, too."

"I think He'll speak to you," said Martis, "if we're patient."

Wytt returned, chattering to announce himself. You might have thought him a rat or a monkey, with golden fur. But he had no tail, he walked like a man, and he carried a little sharp stick. His kind lived in ruined cities. They were the "hairy ones" mentioned in the Scriptures, but few people had ever seen one.

"We're all alone," Ellayne said, translating his squeaks and chitters. She and Jack understood Wytt, and he understood them—not that his kind had any real language as humans understood it. "The Griffs have all cleared out and aren't coming back, and there's no one else around."

"Good. That gives us time to think," Martis said. "We may as well stay here until we can decide which way to go—to Ninneburky, back to Obann, or to the Thunder King."

"He'd only kill us when we got there," Jack said.

"Or worse!" Ellayne added.

"Yes," Chillith agreed. "He'd very likely do much worse."

There was at the same time another journey being made from Obann to the Thunder King: this one by Lord Reesh, the First Prester, and his chosen successor, Prester Orth. Their servant, Gallgoid, rode atop the comfortable coach that carried them. Seventeen more servants of the Temple came plodding after the coach. They had an armed escort commanded by a mardar named Kyo.

Having let the Heathen into Obann's Temple by means of secret passages, and betrayed the city to its enemies, they were traveling east to be installed in the Thunder King's new Temple. That was the agreement they had made with him, through the mardar.

Reesh was too old to make the journey any other way. He would have to be handled with care. Just getting over the mountains in the winter would be more than he expected to accomplish.

"Don't worry, Excellency. We'll take good care of you, and you're under my master the Thunder King's protection," Mardar Kyo said. "Besides, you're too important to die so easily."

"You mean 'too evil'!" Reesh thought.

Truly, what would any man call it but pure wickedness, to accept safe conduct for himself and hand his native city over to barbarians—to consign to flames the Temple he had served so long, in return for preferment at another

Temple? But as far as Reesh knew, there was no one left alive in Obann to call him traitor.

Nevertheless, they were only two days out of Obann when a rider overtook them in the morning. He was of some far-off Eastern nation, like Kyo—stout and swarthy, with a horn bow slung over his shoulder and a quiver of arrows at his hip. His horse was lathered, wild-eyed, and the rider hardly less so. He jabbered at Kyo in a harsh and unknown language.

Kyo's face went hard as stone. He questioned the man at length, his voice rising, growing shrill.

"Something's gone wrong," Orth muttered. He was a big, black-bearded man who looked splendid in the pulpit, but was turning out to be less splendid than he looked: well Lord Reesh had come to know it. Reesh glared at him and Orth fell silent.

At last Kyo dismissed the rider, who galloped off eastward. Kyo walked around to Reesh's side of the coach.

"Tidings, Mardar Kyo?"

"I will tell you, First Prester. The army of my master the Thunder King is no more. It has been driven from the city, scattered like chaff. The Temple has burned to the ground, but the city stands unconquered."

Orth gasped. Reesh clenched his fists. With an effort, he demanded, "How could that have happened?"

"The rider said a monster came out of the river and destroyed the army—a gigantic beast that has no name. A boy rode on its shoulders. It trampled the men by the thousands, and the others ran away. The rider says he saw it all."

Kyo looked Reesh in the eye as if he expected the First Prester to explain the matter. But how could he? It was like some miracle recounted in the Old Books of the Scriptures—only there was no miracle exactly like that mentioned in any of the writings.

"Are we undone, Mardar?" he said. If so, he thought, these men would probably kill them and be on their way.

"No!" Kyo's dark eyes flashed with sudden anger, but then he laughed. "No! What are armies to the Thunder King? As easily as he raised those armies, he can raise others. You do not know my master, Excellency, and yours. He is not a man, that you can defeat him by routing his slaves.

"No, First Prester, we are not undone. There is a new Temple waiting for you at Kara Karram. The fate of armies does not concern us. Come the spring, there will be greater armies marching over the mountains. But by then you'll be in the Temple, and then you will understand. Let us continue our journey." He shouted a command. The escort spurred their horses, and the coach lurched forward.

Inside, Orth's face shone with sweat. "First Prester," he said, "how can such things be? That was the greatest army anyone had ever seen."

"Didn't you hear what Kyo said?" Reesh snapped. "Some kind of beast came out of the river and panicked the army. Superstitious Heathen!"

"But what kind of beast could do a thing like that? There are no beasts that can do such a thing!"

Reesh slammed his palm against the side of the coach, making Orth startle. "What does it matter!" he said. "We've chosen our course, and we must stick to it."

"But when the people find out what we've done—"

Reesh glared at him so fiercely that he didn't finish.

The First Prester settled back on his cushioned seat

and tried to think. Obann should have fallen. The Heathen had entered the city through the Temple and opened the city's gates from the inside. There would have been chaos, the defense demoralized, collapsed. It would have begun just as the coach was on its way east.

Lord Reesh did not believe in miracles. He did not believe in God. He believed in the Temple—in man's great past, and greater future—and had sacrificed the old Temple for the sake of the new.

The servant, Gallgoid, leaned over and looked into the window. It was mildly comical to see his face upside down. "Are you all right, Excellency?" he said.

Reesh nodded. "Yes—thank you, Gallgoid. Just thinking."

"Yes, First Prester. And I'm up here if you need me."

Too bad Gallgoid wasn't a theologian, Reesh thought. He glared at Orth again, then plunged himself into deep cogitation.

CHAPTER 8

Among the Blays

Obst found a seminary student to teach the king to read and write, an hour a day, every day if possible. "I won't always be here for Your Majesty," the old man said. "God has lengthened my days, but who can say for how long? A king should be able to read Scripture for himself, so that he might be guided by God's word."

"I suppose so," Ryons said. He wanted to be able to read, but to have to study every day seemed hard.

"Cheer up, Ryons! You won't be alone in your studies. You'll have a schoolmate—Subchief Uduqu."

So it was that a serious young man named Dyllyd found himself tutoring the boy king and a savage old Abnak who was best known for chopping two Heathen warriors in half with one blow of a giant's sword. Scarred and tattooed, with his scalp shaved except for one long, black lock, Uduqu experienced some difficulty adjusting himself to a desk and a chair.

"What's the matter, Chief?" Ryons had to control the urge to laugh out loud at him; but they'd been friends for a long time now, and he knew the old scalp-taker was fond of him.

"I don't see why we have to have our lessons in a nasty little room where you can hardly breathe," Uduqu grumbled.

They were in a classroom in a part of the seminary that had been spared the fire. "It's not healthy to spend so much time indoors."

Dyllyd watched nervously until the old man finally settled himself. The chief frowned at him. "Well? What are you waiting for? Teach us!"

"Obst says I have to learn to read and write because I'm king," said Ryons. "But why should you have to, Chief?"

"Because I want to. I'm getting too old and stout to run into battle like I used to," Uduqu said. His Obannese was good. "Do you know, no Abnak has ever learned to read and write? I want to be the first. Then I can make my words live on after me. I'll be able to speak to Abnaks long after I'm dead and gone—to men not yet born. There are certain things I want to say to them. I want to tell them how the True God gave us victory."

Ryons looked at him with some awe. He hadn't thought of it like that before—but it was true. Thus King Ozias himself, dead these long ages, still spoke to his people.

Dyllyd finally cleared his throat. "Your lordship is a man of understanding," he said. "Therefore let us begin. First I'll teach you how to read and write your own names."

At the same time, Gurun decided that she liked the Blays and didn't mind being their queen.

For one thing, she was taller than any of them and they had to look up to her when she spoke. That was a good habit for them to start with, she thought. Maybe they'd learn to look up to her in other ways.

For another, these little men were amusingly peculiar. She talked with Shingis constantly, both to learn his language—his Obannese showed scant signs of improvement—and to learn all she could about his people.

They came from a country very far to the east, beyond some Great Lakes that she'd never heard of. She knew what a lake was, although she'd never seen one. Blays carried spears for close-in fighting, but most of them were expert slingers, too: lucky was the bird that escaped them. If they had time, they always spat on a rock before launching it. They liked raw fish when they could get it—a taste that the island girl shared with them, but that revolted Tim the trapper.

"They're every inch barbarians," he said. "I heard Shingis tell you their high chief always marries his sister. And they eat dogs, too. I've seen them eat ants! The sooner we can escape from them, the better."

"But in one thing they are like the people of Obann," Gurun said. "They think they need someone to pray for them, rather than speaking to God for themselves."

"You need a prester to get the prayers right," Tim said. "Everybody knows that. But these people think their gods have all been locked up in a castle."

"We have no presters in the islands where I come from."

"Well, how could you? Only the Temple can make a man a prester. I guess God makes allowances for your people."

As Gurun understood it from Shingis, the Thunder King conquered the Blays and made them his slaves. He took away their idols, all of them, and locked them in a prison: so they had no gods to pray to, and they had to pray to him instead. But now that they had failed him by being defeated before Obann, their god was angry with them and they were afraid. They dreaded he would find them out with spells.

"I will surely pray for you, Shingis," Gurun said, "but not to any Heathen god."

"To Obann god, then?" he asked.

"There is only one God, and He is All-Father, God of all. Not just God of Obann. To Him I shall pray for you."

"How can one god be God of all?"

"I don't know!" Gurun admitted. "He just is, and always has been. I suppose it's because He created the world itself and everything in it. I've never heard of any other God to pray to—although I know that in ancient times, before my people fled into the North, there were false gods and idols in this country and foolish people prayed to them. But if the Blays' gods were truly gods, then no one could have made them prisoners. You must never ask me to pray to false gods."

He puzzled over it. He reported her words to the men, and they had an animated discussion in their own language, which sounded like the squabbling of seabirds in a rookery.

"You'd better be careful not to offend them," Tim said. "Those spears are sharp."

"I won't lie to them. They won't want a liar for their queen. Besides, I'm thinking of a plan for them." Gurun took Tim's elbow, drew him closer: she didn't want Shingis to overhear them. "I'm thinking that these men must settle down. We must find a town for them to live in. Maybe there is a town where the people would like having two dozen armed men to protect them. The sooner they can settle down and lose their fear, the sooner I can go to Obann and see the king."

"There is no king!" said Tim.

"I'm sure there is by now," said Gurun.

CHAPTER 9

Helki on the Trail

When he went to Gilmy to begin his hunt for Jack and Ellayne, Helki took only a single companion—Cavall, the king's dog. A hermit in Lintum Forest had bequeathed the hound to Ryons, and Cavall saw him safely across the plains all the way to Obann. Ryons hated to part with him.

"Bring him back to me safe and sound!" the boy said.

"More likely he'll bring me back safe and sound, Your Majesty," said Helki. "Don't worry about him. He's a wise dog, but he's not used to city life, no more than I am. He wants to be out in the wide world for a while, like me."

"And me!" Ryons said. Helki knew he meant it; but kings cannot go out on adventures like private persons, everybody said.

"Someday, Majesty," Helki said, "when the country's at peace again, I'll take you hunting—just you and me and Cavall in Lintum Forest. It's a promise."

At Gilmy he visited the house where Jack and Ellayne had stayed and did his best to give Cavall their scent. He visited the stable where Martis' horse, Dulayl, had been kept. To hope that Cavall could follow such a cold trail was to hope for much; but when Helki spoke, animals listened. He had no doubt Cavall would understand what was being asked of him.

Helki was most at home in the forest, but this was open country with only scattered isles of woodland. Much of it was farms, from which the farmers had all fled. A day's hike to the south lay the Imperial River. Due north, all the way up to the River Winter, lay mostly empty country, wild and waste. It beckoned to Helki, but he doubted Jack and Ellayne would have gone north.

He was sure they must have gone either east or west from Gilmy. There was no reason for them to try to cross the Imperial. If they'd been seeking to rejoin King Ryons' army, they would have traveled west. Their hometown, he knew, lay to the east; but it was very far away.

Under the grey sky, Helki and Cavall hunted for the children's trail. Two days' journey west of Gilmy, Helki spotted a buzzard in the sky. It led him to a dead man left unburied.

Birds and other scavengers had been at the body, but Helki made a close examination of it. "Let's see what he can tell us," he said to the hound. "There's a hole in his chest—knife or sword, stabbed right to the heart. I think—yes, I'm sure—he's a Griff. Hard to be sure, with his face all eaten away. But what does the ground tell us? Too bad it's been rained on."

Cavall went back and forth, sniffing, keenly interested. Helki studied the ground. A horse's hooves, in spots, had gouged it. And there were other signs that only Helki would have seen.

"This man had two others with him—all three were Griffs, I reckon," he said. "They were attacked by one man on a horse. This one was killed, and his two friends ran away. It was only one man on horseback, one against three." He stood up straight. "That sounds like Martis."

Cavall barked. He had the scent.

"Yes—it all adds up," Helki said. "Let's go." The hound trotted forward, nose to the ground, eastward. Helki followed.

He was sure he knew what had happened. Jack and Ellayne wanted to be back with the army, so they ran away from Gilmy. Martis followed. Three Griffs met the children, but Martis arrived in time to kill one and drive off the others. Then he would have brought the children back to Gilmy—but they never arrived. Why not?

Here and there, Helki saw the horse's prints. Where there were three Griffs, he thought, there were probably more. A scouting party, maybe.

Griffs wandered into Obann sometimes. Often they took service with the army. A few of them used to hunt in Lintum Forest. They'd be valuable to the Thunder King as scouts.

The trail was two weeks old, at least, and likely more. Helki wondered why the Griffs hadn't taken their prisoners back west to Obann. He wondered why they hadn't buried their friend. There must have been a good reason for it.

"Faster, Cavall!" he said. "Don't be slow on my account. I'll catch up to you by nightfall." Even if he couldn't follow the old trail, he could easily follow Cavall's new one.

The hound barked and trotted faster. Helki trotted, too. The gap between the two widened until eventually the dog was out of sight. But Helki followed the trail of grass pressed down by his paws.

Many miles to the east, at the camp deserted by the Griffs, Martis prevailed on Chillith to tell everything he knew about the Thunder King. "I'd like to know," he said, "how a man convinces other men to worship him as a god."

Chillith sat in his blindness, warmed by a campfire that he couldn't see. Jack had always thought blind people kept their eyes closed, but Chillith's were wide open. They peered intently into first one direction, then another, striving desperately to see something, or anything. You would think them the same as anyone else's eyes, until you noticed that they couldn't seem to fasten on to anything. They were always searching, never finding. It must be bad, Jack thought. Bad even for an enemy.

"The Thunder King is not a man," Chillith said, after a long pause. "You are right—it would be foolish to worship a man. But he's not a man. He's not like you or me, or anyone. We call him the Great Man sometimes, but he's not a man.

"I myself have never seen him. But I would have, one day, when I was judged worthy. The great mardars, his trusted ones, he binds to himself. For them it is as if they were in his presence all the time. What they see, he sees. What they hear, he hears—so that he can be anywhere, everywhere, and yet never leave his castle. He causes his trusted ones to think his thoughts, so that they always know his wishes. He causes his power to flow through them. Through them he can stop the rain, turn drinking water bad, make cattle barren and sour their milk, and strike a whole tribe with pestilence. Can any mortal man do that?"

"If he really can do that!" Ellayne muttered under her breath. It all sounded like witches or wizards in the stories of Abombalbap, which Obst always said were fairy tales.

But Chillith heard her. "Yes, he can do those things," he said. "Once they're bonded to him, his great mardars are like gods themselves. That's how they silenced the Griffs' gods and imprisoned them in wood and stone, so that we shamans had no more communion with them. He has done the same to many people's gods.

"I've seen all these things for myself. His mardars make sacrifices to him, of animals and humans. That's how his power is renewed in them. I've seen them make good grazing land go bad. I've seen men who spoke against the mardars sicken and die for no reason at all. There's hardly a man or a woman living east of the mountains who hasn't seen these things with his own eyes. Someday you will see them in the West, too."

No man knew where the Thunder King was born, nor when, nor of what people. He came out of some country yet farther to the east, making miracles and spreading terror. If he had a name other than the Thunder King, no man knew it. Some believed him to be a thousand years old, although he looked like a man in the prime of his life.

His castle at Kara Karram, on a hilltop overlooking the easternmost of the Great Lakes, once belonged to mighty kings. The Thunder King killed the last of those kings and enslaved his people. In dungeons in that castle he kept all the gods of all the nations prisoner. The wealth of all the East flowed in to him. Those who served him at his castle, even the least of them, lived as luxuriously as emperors.

All this, said Chillith, everybody knew. He had never yet been to Kara Karram himself, but he'd spoken to many men who'd been there.

"But do you yourself believe he is a god?" asked Martis.

"What else can he be?" Chillith said, spreading his

palms helplessly.

"A very wicked man," said Martis, "who plays on fear and superstition. I've known a few like that, and served them."

"No man can do the things he does!"

"Or appears to do," Martis said. And he said to himself, "I wonder."

CHAPTER 10

An Omen of Wrath

It was his former master, Lord Reesh, whom Martis was thinking of; and just as Martis thought of him, Reesh was traveling eastward in a cushioned coach.

Mardar Kyo's plan was to cross the mountains in the winter by means of a pass above the source of the Chariot River. If they made good time, he said, they could get there before the snows began in earnest.

"In any case, First Prester, you need only stay alive. My men will see to it that you're kept warm and comfortable and well fed," he told Lord Reesh. "You won't lack for hot drinks, either, when it grows cold. My master's servants will attend your every need. And I'm sure this is a comfortable coach."

"It is," said Reesh. "I couldn't have provided a better one myself."

Prester Orth didn't join the conversation. He could not get it out of his mind that Obann, despite his treason, still stood and that the army to which he had betrayed the city was no more.

"They'll find out what we did," he thought. "We let the Heathen into the city. Everyone in Obann might have been killed because of us." Some enemy prisoner would reveal it all, and Lord Reesh and Prester Orth would go down in history as the vilest traitors ever known. What would happen to them if they ever fell into the hands of the city's rulers, Orth tried not to imagine.

But he couldn't stop thinking about it. Since the news of the city's rescue first reached them, half a dozen of their servants had deserted in the night. What if one of those men should let their secret slip out? What tale might he tell? "Never mind them," Gallgoid said. "If we're traitors, then so are they. Why should they give themselves away?"

"To purchase their own lives by selling ours!" Orth thought.

The First Prester showed no sign of being troubled by it. He had committed himself to the new Temple, and that was that. Reesh would never look back. Orth envied him.

Why, why had he ever gone along with Reesh's plan? Because he was sure the city would fall, and it was the only way to save his worthless skin! What was the use in succeeding Reesh as First Prester in a Temple at the end of the earth, built by Heathen hands and subject to an evil man who called himself a god? Why had he agreed to it? All he would get for it would be a dishonorable grave in a faraway country.

"I must have been insane," he thought. "And as for this miserable journey, who knows where it will end—or how?"

The miles rolled along under the wheels of the coach. To the right, a mile or two distant, flowed the Chariot River down from the northeast. The country through which they traveled was dotted with reedy fens and little streams that wandered east until they found the river. There was no road to speak of: most of the traveling in this country was done by boat or raft. There should have been boatmen, fishermen, and loggers with their rafts, all going about their business here, but the war had driven them to cover. Above the dreary country stretched a dreary grey sky.

Suddenly, the horses neighed, and the coach lurched to a stop. Men cried out in astonishment.

"Look at that!" Reesh said.

Orth looked past him, out the window. He saw a pool with reeds and cattails. And he heard a hoarse, rolling bellow.

Orth's blood nearly froze. Climbing out of the pool on the far side was a creature that might have crawled out from a nightmare. At first he thought it was some kind of gigantic hog, hairless, slate-grey, and black where it was wet. But then it turned to bellow at the men and horses and to shake its head at them.

It was a great oblong box of a head, monstrous, hideous, with big knobbly horns all over it and long, sharp yellow tusks in its jaws. It was like nothing any man had ever imagined. The men with difficulty controlled their frightened horses.

That was all the time it took for Lord Reesh's last eleven servants to throw down whatever they were carrying and race off in eleven different directions, screaming. Kyo's warriors had all they could do just to control their horses. There was no pursuit. And then the creature clumped off into a stand of high reeds, smashing them down. The reeds sprang up again after it and closed their ranks, and the monster vanished. It roared once, and then was heard no more.

"Did you see that, Orth!" said Reesh.

"What was it?" Orth cried. His teeth were chattering. "What in God's name was it?"

Kyo, with his horse still fidgety under him, spurred up to the window.

"Quite a sight, First Prester—eh?" he said. "What do people in Obann call that animal?"

"A hallucination," Reesh said. "I can only say, Mardar, that we have no name for it. I have never seen or heard of such an animal. But I have heard many reports of strange beasts seen in many parts of the country. I never quite believed them until now."

"Whatever it was," Kyo said, "it was wise enough not to attack a band of armed men. I don't think we'll see it again."

Gallgoid hopped down from the roof of the coach. "You saw it, Excellency?" he said.

Reesh nodded. "A most remarkable sight."

"Whatever it was, the horses didn't like it," Gallgoid said. "Another minute, and they would've all bolted. Prester Orth, are you all right? Your face has gone all pale."

"I'm fine—just startled," Orth lied.

"My lord," said Gallgoid, "the rest of our people have run away."

Reesh glared at him. He'd picked those men himself. Now all he had left were Orth and Gallgoid.

"Mardar Kyo, I need those men," he said.

"For what?" Kyo scowled. "No point chasing such cowards. At Kara Karram you will be given better men." His horse fidgeted under him, and he paused to bring it back under control.

"Well, we need not stay here any longer," Kyo said. "We can cover another twenty miles before we make camp for the night."

Their journey resumed. Reesh sat still, thinking. Orth was glad Reesh didn't want to talk: not just now.

He, too, like everyone in Obann, had heard of sightings of unnatural beasts. The ignorant people in the city and the crazed, self-appointed prophets in the streets said the strange beasts were omens of God's judgment, forerunners of God's wrath. For the first time in many years Orth wondered if the Scriptures were true, after all. It had been so long since he'd let God enter into his thoughts, he might as well not have believed in Him at all. But now the monster from the pool had made a wide breach in his indifference; and through it, God came in—an angry God who knew, even if no man knew, that Orth, who presented himself to men as God's servant, was an apostate and a traitor: an angry God who would judge him for those sins.

"I have sinned," thought Orth; and he noticed, for the first time, that his fingertips were cold.

At long last Lord Reesh found something for which he'd been ransacking his memories without knowing what it was.

It was his lifelong avocation to collect relics from the days of Obann's Empire, a thousand years ago—cryptic artifacts, some of them made of materials unlike anything known to living men, for purposes that no living man could know. When he became First Prester, famous and powerful, he let it be widely known that he was interested in such things and would pay good prices for them. People brought him artifacts from all over Obann, and he kept them in a special room in the Temple.

One day, many years ago, a farmer from somewhere in the South brought him not an artifact, but a skull: a dragon's skull, the yokel said. Certainly it was big enough to be a dragon's skull; it took up all the room in his wagon. It had teeth like butchers' knives and was as long as a man was tall. The lower jaw was missing. Reesh marveled at it, but because it was no manmade object, he didn't buy it.

What else could it be, he thought at the time, but some scriptural creature that perished in the Great Shaking, ages and ages ago? The Book of Beginnings named several animals whose identities scholars could only guess at—animals that didn't exist in Obann anymore. Probably the skull had once belonged to one of them. It was interesting, but not what Reesh was interested in. So he'd told the farmer to take it away.

It seemed now that some of those creatures hadn't quite died off. They must have survived in other countries and now for some reason were coming back to Obann. But surely it was nothing to inspire superstitious terror, except among the ignorant.

He stole a sidelong glance at Orth. He would have to watch him carefully. The man had been a useful tool in Obann, by which Reesh had made the presters do his bidding; but taken away from the city, and from Temple politics, he was beginning to look useless.

"Prester Orth!"

The other man's eyes snapped open.

"You weren't praying, were you?" Reesh demanded.

"Praying?" Orth chuckled: there was no mirth in it. "A bit late for that—isn't it, Excellency?"

"I was afraid the sight of that creature, a few miles back,

might have undermined your courage. I hope it hasn't."

"I'm fine, Excellency," Orth said. Reesh knew he was lying, but there was nothing to be done about it. Orth and Gallgoid, that was all he had—an assassin and a milksop. And the milksop would have to be the next First Prester. "At least it's a reason to keep living!" Reesh thought.

CHAPTER 11

The Blays Find a Home

Because they were only two dozen men in a country full of enemies, the Blays took care to scout for miles around wherever they were. Thus they discovered one day that they were within a few miles of a farming village.

"I see it myself," Shingis told Gurun. "Little village, people and cattle and pigs. They have just made harvest of their fields. Easy to surprise them, take food and other things. Maybe take girls, too."

Gurun tried to sound like the queens immortalized in Scripture, imperious and wise.

"No, Shingis—you will not do that," she said. "Winter will be coming soon. What will you eat? How will you keep warm? Will you live by robberies? How can I pray to the All-Father to protect you, if you turn into thieves and pirates? And what will you do when the people send to some big city for help and soldiers in armor come to hunt you? You must be more sensible than that. Tell the men I wish to speak to them."

Shingis called them, and they came. She had them sit on the ground before her, so they'd have farther to look up. This was what she did when she prayed for them, stretching her hands to heaven and praying loudly in the language of the islands, of which none of them understood a single word. She made a display of prayer, like a king or a prophet in the Scriptures. But she prayed sincerely, for she knew these were important prayers. She did this once a day, and the Blays said they were deeply comforted by it.

Shingis stood beside her to translate.

"Listen, you men," she said. "You're strangers in this land, and there aren't many of you. It would be foolish for you to live as outlaws, when there is a much better way.

"I will send Tim to the village, along with Shingis, to tell them that we are nearby, but mean them no harm. Instead, we would like to live among them, if only for the winter. We shall protect them from outlaws: with the Thunder King's army broken up, the country must be full of them. The village will need protection. All we shall ask in return is food and shelter. Tell them we pray to the same God they do. Let Tim talk to them, and then come back and tell me what they say. I am your queen, and those are my wishes."

The Blays discussed it among themselves. By now Gurun had learned enough of their language to understand that they were surprised by her plan, but not averse to it. It was something they hadn't thought of for themselves.

"Queen, we do as you say," Shingis said, when the men had reached a decision. "It is a good saying. It do no harm to try. That's what Blays think."

Gurun treated them to her most radiant smile and curtseyed to them. "Tell my people that their queen is pleased with them, and the All-Father will be pleased, too. They shall earn His favor by this."

Shingis bowed. "We always try to please All-Father, while we are in His country."

"All countries, Shingis, are His," she said.

Gurun said a silent prayer, asking God to forgive her for acting like a queen and a prophet, when she was no such thing. "I know these Blays are skreelings, ignorant Heathen," she prayed, "but I can't see that they are evil. They are the protection you have given me in this strange land. Please, All-Father, help me to do right."

As poor as the people were in the northern islands, they were rich in Scriptures. They'd made very many copies on sheepskin, although they were not rich in sheep. There were True Copies, which only sages knew how to read, and Common Copies, rendered into the people's own language so everyone could read them. Bertig owned common copies of all the books of Scripture. When the reciter visited, he taught Bertig's children out of those books. But of course only the true copies were authoritative, and sometimes common copies had to be burned because a copyist had deviated too far from the original.

Before the end of the day, Tim and Shingis returned from the village.

"They've invited us to stay the night with them," Tim said. "They want to meet you and to question you. I suppose that'll be all right."

"Nice village," Shingis said. "Like villages back home."

They all went down to the village. It had a mill on a stream that would eventually find its way south to the Imperial River, barns for the cattle, chicken coops, and little thatch-roofed houses. As small as it was, it was bigger than any settlement on Fogo Island. Low, forested hills looked over its fields.

The people were gathered to see them, the men all holding rakes and scythes—meant as weapons, Gurun thought. There were more of them than there were of the Blays, and the women and children stood in a crowd behind the men. If Gurun had known anything about warfare, she would have recognized the villagers as easy prey. The Blays did.

An old man with a wispy white beard stepped forth to greet them.

"Welcome to Jocah's Creek," he said. "We are told you come in peace. We would not have believed this, but the man of Obann swore that it was true."

"Of course it's true," Tim said. "This is Gurun, who comes from a far country in the North that I never heard of. Came here on a boat, across the sea, if you can believe it. And these men are the Blays, who come from far away in the East. We've been with them for a while, and they've done us no harm."

"I can see the girl is as you said: not Obannese," the old man said. "My name is Loyk. I'm headman here. There's no one else to speak for us. The nearest chamber house is in a town called Humber, fifteen miles down the creek. The reciter hasn't come here for two weeks. No one knows when he will come again."

"What's the nearest city with an oligarch and a militia?" Tim asked.

"You'd have to go all the way to Trywath."

Gurun spoke up. "Loyk, my people come in friendship. If you let us stay, you may have need of us someday. My Blays can work, but they can fight, too."

"They came to Obann as enemies," Loyk said. "They

came here in the army of the Heathen."

"They're on their own now," Gurun said.

Loyk gave her a cold, hard smile. "I'm afraid we all are, these days."

Gurun, Tim, and Shingis supped with Loyk and his sons and their wives and children. There was hardly room for all of them in Loyk's house, although it was the biggest house in the village. The rest of the Blays, by twos, were guests at other houses. Shingis promised Gurun they'd behave themselves.

"Usually it would be impossible for us to feed so many guests," Loyk said, "but this year's harvest was the best we've ever known. We have more than enough to carry us through the winter."

"Provided we're not burned out by brigands," Loyk's eldest son said.

Already several villages that they knew of had been wiped out by marauders. From Obann, the Thunder King's host had fled in all directions. There wasn't enough militia to protect any but the biggest towns.

"We've heard the Temple's gone—destroyed by fire, and the First Prester killed," Loyk said. "How such a thing could happen, no one knows. The great city still stands, but how long can it last without the Temple? The heart of Obann has been cut out.

"We have no one now to lead us in our prayers. No prester will set foot outside a walled town. Nor can we farmers leave our lands. But we have heard, Gurun, that you lead prayers and know the Scriptures like a prester. Tim said that where you come from, there are no presters. You pray now for these Heathen men. Maybe you can pray for us."

"In my country we all pray for ourselves," Gurun said. "My father leads the prayers when our family prays together, but anyone can pray whenever he pleases. God hears everybody's prayers."

"She ain't a Heathen, though," Tim said. "That's just how her people do things, not knowing any better. But their Scripture is the same as ours. Recite the Song for him, Gurun."

Many of the islanders memorized verses as laid down in the true copies of the holy books, even if they didn't understand the ancient language. They had the Sacred Songs exactly as King Ozias wrote them, centuries ago. Anyone who'd ever attended services at a chamber house would recognize Ozias' Song of the Lion, as Gurun spoke it:

> When I was alone in an uninhabited land,
> The lion caught my scent and roared.
> Behold, I had no hiding place,
> Far from the forest where my mother raised me:
> Nor could I return, for fear of my enemies.
> I called upon my Lord, who heard my voice:
> Who preserved me in the desert land;
> Who made the lion to flee before my face.
> My every hope is in my Lord, and my salvation.

That was as far as Gurun had learned the Song. The ancient language was difficult. But Loyk and his family listened reverently and bowed their heads over their table.

"The prester himself, in the chamber house in Trywath, couldn't have spoken it better!" Loyk's wife said.

"We will assemble tomorrow to decide whether you and your men can stay with us all winter," Loyk said. "As for me, I think that would be a good thing, and I'll say so. I have heard your recitation of the Song, and it is good."

"What else can we do?" said one of the sons. "There's no Temple anymore. There could be fighting here tomorrow. If these men will fight for us, we'll need them."

"You feed us, we fight," Shingis said. He'd been fed roast chicken, and he liked it. "Our Queen Gurun, she will pray for you. Pray to the All-Father."

Loyk shook his head and sighed. "These are evil times we're living in. Some of us believe the harvest was so good this year because it was the very last one we'll ever have. We shall need prayers as much as we'll need fighting men—and maybe more."

Gurun didn't understand why so many people in Obann had a notion that the world was coming to an end, but at least now she would have a place to spend the winter. She wondered how these above-ground houses would stand up to the winter. It seemed foolhardy not to plant one's dwelling deeply in the ground.

An inner voice reminded her, "Don't forget what the filgya said. You are to go to Obann and see the king. You can't sit here all winter."

She wondered when the Blays would let her go.

CHAPTER 12

Into the East

The trail Helki was following ended at an abandoned barn, where it was erased by the scuff-marks of at least a hundred men. There was no telling whose those were, but Helki thought they must have been Griffs.

"Martis let those two men get away," he said to Cavall, "and I guess they ran for help. Looks to me like this bunch must have grabbed Martis and the kids. But look here—their trail runs east. Funny they didn't head back to Obann, where their army was."

The hound looked up at him. Helki always talked to animals, probably more than he talked to people. It didn't bother him that they never talked back. He usually knew what they were thinking.

"What do you say, boy? Should we follow this crowd?"

Cavall wagged his tail. Helki nodded to him, and they trotted after the hundred men. What he would do when he caught up to them, he'd decide later. It was an old trail, rained on once or twice, but to Helki it was as plain as a highway. He and Cavall would have to push themselves hard to gain ground. But at least it looked like only one of the men was on horseback, the rest on foot. A hundred men can't go as fast as one, he thought.

Crows cawed at him from a nearby tree. "We see you,

we see you!" was the meaning of their call. "We know you're a stranger here." Helki grinned at them and saluted them with his staff. He answered with a crow-call that no one could have told from the real thing.

It was good to get away from cities!

Back in Obann, King Ryons would have agreed with that sentiment.

He was busy this morning receiving an oath of allegiance from several dozen Wallekki who'd surrendered to his cavalry. Chief Shaffur spoke up for them.

"These men are of the Serpent Clan of the Wal Hazoof, my king," he said. "Their obedience to the Thunder King was forced: he was drying up their wells. But the Wal Hazoof have never been known as oath-breakers. I believe they'll be true to us."

There was no royal palace in Obann. The surviving oligarchs had given up their administration building, and the king now held his audiences in its assembly hall. Ryons had never dreamed so much space could be enclosed by four walls and a ceiling. There were paintings on the walls—gigantic men and horses—and even on the ceiling: gilded suns and many-colored clouds. Sitting on an ivory throne that was much too big for him, looking up at the warlike pictures, Ryons wondered if he were dreaming. This great hall, he thought, made people look unnaturally small. It gave him a very funny feeling.

Obst asked Shaffur, "Do these men understand that they will be fighting in the service of the living God, as do we all?"

"They've been told we serve the Great God," Shaffur said. "Of course, they know nothing of Him yet. At home they worshipped the sun god and the moon. The sun and the moon are still in the sky, but the gods who inhabited them have been taken away. Except for the Thunder King himself, who is no god, these are men who have no gods. This distresses them, and they are eager to know the True God who cannot be taken away—who sent a beast to route the strongest army in the world. That they saw, and they remember."

Obst turned to Ryons. "It then remains for Your Majesty to accept their oaths and grant them amnesty for all they've done against Obann, on condition that they serve God loyally."

"I do," said Ryons, as he'd been coached to say, "in God's name."

Lord, he prayed silently, am I to be doing things like this for the rest of my life?

He was sure he didn't want to.

Hlah, the son of Spider, had a long, long way to go before he reached his home. The Abnaks lived among the foothills and forests on the east side of the mountains, so he would have to traverse nearly the whole breadth of Obann.

Young and strong, he could trot all day, eating up the miles. He traveled south of the Imperial River, parallel to its course but not in sight of it. He ate and drank what he could find each day. The land would be full of stragglers from the Thunder King's army, many of whom had turned bandit. To a city man, it would have seemed a hopeless journey; but the Abnaks have no cities. His only shelter, most nights, was a leather bag lined inside with wool, in which he wrapped himself: it had been treated with deer fat to shed water. For weapons he had his stone tomahawk and a long, curved knife.

He didn't fret about the dangers he could expect to encounter on the way. "If it's God's will that I get there, I'll get there," he said to himself. Time and again God had saved King Ryons' little army, and from such desperate dangers, that it now seemed natural to Hlah to put his trust in Him. Besides which, he thought, "Anyone who wants my scalp will have to earn it!"

With no such hopes did Prester Orth continue on his eastward journey. He was losing his nerve, and he was sure Lord Reesh knew it.

"Play the man, Orth," Reesh said. "I've chosen you to succeed me as First Prester. There's no one else.

"I won't live much longer. And the Thunder King, for all his people believe him to be otherwise, is mortal. But the Temple will endure forever."

Brave words, Orth thought. But even the First Prester's nerve was challenged one day, when their escort caught a young man, hardly more than a boy, trapping eels among the reeds.

"It's time we offered a sacrifice," Mardar Kyo said. "You and your people, Excellency, will not want to witness it. I'll leave the coach here and go on ahead a little ways. A few of the men will stay with you."

All the Scriptures condemned human sacrifice as an

abomination. It had not been practiced in Obann since the days of the apostate kings put down by Ozias.

"It's necessary," the mardar said. "By this sacrifice we shall discover whether we are to cross the mountains in the winter or wait until the spring. I'd hoped to cross this winter, but there are already clouds on the mountains that mean snow."

Reesh only nodded. Leading their captive with a rope around his neck, Kyo and his men rode off. Gallgoid came down from the roof of the coach.

"What are we going to do?" Orth said.

"Do? There is absolutely nothing we can do!" Reesh answered.

"But it's an abomination! And what if they expect us to do the same, in that new Temple that they've built for us?"

"No sense howling before we're bitten," Gallgoid said. "Be thankful it's not one of us, Prester."

From somewhere in the distance, screams rang out. They wouldn't stop.

Orth clenched his eyes shut and pressed his hands to his ears, but he couldn't shut out the screams. Nor could he shut out the knowledge that he had sinned, that he was a party to this worst of all abominations. The young man being murdered was his countryman, a member of a congregation of a chamber house.

For the first time in his life, Orth sensed the vastness of the living God, like a great mountain cloaked in darkness. "I was wrong, I was wrong, I was wrong!" he thought. He had sold himself to evil, and God knew it. The mountain that was God was everywhere.

The screams went on and on. Inwardly Orth screamed,

too. The prophets that they'd hanged in Obann's public squares rose from their graves to accuse him. Yes, he'd given his consent to that—and preached in favor of it from the pulpit. How grandly his voice had resonated in the chapel! How the people had hung on his words! Yes, those people, his congregation—the people whom he and the First Prester had betrayed. And the God he didn't believe in sent a monstrous beast to save the city. His treason had been all for nothing.

Damned, damned, he was damned—

"Prester Orth!"

Reesh seized Orth's elbow and shook it, hard. The screams had stopped. Orth opened his eyes. He and Reesh were still sitting in the coach, on cushions.

"It's over, Prester," Gallgoid said. "At least we didn't have to see it."

"Pull yourself together!" Reesh said.

Sweat poured down Orth's face, "My lord," he said, controlling himself with grievous difficulty, "we have sinned an abominable sin."

"Save it for the seminary," Reesh said. "Do you think anyone can be First Prester without sinning? Don't be a fool.

"Man cannot attain his rightful greatness without the Temple, and that's all that matters. I thought you understood."

Folly, Orth thought. You collect bits of rubbish from the ruins of the Empire and treat it like fine jewels, and you delude yourself. If the men of that age were so great, why is there nothing left of their greatness but useless pieces of trash? Why did they perish? You say they flew through the air, and sailed the seas, and spoke to one another over great distances as if they sat across a table from each other—but did any of that save them? Where are they now, First Prester? Why should we try to emulate a civilization that has utterly died out?

But of course he couldn't bring himself to say any of those things: not to Lord Reesh, of whom he was now mortally afraid.

"Abomination!" he muttered.

"Yes, yes, to be sure," Reesh said. "But it must not be imagined that bloody pagan practices shall long outlive the Thunder King. The future, Orth, the future—fix your mind on the future. It's all that matters. It's all there is. Live for the future of mankind. We are the keepers of that future. There's no one else, and we must succeed—so brace up!"

Orth nodded—anything to stop all this talking. He didn't want to hear any more. So he pretended to understand and to agree, and Lord Reesh let him.

CHAPTER 13

Oziah's Wood

In the end they decided to seek refuge in Oziah's Wood.

It was Martis' idea. "From all I've heard," he said, "there are no enemy warriors in the wood. No Heathen army ever went into it. Anyone we meet in there is likely to be a friend. And whether we decide to go to Ninneburky, or on to the mountains, we'll be safer going through Oziah's Wood."

"Yes—let's go there!" Ellayne said. "That was where King Ozias himself stayed, after they drove him out of Obann City. His enemies couldn't get him there. Ever since then there's been a blessing on the wood, my father says."

"I've been there with Van," Jack said. His stepfather, the carter, often had errands that took him a short ways into Oziah's Wood. "It's different from Lintum Forest. You don't feel scared by anything in there."

Chillith didn't care. "Where can I go, but where you lead me?" he said. He'd now been blind for two nights and a day. "Your people in the wood will probably kill me."

"No one's going to kill you," Martis said.

It was with a sense of homecoming that the children followed Martis across the Chariot. He knew a ford where the water was only ankle-deep. From the southern border of the wood, it was only a day's journey to Ninneburky, provided you could get a ferry across the Imperial.

The bed of the Chariot was stony. Chillith would have stumbled and fallen many times without Martis' help. Jack and Ellayne rode Dulayl, with Wytt perched atop the load on Ham the donkey's back.

"We're going home!" Ellayne said. "I feel like I've been away forever, and yet it hasn't even been a full year. My mother will scream when she sees Wytt! She might even faint."

But for Jack there was only Van to come back to, and he wasn't looking forward to that. He hadn't once missed Van, and he was sure Van hadn't missed him. On the whole, he'd rather go back to Obann where Obst was and Helki.

"I know what you're thinking," Ellayne said. "Cheer up! Do you think you're going to go back to that old pill of a carter, after what we've done? Don't you know we're going to be famous? More famous than Abombalbap!"

Jack didn't even know what "famous" meant. There weren't any famous people in Ninneburky. He was just the carter's stepson. He and Ellayne had carried out the mission God had given them, and now it was over.

"First thing," Ellayne said, "you're going to come and live with us. Once I tell him about you, my father will want you to. Martis can live with us, too, if he wants."

"And what about Chillith?" Jack said. "Won't it get kind of crowded in your house?"

"No—not Chillith. Martis can figure out what to do with him."

Hard on Chillith, Jack thought. But then the whole business was just silly.

"I'm not going to let you be unhappy, Jack."

"I'll be unhappy if I want to."

"You'll see what a fool you are, when they have a parade for us."

Jack didn't bother to answer.

Martis hurried them along, and by noon the next day they were under the eaves of Oziah's Wood. It was mostly oak trees, and all their leaves were gold. Jays greeted the travelers with raucous music. Helki would have said they were complaining.

"We have woods like this in my country," Chillith said. "I remember the smell of them, and the birds sound just the same. But I'll never see any of it."

"You have to trust in God," Ellayne said. "You've been a bad man, Chillith. God could've struck you dead, but He didn't. And that makes me wonder if He's saving you for something else. Something important. You may be blind, but you're not dead."

"The blind man is rebuked by children," Chillith said. Ellayne wanted to say she was sorry, that she hadn't said it to be mean; but something made her hold her peace. Even so, she believed in what she'd said. Hadn't God sent her and Jack up to the top of Bell Mountain? And to all kinds of other places she never would have dreamed of going to. Why shouldn't God do things like that with Chillith?

"Someday, Chillith, I'll tell you the story of my life," Martis said. "Whatever you've done, I've done worse. I didn't believe in God for most of my life; but now I know I never take a breath without Him. That's how I live."

"When didn't you believe in God?" Jack asked.

Martis smiled. "When I was a servant of the Temple!"

There were paths all throughout Oziah's Wood, some of them nearly as wide and well-traveled as country lanes. Hunters, trappers, and loggers used them. Martis stuck to a beaten path that led toward the center of the forest. When the day drew to a close, they made camp on it.

They'd just gotten their fire going when two buckskin-clad woodsmen came up the path from the opposite direction. Martis waved to them.

"Come and sit with us," he said, "and tell us the news of the wood."

"We will, once you tell us who you are and what you're doing here," said the elder of the two men, a greybeard.

"Not much to tell," said Martis. "There's a war on, and we've come here to get away from it. We're from Caristun. My name is Martis, and these are my grandsons, Jack and Layne." They kept Ellayne's bright blond hair cut short and said she was a boy. It was safer that way: Jack and Ellayne had come to that conclusion themselves long before they'd met Martis.

"What about him?" said the younger woodsman, clean-shaven. "He looks like a Griff to me." The hair on Chillith's head was growing back.

"He is," Martis answered, "but there's no harm in him. God has stricken him blind, so we've been taking care of him. His name is Chillith."

The two strangers exchanged a look. "You won't mind if we're careful about this," the older man said. "All of us here in Oziah's Wood have sworn an oath together to keep the enemy out. If any Heathen do get in, we make sure they don't get out again. My name is Bibb, and this is Deffit. We're scouting for a band of rangers camped not far from here."

They sat down by the fire, declining offers of food. They had plenty of their own, they said, without borrowing from travelers. The wood fed them in abundance.

"We caught a Heathen rider, just the other day," Bibb said, "but we can't get any sense out of him. He doesn't understand our language, and we don't know what he is—not a Griff, not a Wallekki, nor any kind of Heathen we've ever seen before. We'd string him up, but first we'd like to know what he was doing here."

"I speak Wallekki," Martis said. "I might be able to get something out of him, if he speaks it, too."

"I speak many of the languages of the East," Chillith said.

"Well, then, that's a piece of luck for us," Deffit said. "We won't ask you to break camp, after you've been hiking all day and you're all settled down for the night. But tomorrow morning you can pay us a visit."

"We'll be happy to," Martis said.

"Good!" Bibb said. He got up again. "Just keep to this path, and we'll meet you and guide you to our camp. Some of our lads will be on patrol during the night, so you and your kids can feel safe. We'll go on ahead now and tell our friends about you. Come on, Deffit."

After the rangers left, Chillith said, "They'll probably want to hang me, too, along with their prisoner."

"We won't let them," Martis said.

"And anyhow, they're not like that!" Ellayne said. "My brother is a logging foreman, and he comes here all the time. So I ought to know."

Chillith shrugged. "War is war," he said.

They spent a peaceful night. In the morning Bibb met them on the trail and led them up a side path.

Ten rangers had a camp in a clearing by a little brook, living in tiny makeshift cabins. A few deerskins were stretched on frames to dry. A couple of donkeys and a horse were tethered to a line between two trees. Ham, the donkey that Jack and Ellayne had taken from a tinker who'd tried to sell them into slavery, brayed a greeting to the other donkeys.

Somewhere nearby, Jack and Ellayne knew, Wytt was watching over them from a hiding place in the underbrush. It was a good thing, Jack thought, that the rangers didn't have a dog.

The men, having been told to expect visitors, were all waiting for them and for news of the outside world. Sitting on the ground with his wrists and ankles bound was the prisoner, silent and impassive. Bibb introduced the newcomers.

"We have trappers' tea, if you'd like a cup," he said. "And then we can get down to business."

It was good to be here, Jack thought, as he sipped his tea—better than home. Maybe when the war was over, he'd become a ranger. It was good to hear men talking who sounded like they'd grown up in Ninneburky, and a few of them probably had.

"Are you ready to try to talk to the prisoner?" Deffit said, after they had all had tea. "I don't think he's in a chatty mood; but then he never is."

"If I could see him, I would know what he is," Chillith

said. "Men of many nations have come west over the mountains. He must belong to one of them. Take us to him."

Martis and Deffit led him to the prisoner, Jack and Ellayne following with the rangers. The prisoner glared up at them. He was a small man, dark and wiry. Chillith sat down in front of him.

He tried several languages, and then one of them turned out to be right, and the prisoner replied. They exchanged some words together.

"He is of the Shoto people," Chillith said, "from the western shores of the Great Lakes. His name is Arvaush."

"Ask him what he was doing in the wood," Bibb said.

Chillith asked and got an answer. Then their talk became more lively—back and forth at first, but soon the prisoner was doing all the talking, and Chillith all the listening. The Griff sat as motionless as a stone, taking it all in.

Sweat began to show on his face. The muscles around his jaws clenched themselves. The rangers grew impatient.

"For heaven's sake, what is it?" Deffit cried. "What's he telling you? Out with it, man!"

Chillith seemed not to hear him. Martis knelt beside him and grasped his shoulder. The Griff flinched, then turned to him, wide-eyed even in his blindness.

"Martis! The boy's dream—it was even exactly as he dreamed it—"

"Tell us what the man was saying, Chillith."

Chillith shuddered. He licked his lips, which had gone dry.

"This man, Arvaush, was at the siege of Obann," he said. "The Thunder King's army is no more, even as Jack dreamed it the night I was struck blind. This man saw everything. A monster like a walking mountain came out of the river and destroyed the army. Thousands were killed, and thousands more scattered in all directions. Arvaush was bringing the news eastward, and he entered this forest as a shortcut.

"The city stands. It is a miracle! Our troops were in the city, thousands of them. They opened the gates to the army. They burned the great Temple of the Obann God. And yet the city stands, and the great army is no more."

He stopped to take deep breaths. His face had gone deathly pale. Around him the rangers stood as men transfixed.

"What do you mean, they burned the Temple?" Martis said.

"The rulers of the Temple let our warriors in by secret passages: that was how they got into the city. That was the plan. To create panic in the city, they set fire to the Temple. Then they opened some of the city's gates from the inside. Warriors came storming in. The city should have fallen. But the great beast came out of the river and made the army mad with fear. It had a boy riding on its back—at least that's what Arvaush thinks he saw. Warriors slew each other by the thousands, trying to escape."

"Wait!" Martis cried. He looked as though he was going to faint, Ellayne thought. "The rulers of the Temple let the Heathen in? Is that what you said?"

"Arvaush says so," Chillith answered. "And a week ago he overtook a coach traveling east, protected by riders under the command of a mardar. In that coach was a passenger. Arvaush saw him: an old man, fat and white-haired, with a wrinkled face. It was the First Prester of Obann—the mardar said so. They were taking him to Kara Karram, where the

Thunder King has built a new Temple. It's been many years in the building and is finished now. Maybe the old man is to be First Prester there and a servant of the Thunder King. That would be his reward for betraying the city."

The rangers stared at each other, speechless. Jack and Ellayne stared at each other, too. Many times had Martis told them that the First Prester was a wicked man. Ellayne had never quite believed it. After all, the First Prester—the holiest of all God's servants in Obann—how could it be?

"Tell us the rest," Martis said.

Chillith wiped his face with both hands and spoke to Arvaush. The prisoner answered: he would have waved his hands in sweeping gestures, had his wrists not been tied together. When he'd finished, Chillith translated.

"He says the fire in the city, where the Temple burned, rose all the way to heaven. But when he looked again from a hilltop some miles distance, a heavy rain was falling and the fire had gone out. The city was saved. Arvaush heard from other fugitives that the Temple was completely destroyed, but that the fire hadn't spread to the rest of the city.

"That's all he knows. All he wants now is to go home, and never come again to Obann. He believes the Obann God has cursed the Thunder King. He's very much afraid."

Silence fell over the rangers' camp. At last Bibb said, "These are the worst tidings that were ever heard in my time. No Temple! What shall we do? It's not the Heathen that God has cursed, but us."

The men murmured their agreement. Martis stood up, steadied himself with a hand on Chillith's shoulder. The Griff sat with his head bowed, as one who mourns.

"There's no call to lose heart, friends," Martis said.

"There may not be a Temple anymore, but God has saved the city, and He has true servants everywhere—never more than now. Obann the city has survived, and the enemy is broken. You'll be hearing from God's servants, and they will know what to say to you. But I know now."

He looked beaten, Jack thought, like he was when they'd led him down from the summit of Bell Mountain.

Ellayne squeezed Jack's hand. "I wish Obst were here!" she said. "He'd know what to say."

Jack wanted to tell these men that it wasn't as bad as it looked, not by a long shot, that they'd found missing books of Scripture, written by King Ozias in his own hand. But it was too much to tell at this time. Maybe later.

"Gentlemen," said Martis, "we have given you this prisoner's tidings. I would recommend you don't hang him. But for the time being, I want to be left alone—except for Chillith." He prodded the Griff's shoulder. "Come, friend. I need you."

Puzzled, Chillith let Martis help him up and lead him away. Jack and Ellayne tried to follow, but Martis didn't let them.

"Not now," he said.

He and Chillith passed out of sight of the camp. "Let them go," said Bibb, "and God have mercy on our country! How are we to live without the Temple?"

No one answered. No one knew.

Out of sight and earshot of the camp, Martis told Chillith the story of his life: how Lord Reesh took him in, a young cutpurse from the streets, taught him to read and write, made him an assassin in his service and the Temple's, how he committed murder, suborned and corrupted witnesses—anything the First Prester asked of him, he did.

"It was for the greater good, always," he said. "I let my master decide what that greater good was, and did whatever he required of me. It was all for the Temple, and the Temple was everything. And then he sent me to Bell Mountain."

Chillith interrupted. "Your grandson, Layne, is a girl," he said. "I don't suppose either of them is your grandson, or any natural kin of yours."

It took Martis a moment to recover from surprise. "How do you know that?" he said.

"I know. It's clear to me now. You've never had a wife, never any children of your own. You have no family, Martis. All you ever had was the Temple."

"It's true," Martis said. "If any man could be called my father, it would be Lord Reesh. He was my master, the First Prester: the servant of God, God's steward, the keeper of the Temple. And he destroyed the Temple. All those terrible things we did, he and I, all in the service of the Temple—and all for nothing. He has betrayed the Temple."

"You loved him very much," Chillith said. Those words were like an arrow coming out of nowhere to slam quivering into the target. Martis flinched.

"Yes," he said. "That's true, too. I did love him. I never thought of it, but I suppose I did. But hear the rest of my story, while I have the nerve to tell it."

He told Chillith how the First Prester had sent him to find the children who were going to Bell Mountain, to follow them up the mountain and stop them from ringing the bell, if indeed the bell was there. He was to kill them, if that was the only way to stop them. Otherwise he was to capture them and take them back to Lord Reesh, where they would be murdered when the First Prester had finished with them.

"But I couldn't complete my mission," he said. "God laid His hand on me. I was given a reprieve. And yet God's noose is around my neck, and I am conscious of His mercy every day. I protect those two children now and would give my life for them. That's what my new master requires of me."

Chillith tried to see him, but of course he couldn't.

"So they rang the bell, those two—the bell that was heard in all the countries of the East," he said. "No man knew what it was or what it meant. The Thunder King's mardars forbade anyone to speak of it."

"God's bell," Martis said. "Ozias put it there, so that God would hear it someday. And I believe He has. The world is changing."

"And meanwhile the Thunder King has given your old master a new Temple," Chillith said.

"So it seems!" Martis clenched his fists. "I want to follow Reesh there, to his new Temple," he said, "and there, to his face, perform my last act as an assassin. Let him be destroyed by the weapon he himself made."

They sat in silence for a little while.

"Why have you told me all these things?" Chillith asked.

"Because the hand of God is on you, as it is on me."

"If you go to Kara Karram, how will you protect the children?"

"Drop them off at Ninneburky, where they belong, and

go on without them," Martis said. "Alone, if I have to. But I thought you might come with me."

Chillith smiled, and this time there was warmth in it.

"I will," he said. "Do you remember when we first met, and I said we might be friends, were it not my duty to put you to death? There was always something that drew me to you, as a friend. We shall go to Kara Karram as brothers, you and I. Probably the Thunder King will kill us both."

They shared a quiet laugh over that.

"Tell me one thing, though," Martis said. "Do you still believe the Thunder King to be a god?"

Chillith shrugged. "If he is," he said, "he is an evil god, and the world would be a better place without him.

"The God of Obann performed a miracle to save His city. He let the Temple be destroyed because it was rotten at its heart and served itself, not Him. He made me blind; but here in the country of my enemies He has raised up friends and protection for me. It shames me now that I ever served the Thunder King. Your God now shall be my God."

CHAPTER 14

The Blays in Battle

No sooner had the Blays been accepted by the people of Jocah's Creek, and given space in several families' houses and barns until some new houses could be built, than they started scouting the countryside. They needed to learn the lay of the land, and it was needful to patrol for enemies.

"These people lucky nobody come and kill them yet," Shingis said to Gurun. "Easy to take this place. We could, if we want. They make no protecting for themselves."

"You will have to teach them how," Gurun said.

"You bet! My country, bad men always try to steal food and girls. Village people always have to fight."

Some of the young men went out patrolling with the Blays. They couldn't speak with them, and they were hard-put to keep up with them.

"Those men run like deer!" they complained to Loyk, after the first day. Their legs and feet were sore, but most of them went out again the next day.

Meanwhile, the women and the older men were putting up a fence around the village. Shingis would inspect it in the evening when he came back from patrol and explain to Loyk what more would have to be done, or undone.

"Make fence so horses can't come in too fast," he said. "Also, men can move behind fences and enemy outside can't see them."

The fence went up quickly, but after three days' work, Tim didn't think much of it.

"Look how flimsy it is," he said to Gurun. "Anyone could knock it down."

"I know nothing of these things," Gurun said, "but Shingis does. Leave it to him."

In the evening she recited Sacred Songs for the villagers and prayed for them. A few of the old men and women said it wasn't right to pray without a prester, and didn't attend the services.

"Don't mind them," Loyk said. "I've never known anything to make them happy. Everyone else is very pleased."

The Obannese had very peculiar ideas about prayer, Gurun thought. But in light of the ancient traditions of the wickedness of the South, it was something that they believed in God at all.

A few of the Blays slept during the day and patrolled all night. When they woke, they helped supervise the building of the fence. In three days the villagers knew all the Blays by name, and the Blays knew many of the villagers' names. The children followed them around at every opportunity. When they weren't following the Blays, they followed Gurun. She told them stories of Fogo Island; and as she had grown up with three younger brothers, the children's company made her happy.

Three days they had to strengthen the village. As dawn was breaking on the fourth day, one of the scouts came running with an alarm. Tim woke Shingis to translate, and Shingis woke Loyk, who sent his sons to rouse everybody else.

"Wallekki riders coming," Shingis said, "eight of them.

They look hungry, dirty. Bad men."

He made most of the women and all of the children hide in the houses closest to the center of the village. The men were to take farm implements and hide behind the fence.

"Any horse come in," he said, "you men must fight, all at once."

"But the bandits will be on horseback!" one of the men protested.

"No matter," Shingis said. "Five, six men with rakes fight one man on horse, they kill him quick."

The sun was just rising when the riders emerged from a stand of trees and came clattering down a hill, heading straight for the village. They brandished spears and whooped.

Gurun, with a sturdy hoe in her hands, waited to see what the Blays would do. She'd never been in a fight before, but island women were expected to defend their homes from outlaws, side by side with their men. It didn't happen often, but there were many historical songs and stories about it.

On came the marauders. The villagers trembled. The Blays crouched behind the fence, uncoiling their slings, checking their supplies of stones. When the riders were within fifty yards of the fence, the Blays ran out through the gaps, cheering, whirling their slings above their heads.

It was over fast. The slung stones flew through the air, and the eight saddles were emptied in a moment. Two of the bandits never rose again. The rest of them died before they could collect themselves and make a stand, brought down by the Blays' short, stabbing spears. The victors then scattered to catch the horses, which took longer than the battle. They led the horses back in triumph, singing barbarous songs and dancing little jigs.

"We've won!" cried Loyk's eldest son. "The bandits are all dead!"

"Did you see that?" cried another man. "The bandits never had a chance. My, how those stones did fly!"

The whole village rejoiced, the children coming out to dance around the Blays, the men cheering and thumping them on the backs and shoulders. Gurun laid down her hoe and joined the headman.

"There, Loyk," she said. "I told you they could fight, and now your village is richer by eight horses. But someone will have to bury the dead."

"That task won't distress us," the headman said. "But what if it had been twenty horsemen, or thirty? This country isn't safe anymore."

"My men will teach your people how to fight," Gurun said. "The rest is in the hands of God."

CHAPTER 15

The Legacy of the Temple

Back in Obann, Obst did not know what to do.

An entire seminary class had just walked out on him. As the young men pushed their way out of the lecture hall, he heard them mutter words like "heretic" and "blasphemy" and "crazy old fool."

"What you say is out-and-out paganism!" a student spoke up, as Obst tried to finish his talk. "The only thing to do is to rebuild the Temple, and the sooner, the better. As for your so-called rediscovered books of Scripture"—the student snapped his fingers loudly—"you'll have to do a lot better than that to fool anybody here!"

Another young man stood up from his seat and shook his fist. "You made up that story about the First Prester—didn't you! As if you could be First Prester in his place!"

"You aren't even ordained," said another. And then they all got up and left.

After a few minutes of standing alone in the hall, Obst went outside and sat alone on a bench by the door. That was where Uduqu found him.

"You look a bit glum, Teacher," the old savage said. He sat down beside him and belched. "At least it's a sunny afternoon. At our age, that counts for something. Much too nice a day to be indoors. But what's the matter?"

Obst tried to tell him. "Ironic, isn't it?" he said. "The people to whom God first delivered His Scriptures have closed their ears to His message; but men who were born Heathen, knowing nothing of God—they listen. Now the seminarians are accusing me, not the First Prester, of betraying the Temple to the Thunder King. I knew nothing about it until I heard it from the lips of prisoners taken in the city. That's how they got into Obann—through the Temple. Lord Reesh let them in. But it seems fewer and fewer of the people are able to believe it."

"Why should the prisoners lie?" Uduqu said.

"They're telling the truth, of course. But the seminarians won't listen."

"Take the scalps off a few of them, and the rest will be more attentive."

"You'll be First Prester before I will, Chief!"

Uduqu's throaty chuckle raised Obst's spirits.

"It's hard for people to change their ways," Obst said. "The Temple lies in ruins, but it still rules the people's minds. All their lives they've been taught to believe that only a prester ordained by the Temple can present their prayers to God. There's nothing about that in the Scriptures—but it's been a long time since the Temple accurately taught the Scriptures. That's why I left the Temple and became a hermit. The people were allowed to believe they couldn't know their God, except through the Temple."

"But that's just foolishness," Uduqu said. "You taught us to pray before we ever set out for Obann. You taught us God would hear us; and we believed you, because we knew that only God could have saved us from our enemies those many times. We all pray to Him now, every day.

"Soon I'll be able to read the Scriptures for myself—me, an Abnak! If I can, surely all these city people can. What's the matter with them?"

"Nothing that's their fault," Obst said. "But I was counting on those seminarians to make copies of the Scriptures, especially of those that Jack and Ellayne found in the cellars of the First Temple, written in King Ozias' own hand and missing for so many centuries. Those must be copied as soon as can be.

"The seminarians say we must rebuild the Temple. And so we shall, but not in stone. God's word itself must be our Temple—preached everywhere, taught everywhere, read and studied everywhere. That's the kind of Temple that can't be destroyed."

Uduqu shook his head. "Even if I'd never seen anything else," he said, "when I saw that gigantic beast trampling the Thunder King's army, with little Ryons on its back—why, that would've been enough to make me believe. I don't understand these city people. God makes a miracle to save them from certain death, and they all see it with their own eyes, and all they can do is cry buckets over their cusset Temple—when it was the Temple that betrayed them! Good riddance, if you ask me."

A few children came walking up the street. When they spied Uduqu, they ran to him, faces shining with delight.

"Uduqu, Uduqu!" they cried. "Two men with one blow!"

The old chief growled and made a ferocious face at them. Squealing with pretended terror, they fled back down the street, laughing, giggling, and growling ferociously at each other. It made Obst smile.

"At least the children are with us!" he said.

"And they'll be grown up someday," said Uduqu, "when all these fools are dead and gone."

By Obst's direction, Dyllyd taught King Ryons from the Scriptures, reading to the boy until he could learn to read them for himself. "A king must know many things," Obst said, "but the most important thing for him to know is God's word and the laws of God. A king who does not submit himself to God's laws will only be a tyrant."

Every day Dyllyd read him a fascicle out of the Book of Beginnings and taught him how to write the names of whatever important personages were mentioned in the text. So Ryons learned his letters.

He also learned how God made the heavens and the earth, and all that was in them—the mountains and the trees, sun and moon and stars, all living things, and man himself. "He made the things that are out of things that are not," Dyllyd read. "He uttered His voice and the sun shone, and gave warmth. He set the limits of the sea, and raised the mountains out of dust."

Ryons was born a slave among the Wallekki and grew up without even a name to call his own. The masters' gods were not for slaves, but often he saw the masters burning incense or sacrificing doves to one or another of their gods. It might be a figure carved from wood or stones, or a tree, or a pile of rocks. They asked these gods to increase their herds, to give them many sons, and for revenge upon their enemies. When such gifts were not forthcoming, they would turn to yet another god.

No one taught the slave child about the gods, any more than they would have taught a goat. He was more interested in finding food and avoiding beatings than in learning about the gods. There were so many of them, and it never seemed to him that any of them were very important. He certainly never heard that they created the earth itself. It never came into his head to wonder where the world came from, or anything he saw in it. It was all just there.

But this God was important! This God, Obst said, created him and knew him by his name. This was a God that even a slave could pray to—indeed, that even a slave must love and honor, and fear. And certainly—Obst said so—this God had plucked him out of slavery and made him King of Obann, had saved him from a hundred perils, and had put him atop a giant beast that had no name to save the city at the moment it was about to be destroyed. It made Ryons dizzy just to think of Him.

With his mind awakening to questions that he'd never imagined could be asked, Ryons ventured one to Dyllyd.

"Where did God come from?" he asked. "I mean, if God made the world, and everything else, where could He have been before there was a world?"

Dyllyd smiled. "I used to ask that very same question, Majesty," he said, "and my teacher told me this: there never was a time when God was not God. Before God created it, there was no such thing as time. God had no beginning, nor will He have an end. He created beginnings and decrees the end of each created thing.

"We are flesh and blood, but God is spirit. The whole world ages, but not the God who made it. If you could look down from God's throne—just in a manner of speaking!—

all times would seem like now to you. God never changes, although everything else does.

"So it's no use to ask where God came from—until God made all places in heaven and on earth, there was no where. I know that's hard to understand. Most things about God are."

Ryons wondered what Uduqu would say about a thing like that; he'd skipped his lesson today.

"It's not hard to understand," Ryons said. "It's impossible!"

"It can't be helped," said Dyllyd. "It would be easier for a fly to understand what it means to be a human being, than for a human being to understand God. He is unimaginably greater than anything we know. That's why all Scripture teaches us to love Him, and to trust Him, and to walk by faith and not by sight."

"What does that mean!" Ryons cried.

Dyllyd rubbed his face and sighed. "Whew! You'll make a theologian of me yet, Your Majesty! If I can explain these things, and you can understand them, by the time you grow to manhood, we will have both done well. In the meantime, the best thing you can do is learn the Scriptures."

When he next saw Uduqu, Ryons tried to tell the sub-chief what he'd learned that day—or rather not quite succeeded in learning.

"I won't live long enough to wrap my mind around such things," Uduqu said. "God is God, that's all I know. It's good enough for me."

"Easy for you to say, Chief. You don't have to be a king."

"God is wiser than to make a king of me," Uduqu said.

CHAPTER 16

Two Angels

Helki met a man who'd seen the Griffs pass by. The fellow was a swineherd, but he had no pigs.

"Heathen took 'em, every one," he said. "Don't know how I'm going to make it through the winter. They burned my master's house and made off with his daughters, too. I've been hiding out, eating scraps. It's too dangerous to travel anywhere, and there's nowhere to go, anyhow.

"But I remember that bunch because they were going east instead of west, and it was before their whole army got chased away from Obann. There was a whole herd of 'em, and they were Griffs, all right. It's Griffs who do fancy things to their hair. I was up on that little hill, right up there"—he pointed to an isolated hillock crowned with trees—"and they went by right past me, down below. Good thing they didn't see me!"

"I'm looking for a man and two children," Helki said, "taken by the Griffs. Did you see them?"

"Clear as day," the swineherd said. "A man and two kids, with ropes around their necks, poor devils. But there was nothing I could do to help 'em. I don't see what you could do, either."

"I'll think of something," Helki said.

He now knew he was only a week behind the Griffs; he

and Cavall had gained several days. Griffs were pretty tireless walkers, so he was pleased with that. If only he had a horse—but then he'd never learned to ride one. He wished the swineherd luck and went on his way.

There wasn't much game in this country, and both man and hound had lost weight since beginning their chase. "It won't hurt me to tighten my belt a bit," Helki said, the next time he and Cavall stopped for a drink of water. "Life with the army was getting to be too easy, making me soft. If we starve, it'll be our own fault." Cavall wagged his tail.

Later that day, they came upon the burned-out shell of a country house. Examining the site, Helki concluded the estate must have been sacked a month ago, at least. House, stables, and sheds were all in ruins.

In the charred skeleton of one of the outbuildings, he found a brown hawk finishing off the remains of a squirrel. The hawk should have flown away as soon as it saw the man and the dog, but this one didn't. The remains of a leather strap still dangled from one of its legs. Helki whistled at it, and the hawk paused in its feeding to look at him with piercing yellow eyes.

"You're a tame bird, aren't you?" Helki said softly. "I reckon this was once your home. Not much of a home anymore, is it?"

He stretched out his arm and made a peculiar kind of high-pitched whistle: a call only known to master falconers, or to someone who'd lived in Lintum Forest all his life and several times raised baby hawks left orphaned by some misfortune to their parents. This hawk flapped its wings noisily, craned its neck, and then flew over to roost on Helki's forearm. Cavall, who'd lived his life with a solitary crone who made friends of birds and animals, held his peace. He knew how to behave with hawks.

"There, there—good girl!" Helki spoke softly to the bird, and even more softly stroked her head and breast. Her feathers were like silk. He made some other sounds that hawks make to chicks in their nests. The bird shut her eyes.

"You'll come with us," said Helki. "I might have need of you. There's nobody left for you here. And who knows? Maybe someday I'll present you as a gift to a king."

The hawk must have been hand-raised and skillfully trained by someone who'd loved her. When Helki and Cavall resumed their hunt, the hawk went with them—sometimes flying overhead, sometimes perched on Helki's forearm.

He called her Angel.

The mountains loomed in the east, and by now Prester Orth knew he would do anything rather than to cross them into the country of the Thunder King.

Orth had an angel with him, too—not a companion that he desired. He couldn't escape from it and couldn't get rid of it. He couldn't see it, but it was always there.

This was an angel from the Scriptures—from the Book of the Prophet Naiah, to be precise. Naiah saw a vision of a shadowy form, dark, with a slaughter weapon in its hand, and heard a voice from Heaven say, "Behold, a dark angel shall execute my judgment on the cities of the coast, and there shall be none that escape him." The Scripture never gave the angel's name; but Naiah prophesied against those ancient cities on the coast, and they succumbed to fire and to plague. This was in the days of King Andrech, an evil king of ancient Obann.

It had all happened a very long time ago, and men like Orth and Reesh nowadays didn't believe in angels anymore. But Orth had believed in this one, as a boy; and now, to his horror and his dread, he believed in it again. The dark angel with the slaughter weapon was waiting for him beyond the mountains. Every step they traveled into the East was a step closer to that meeting. And then the angel would slay his body, and his soul would be cast into the Pit for all eternity.

He dared not speak a word of this. Reesh would despise him for a superstitious fool. "Never mind," Reesh would say: "You'll either come to your senses when we get to the Temple, or die." And Orth would be carried by force to his meeting with the angel.

But if he could escape into the fens before they got there—into the watery fens, where he would leave no trail that could be followed—yes, that's what he would do. The other seventeen men had run away, and no one brought them back. They'd escaped. He could do the same.

He would have to be careful. Kyo posted sentries at night. But since they'd captured and sacrificed the young man with the eel pot, they hadn't seen another living soul in this country. Orth was having trouble getting any sleep at all, so he knew the sentries were dozing: there was no danger around to keep them awake. If he were quiet enough, he ought to be able to get past them. Once into the marshes, they would never find him.

If it were raining, or particularly cold, the passengers would sleep inside the coach under luxurious furs. But on warmer nights Orth and Gallgoid preferred to stretch out on the ground, cushioned on and wrapped in furs. Tonight would be seasonably cool, but by no means frigid, clear, with a full moon. "Tonight it is, then," Orth decided. "They think I've lost my nerve; they won't be watching me." Besides, Gallgoid slept like a hibernating bear, and snored.

Having made his decision, Orth felt calm and capable. When the party made camp for the night, he ate a hearty meal and laughed at Gallgoid's story of a fat and shrewish fiancée who inspired him to take service with the Temple.

In due time the camp settled down and everybody went to sleep. Orth lay huddled in his furs, feigning sleep and waiting for the sentries to doze off. Somewhere far away an owl hooted mournfully. Overhead the moon hung like a silver coin in the sky. Even the horses were quiet. Kyo worked them hard all day, and they slept soundly.

When he was satisfied there was no one left awake, Orth carefully crept out of his furs and rose to his feet. Slowly he stood erect, listening; but there was nothing to hear but the owl, and Gallgoid snoring.

Orth was a big man, but he had a gift for stealth. One step at a time he advanced toward the nearest stand of reeds, behind which he knew he'd find water. He would leave no tracks for anyone to follow.

Closer, closer; behind him, no one stirred. Orth proceeded slowly, making only little movements. He reached out with his hands to part the reeds before him. They rustled only slightly, but enough to make him go even more slowly. He would have to be especially careful about picking up his feet and putting them back down. A snapped twig would be fatal to his hopes.

But he didn't snap any twigs, and no one woke while he

made his way through the reeds. Soon enough he found the water stretched before him, inky black but shimmering all over with moonlight.

When he first stepped into it, the water was so cold that he almost cried out loud. He clamped his jaws together and went on. Careful, careful—don't stumble! Take tiny steps. There was another piece of reed-grown, mushy land just a few yards ahead, and probably another stretch of water beyond it. He would have to put as much of it as possible between him and the camp. But if a massive beast with horns could disappear into the fens, then he could, too.

Carefully he climbed out onto land again. It was only a little strip of boggy ground. By now his teeth were chattering, but Orth went on. Into the water again, and back out, and in again, deeper and deeper into the shelter of the fens, where no dark angel was—

By some miracle, no one in the camp woke up till sunrise; and by then it was too late to find any trace of the missing prester. Kyo stormed at his negligent sentries, but to no avail.

"We must continue our journey," he told Lord Reesh. "I'm sorry we can't spare the time to find your friend."

The First Prester took it well. "Better he fail us now," he said, "than after we're installed in the Temple. I'll find someone else to take his place."

"Don't look at me, my lord!" said Gallgoid. "I'm not even ordained, and my reading's none too sharp."

"Then I hereby ordain you, here and now," said Reesh. "Ride with me inside the coach today, Prester Gallgoid. You have a lot to learn before we reach the Temple."

CHAPTER 17

A Heathen Prophet

So they were going back to Ninneburky: going home. Their part in God's affairs was over.

"But what will you do now, Martis?" Ellayne wondered. "And what will Chillith do?"

They were going to journey through Oziah's Wood and come out on the banks of the Imperial, across from Ninneburky. The rangers made a map for Martis, showing the trails he ought to follow. The forest was safe, but there was no point in getting lost.

"I suppose I'll go back to Obann to serve King Ryons," Martis said. "Chillith, too. I'm sure there's much to be done."

"Now that the war's over," Ellayne added.

Jack just shook his head. How could it be over? The Thunder King still ruled the East. He'd pledged himself to take Obann. Someday he'd send another army over the mountains—a bigger one. Chillith had said so, and he would know.

"Besides," Jack thought, "Martis swore to protect us. He can't just go off and leave us. Things can't just end like that."

Ellayne went on and on about what a fine time they were going to have in Ninneburky, with everybody treating them like heroes—not to mention hot baths, feather beds, and crawfish chowder. Jack wished she'd just shut up and let them all march through the woods in peace. He liked to hear their feet swishing through the fallen leaves, and the rat-tat-tat of woodpeckers, the squawking of the jays. He should have been happy about going home, but he wasn't. This was more like being taken away from a story before you heard the ending.

When they were some hours out of camp and paused for a bite to eat, Chillith said, "I think we ought to tell the truth to these two children. They aren't ordinary children, and they ought to know what we mean to do."

"I knew there was something!" Jack said; but Martis gave him a look that stopped him from saying more.

"What are you going to do?" Ellayne said. She already didn't like the sound of this.

"We aren't sure," Martis said. "But we mean to travel East, Chillith and I, until we come to the Thunder King's new Temple. My old master, Lord Reesh, is to be First Prester there. It's an abomination. I can't bear the thought of it."

"What'll you do, just you and Chillith?" Jack said. "He can't even see!"

"He's going to try to kill Lord Reesh," Ellayne said. "Aren't you, Martis?"

"That was my thought."

Jack laughed: not that there was anything funny about it. "Don't you think that might be kind of hard to do?" he said.

"Impossible to do," said Chillith. "There will be more armed guards in that Temple than there are trees in a forest. Nevertheless, we will go."

"But why—if it's impossible?" Ellayne cried.

"That I don't know," Chillith said. "I just know we ought to go. I'm thinking maybe you and Jack ought to go with us, too."

"That's not what we agreed!" Martis snapped. His glare was wasted on the blind man. "As for armed guards, there's always a way into the Temple. There's a way into anywhere. So it was in Obann. No one was safe. At Lord Reesh's command I murdered people in their beds. But to bring you children with us—no! It's time you went home."

"Oh, this is all rot!" Ellayne said. "It'd take the biggest army in the world to drag Lord Reesh out of that Temple."

Chillith shook his head. "It won't be done by any army," he said. "You don't understand the power of the Thunder King. He holds the whole East captive, lands and people that you've never heard of. His mardars are everywhere. He intends to stretch out his hand and seize the world.

"Even so, your God is calling us to go. What we are to do when we get there, I don't know. Die, probably."

"How do you know God is calling you?" Martis said.

"I don't know how! How does the seed know when it's time to sprout? It's not as if I've heard God's voice speaking words to me. Not like that. Maybe it's another way of seeing, now that the eyes in my face are darkened. But I do know."

Martis let out a long, deep sigh and shook his head.

"God's not done with us yet, is He?" Jack said. "He sent us up Bell Mountain, and we rang the bell. He sent us to Obann, and we found King Ozias' books. And now this!"

"What? Because he says so?" Ellayne cried, pointing at Chillith. "We're supposed to hike to the ends of the earth and get killed, because this man says so?"

"We'd go if God said so," Jack said, very softly. But God had not said so—not yet. Not like the way He sent them up Bell Mountain, with dreams and visions—nor had He spoken to them through a prophet, unless Chillith were a prophet.

But a Heathen prophet? Who ever heard of such a thing?

Orth was a city man, born and bred. He didn't hunt or fish, not even as a recreation. He liked elegant dinners at home, with elegant guests and expensive wines. He liked to wash his hands in perfumed water and sprinkle it on his beard.

Now he was wet from head to toe, and bits of mud and weed clung to his hair and beard. Several times he fell, once face-first into a pool of stinking muck. Well before the moon went down and the first intimations of the new day tinted the sky, he was chilled to the core. His teeth chattered like castanets.

He was going to die in this forsaken wilderness. Of that he was quite sure. Disgusting animals would feast on his carcass. He didn't care. The thought of the dark angel with the slaughter weapon, waiting for him in the East, drove him deeper and deeper into the fens.

By dawn he was too exhausted to go another step. Panting, he sank onto a tussock of coarse yellow grass, with water squishing underneath, as the sky turned grey and then reddened with the sunrise. Birds with harsh voices greeted it. Orth wished he could burrow into the grass and cover himself with mud, but he lacked the strength to try. He was too tired even to think.

CHAPTER 18

The Village and the City

For part of every day, the Blays taught the villagers how to fight. The farmers had no proper weapons, "but farm tools do just fine," Shingis said. A man could be knocked off a horse, or off his feet, just as well with a hoe or a rake as with a spear.

The most important thing was that the men should act together. "Never alone," Shingis said. "Bad man come in, three, four, five of you fight him. Kill him pretty quick."

With the harvest already in, the people of Jocah's Creek had little else to do; they took to their training eagerly. Some of them made slings and were learning how to use them. A Blay named Ghichmi taught them, with a scarecrow for a target. He could knock its hat off from fifty yards away, and the children loved to watch him do it.

"I hope we'll be ready for the winter," Loyk said to Gurun. "That's when the bandits will be desperate. They'll have nothing to eat."

"Maybe by then some of your people will be able to hit the scarecrow," Gurun said. She'd tried it with a sling but couldn't get the hang of it. "But when Shingis comes back from patrol, I want to talk to you and him together."

Shingis had dinner with Loyk's family that evening, along with Gurun and Tim. Loyk's wife served a fine fish stew. "The trout in the creek this year," she said, "are more plentiful than anybody's ever seen them. And fatter, too."

When they'd had their fill, and the table was cleared, Gurun spoke her mind.

"I hope we've learned to trust each other," she said. "This is a good place for my men, and they've been good for the village."

"No one would deny that, Gurun," Loyk said.

"We like it here," said Shingis.

"We shall stay here through the winter," Gurun said. "But in the meantime, there's something that I want to do, and I hope you'll all approve.

"I want to send Tim to the city of Obann, along with one or two companions, to see how things are—and to see the king. Then they must come back and tell us what they've seen."

"She thinks there's a king in Obann now," Tim said. "That's why the two of us were going there—to see the king. I've told her that there is no king, but she won't listen."

With the country in an uproar, it had been some time since Jocah's Creek had heard any news from beyond their own little valley. From the Blays, of course, they knew that the Thunder King's host had been driven from the city. But that was all they knew.

"Why do you think there is a king in Obann now?" said Loyk.

"When I first came to this country, from across the sea, a man told me I must go to Obann and see the king," Gurun said. "He was not a man of Obann. He spoke to me in the language of my own people, and there are none of my people in this land. By that I knew he was a filgya."

She had to explain what a filgya was. Neither Loyk nor Shingis had ever heard of such a thing.

Shingis listened intently. "You never tell us this before!" he said.

"I knew you wouldn't let me go to the city," she answered. "But at least you should let me send Tim, while I stay here with you, as I have promised."

"No one has asked old Tim if he will go," the trapper said. "Not that I'd mind a visit to the city."

"Maybe you will get a chance to speak to the king," Gurun said. "You must tell him about us, and tell him that I want to see him."

"If there is a king!"

"A filgya doesn't lie."

Loyk shook his head. "I wonder if it was an angel that you saw," he said.

"Perhaps my filgya was a kind of angel," Gurun said. "If he was, it would be well to do as he said."

"What is angel?" Shingis asked.

"A servant of God," said Loyk. "Sometimes they come down from Heaven, and people see them. So the Scripture says. Angels can appear as men or women, but they aren't really men or women. They are spirits."

Shingis stared at Gurun, and she saw fear in his eyes; yet she knew him for a brave man. She hoped he didn't fear her. It wouldn't be right.

"You send Tim—yes!" he said. "But you stay, make prayers for us. We much fear Obann's God."

"The fear of God is the beginning of wisdom," Loyk said.

Tim set out the next day, accompanied by a strong,

young plowman who'd been to Obann once and knew the way. Shingis wouldn't let any of his own men go. He was sure that any Blay who set foot in Obann would be killed. He made Tim swear not to mention them.

"I don't think they'd bother to send an army out to Jocah's Creek, just for you," Tim said. "Anyhow, there ain't going to be a king in Obann, no matter what anybody's filgya says. But Osker and I'll come back and tell you everything we see and hear. It'll be good to know what's been happening in the rest of the world."

Thanks to the Blays' slings and spears, Tim and Osker would be able to make the trip in style, on horseback. No one in the village could tell them much about the art of horsemanship, but they would have a journey of a hundred miles in which to learn it for themselves. The whole village turned out to wave them good-bye and wish them luck.

"If there is a king in Obann," said Loyk, when the riders had passed out of sight, "it means that everything has changed. Whether the change be good or bad, we'll see."

"They'll be back inside a week," Gurun said. "And then we'll know."

In Obann, Captain Hennen—now General Hennen— had just returned from breaking up an angry mob that had gathered before the ruins of the Temple. Now he was reporting to the king and his advisers in the private council chamber of the oligarchs' administration building.

"We were able to move them along without breaking any heads," he said, "but it might be harder, next time. I don't like what I'm hearing in the streets."

"It's the seminary students, isn't it?" Obst said.

"They do most of the talking," Hennen said. "They're angry, and anybody can see what makes them so. They went into the seminary so they could be ordained as presters someday and rule over chamber houses. But if there's no Temple, they can't become presters. They want everything back the way it was."

Obst translated. He only had to speak, and every man present heard it in his own language: that was the gift God gave him when he climbed Bell Mountain. Most of King Ryons' chieftains still hadn't learned Obannese.

Old Chief Spider was ailing and had been brought to the meeting on a litter. His attendants had had to move him into a chair and stand beside him to make sure he didn't fall out of it. His head kept nodding; but now he propped it up with his hands and spoke.

"It would be too bad if God saved this city, and its own people destroyed it. We asked them if they wanted a king, and they said yes! If they'd said no, we'd have all gone back to Lintum Forest.

"These are very foolish people here in Obann. They know it was King Ryons who rode the great beast and scattered their enemies like dust. That was a miracle. Only the power of God could have made it happen."

He coughed, hard, and it was some moments before he could continue. His shaved scalp gleamed with sweat. The scars on his face were pale against his skin.

"I won't live much longer," he said. "I don't mind. My eyes have seen great things. I've taken many scalps, and I have three strong sons. Best of all, I've lived long enough to come to know the true God, whose mercy endureth forever.

That's the battle anthem of our army, and I hope it always will be. So I depart with no regrets. Soon I'll worship God before His face. Even so, I'd like to see these troubles all cleared up before I go. Two things I advise.

"First, let these people see their king more often. Let them hear his voice. Among us Abnaks, great chiefs don't seclude themselves in palaces. These city folk must see their king and be reminded how he came to them, riding on a giant's back.

"But also, as soon as may be, send back to Lintum Forest for the little girl who is a prophet. God speaks through her. We've all heard this with our own ears. Let Obann hear it, too. Bring her to this city. If nothing else, maybe that filthy bird that follows her around will scare these people to their senses."

"Yes, yes—he's right!" In a dozen different languages, the chiefs barked their assent. It was Jandra who'd told them, in a voice that was certainly not her own, that Ryons was to be their king, and king of Obann. It seemed like lunacy at the time, but it had come to pass.

Obst turned to the boy king. "Your Majesty?" he said.

"Oh, yes—bring Jandra!" Ryons answered. Just to hear her name again reminded him how happy he'd been, for the little time he'd lived in Lintum Forest. It made him think of Jandra, who used to toddle after him in play, and of Szugetai, who'd bequeathed his men to him. Szugetai fell in a battle, but it'd be good to see Jandra again. And going back to Lintum Forest would be even better, Ryons thought.

"But we already have a prophet—Nanny Witkom!" This objection came from Zekelesh, chief of the Fazzan—fleet-footed men who wore wolf's heads when they went into battle. Zekelesh spoke not a word of Obannese, but he was a friend to Nanny Witkom. "Why don't we ask Nanny what we ought to do?"

Nanny didn't attend meetings. She spent most of her time now resting in her old rocking chair at the house of the late Lord Gwyll, where she'd been nurse to the general's children. She wanted to be there when Gwyll's wife returned. Since the rescue of the city, Nanny had made no prophetic utterances.

"Yes, let's hear Nanny," Chief Shaffur said. "Maybe God will speak to us through her, like He did before."

Zekelesh ran off to fetch her; he knew the way. While they awaited his return, the chieftains discussed the problem posed by the seminary students. "We ought to drive them out of the city—ungrateful dogs!" Shaffur said; but Obst argued against it. "They don't understand what God has done," he said. "They need more time." But he could not say how much more.

Ryons tried to follow the discussion. He didn't understand much of it, but he did understand that whatever the chieftains decided to do would be done in his name—whether he understood their decision or not.

Wherever he went in the city, his bodyguard went with him—fifty horsemen from the far, far East, Ghols, Szugetai's men, who addressed the boy king as "father." Ryons loved them; but lately he'd seen very little love for them in the eyes of people in the city. The same could be said of all the four thousand men of his army. The people of Obann didn't like them.

"Soon they won't like me, either," Ryons thought. But Obst and Jandra both said it was God's will that he should be king in Obann, and there was no going against that.

His ride on the shoulders of the giant beast seemed like a dream to him now. Sometimes he found it hard to believe that such a thing had really happened.

Zekelesh and a few of his men came back with Nanny Witkom, carrying her in a chair affixed to poles. She looked old and frail, Ryons thought, and half-asleep. Maybe she should have been left alone.

"Nanny, we're sorry to disturb you," Obst said, "but the chieftains wish you to inquire of the Lord for them." He told her about the disturbances in the city, but she didn't let him finish.

"Yes, yes, I know all about that!" she said, waving him to silence. "Servants tell me everything. The people want their Temple back. They're afraid God won't hear their prayers without the Temple.

"But how many times do I have to tell you? I'm not a pump—jerk the handle up and down, and out comes prophecy like water. I know the Lord sent me to you and spoke to you through me while we were marching to the city. I can even remember little pieces of it. But that's all over now."

The chieftains fretted, but she paid no heed to them.

"I was dozing in my poor Lord Gwyll's garden," she went on, "and I was having such a dream! It was a funny kind of dream—I wasn't in it. But I dreamed I saw a great hall, as great as anything in Obann—but I don't know where it was—and in the middle of it was a table. There's no table like it anywhere. You could drive a horse and a cart down the middle of it. And there were great lamps burning everywhere, a thousand lamps, and the wood of the table shone like polished copper.

"And all around the table there were chiefs, like you, in big, fancy chairs—men in such finery, you could hardly bear to look at it. And at one end of the table sat Lord Reesh, the First Prester. He used to come to Lord Gwyll's house sometimes, so I knew him right away. And there he was, alive. I didn't know any of the other people there. Just him.

"They were all feasting and drinking; and behind them, all around the table, there were statues, some of wood, some of stone. They were very queer-looking statues, and I couldn't tell what they were. Idols, maybe. But it was quite a feast those men were having—and then Zekelesh came along and woke me up, before I could find out what it was all about." She sighed and closed her eyes. Obst nodded, and Zekelesh's men carried her out of the council chamber.

"So much for that!" said Shaffur. "We'll need the little girl, after all, if we're to have a prophet."

"I don't know," Chief Spider said. "Dreams may often tell us secret things. We Abnaks set great store by them."

"She dreamed of Lord Reesh," Obst said. "I do wonder what that could mean, if anything. His bones lie mixed with the rubble of the Temple, and yet she dreamed of him alive."

Uduqu laughed. "If half of what I've heard of that old toad is true," he said, "then he's feasting in Hell with all the other sinners!" They all laughed at that; but Ryons noticed that Obst didn't laugh. He didn't even smile.

CHAPTER 19

Helki on the Trail

Helki and Cavall pressed on, following the Griffs' trail. Helki set a fast pace, gaining on them day by day. Soon he would see whether they'd crossed the Imperial River or turned northeast to march along the Chariot.

Toward noon one day the hawk, circling overhead, came back to him with a piercing cry. Helki held out his arm and she landed on it.

"Good, Angel, good! Strangers up ahead, eh? Too bad you can't tell me how many of them." Whatever men these were, he thought, they were downwind. That was why Cavall hadn't yet scented them. But Angel saw them: very good, indeed, he thought.

"We'll creep up on them, careful-like," Helki told the hound. "I'd like to parley with them. Maybe they've seen those Griffs."

The land rose gently, just ahead, crowned with clumps of waxbush: good cover. Helki sent Angel aloft again, squeezed the scruff of Cavall's neck to keep him close and quiet, and advanced at a walk. His feet made no sound. As he neared the top of the rise, he dropped to hands and knees. He crawled just as silently as he walked.

He peered down from the bushes and got a surprise—there were Griffs down there. He knew them by their hairdos: only Griffs took such trouble with their hair. There were only a dozen of them, so they might not be the same Griffs he was following.

"A round dozen," he muttered. "Shouldn't be too many for us, Cavall, if they're in a mood to fight. But talking would be better." He stood up. "Come on," he said.

With the big dog loping alongside, and the hawk circling above, Helki strolled down the slope, handling his staff like an ordinary traveler's walking stick. He spoke Griffish passably, but if these Griffs didn't wish to talk, he trusted in the eloquence of his staff. When the men looked up and saw him, he waved to them and kept on coming. The Griffs drew swords and knives.

"Rest easy, boys—I come in peace," he said. The Griffs seemed not to believe him. Cavall growled. But before any blows could be struck on either side, one of the Griffs shouted at his fellows.

"Stop, you fools! Don't you know who that is? It's the man who killed the giant! Don't you remember Shogg, the son of Sezek—that Zamzu man-eater? I was there, I saw it! This man killed Shogg as easy as you'd swat a fly! Haven't we trouble enough, without picking a fight with him?"

The others were quick to see reason. Shogg had been a legend in the Heathen army, its champion. They thought he was worth fifty ordinary men.

"Relax, I'm not here to fight," said Helki. "Sheathe your weapons; let's be friends. You're going to need friends, if you stay in Obann."

The Griffs sheathed their blades and honored Helki with salutes and bows, which from them was a pledge of peace. Knowing that they wouldn't break the truce now,

Helki went to their campfire and sat down among them, Cavall beside him.

"Don't mind my hound," he said, noting some uneasy glances. "He knows his manners as well as you or I do."

There were formalities to endure before Helki could bring up the purpose of his visit. These Griffs were uneasy, and it took some time before they were ready to talk.

"I'm looking for two children and a man," he said, and described Jack, Ellayne, and Martis. Before he could get much farther, he had his answer.

"Those three were our prisoners," said the man who'd seen his fight with Shogg. "We captured them. Our mardar meant to take them East. But then—!" he shook his head.

The band of a hundred Griffs were now scattered. The God of Obann had struck their mardar blind. If the men had stayed with him, they would have been blinded, too. They'd left the prisoners, wanting nothing more to do with them: indeed, they were afraid of them. Unable to think of any better plan, these dozen men were traveling back to rejoin their army at Obann.

"It's too late for that," Helki said. "Your army doesn't exist anymore: God saw to that." And he told them how the great beast, with the boy king on its back, routed the host of the Thunder King. Their eyes went wide with fear and wonder.

"Then it's even as the boy dreamed it, the night Chillith's eyes were darkened," said one.

"What shall we do?" cried another. "We're cursed. Obann's God is stronger than the Thunder King. He will destroy us all."

They wailed together, as Griffs sometimes do, and

Helki was hard put to quiet them.

"There's no need to mourn yourselves," he said. "You're not dead yet, nor blind, and you don't have to be. Obann's God is stronger than the Thunder King, and He'll take care of him like He took care of Shogg. Don't think I killed Shogg by my own strength! It was God who killed the giant. Anyone who tries to stand against God isn't going to stand for long.

"But I have good news for you! Obann's God is not just Obann's, but the God of all the nations. And He's not just strong, but merciful—a lot more merciful than any man. If you turn away from the Thunder King and put your trust in God, and serve Him, God will be merciful to you, too. He'll accept you as His own. Four thousand Heathen already belong to Him, and they're mighty glad they do."

"But how can that be?" a Griff asked. "Why should Obann's God be merciful to us?"

Helki made a face. "Now you're asking me to explain things, and I'm no teacher," he said. "But there's a teacher in Obann who can teach you all you need to know. In the meantime, you can start serving God right away. You can join up with me and help me: I reckon that's why the Lord brought us together today. But you'll have to decide for yourselves."

Twelve men in a land of enemies, with their great army miraculously destroyed, and their own captain smitten blind, and a divine curse hanging over them—they didn't need much more encouragement than that. They all stood up and bowed to Helki.

"We are yours to command, Giant-killer," said one. "From now on, we serve the God of Obann. My name is

Tiliqua, son of Thurr, and I give you my word, freely, of my own free will."

"And I, your honor!" said another.

"And I—Shalamac, son of Thilonoc!"

They all twelve pledged themselves to Helki, and to Obann's God. They did it with much ceremony. Helki sighed. This was not the kind of thing he'd ever expected to be doing in his life. He'd been happy in the company of hawk and hound, and wanted nothing more. Now he had twelve men who would pester him to make decisions. But he supposed it was what God wanted—no telling why.

CHAPTER 20

Hlah's Holy Man

Somehow Orth didn't die. He blundered around and around the fens, not even knowing that he'd crossed and re-crossed the Chariot River. By the grace of God he stumbled upon a deserted cottage, and there he stayed. At least now he had a roof over his head and four walls between himself and the wind—between himself and the unknown, unseen beasts and birds that wailed, roared, shrieked, whistled, and rumbled all day and all night long. At least he hoped they were only beasts and birds, and not devils.

He ate raw eggs when he could find them, raw fish when he could catch them with his hands, the remains of a big cheese that he found in the cottage—but mostly he starved. Every waking moment, he was hungry. Every day he foraged for food around the cottage, never daring to wander out of sight of it. As a city man, ignorant of the wider world, he went hungry where a marsh-man would have found ample food. But Orth knew nothing of trapping, fishing, or digging up edible roots and tubers.

So Hlah, the son of Spider, hurrying up the Chariot, found him late one morning—a trembling scarecrow of mud and filth who screamed when he saw Hlah and tried to flee, but slipped in the mud and fell. He skidded on all fours, moaning, until Hlah grabbed him by the hair and put a stop to that.

"Here, now, stop that noise!" Hlah shook him. "I won't hurt you! But who are you, and what's the matter with you?"

Orth goggled at him with fearful eyes, and Hlah knew he was talking to a madman. "Can you tell me your name?" he asked.

Orth hadn't been in the fens long enough to forget his name, nor what he used to be. But this stranger was a savage, with a shaved head and tattoos all over his skin: a barbarian who was likely to kill him, no matter what his name was. But Orth didn't want to speak his own name. He didn't want to utter it ever again. An angel might be listening.

"Leave me alone!" he answered. "God's curse on me! The slaughter-angel is hunting for me. Go away!"

Hlah saw the cottage, pointed to it. "Is that where you live?" Orth nodded. Hlah helped him to his feet. "Let's go sit in your cabin and have a bite to eat." He'd learned to speak good Obannese, and the madman understood him.

"Don't be afraid of me," he said, as he pushed Orth toward the cottage. "I'm King Ryons' man: he's king in Obann now." But at those words Orth broke down with shudders, and Hlah couldn't keep him on his feet.

Abnaks make shamans of their madmen, and for as long as they are harmless to others, treat them well. It never entered Hlah's mind to harm this madman. Besides, he was Heathen no more, and he'd been taught that violence and cruelty offended God. Even so, it took all of his patience to maneuver Orth into the cottage and set him down on the rough bed he found there. Then Orth began to blubber like a child, so Hlah shook him by the beard and had to slap him once.

"Talk like a man!" he said. "And tell me your name."

"I won't!" Orth shook his head. "I dare not. I will never speak my name again."

"Won't you tell me anything?"

"Let everything about me be forgotten!" Orth said.

Hlah shrugged. It was no use arguing with a madman. "Under those rags you wear," he said, "and under all that mud, you're skin and bones. You don't know how to take care of yourself. If I go away and leave you, you won't live to see the winter."

"Better, that way," Orth said. "God's curse on me!"

Wishing to do the man a kindness, Hlah gave him a drink from his waterskin and a strip of jerky from his bag. Orth gnawed it like a wolf. Hlah gathered some wood and built a fire in the cabin's little hearth. He gave the poor madman the last of the bread he was carrying, too. Tomorrow he would have to hunt. Finally he wet a rag and wiped several layers of mud from the man's face. Kindness to strangers, Obst taught, pleased God. It made a change from scalping them, thought Hlah.

"Will you tell me why a curse is on you?" he asked.

"I cannot."

"You don't know?"

"Oh, I know!" Orth said, gnashing his teeth. "I've sinned great sins."

What should he do with the man? Hlah pondered it all day, and on into the evening. Just before it was time to curl up in his bag and go to sleep, he decided.

"Hear me, whatever your name is," he said. "I can't just leave you here to die, but I'm on my way to Abnak country. I have to go there so I can teach my people to worship the true God—we shouldn't be heathens anymore. So I suppose I'll have to take you with me and hope your wits come back to you along the way. Maybe you can help me teach my people. You're Obannese. You must know more about God than I do."

Orth stared at him, then threw back his head and laughed out loud, laughed until he cried. The whole marsh rang with it.

"Mad as a magpie!" Hlah thought. "And therefore very holy. Like as not the people will kill me and make him their shaman."

It wasn't an easy night. Several times the madman woke Hlah, babbling in some language that sounded like Obannese but which Hlah couldn't understand. He wondered if maybe it was praying of some kind. Hadn't Obst said the Scriptures were in an ancient language? Maybe this poor devil knew the Scriptures. That would make him useful.

The next day Hlah spent collecting food for another two or three days' traveling. He'd changed his plans for traveling along the Imperial: from what he'd heard along the way, the upper reaches of the river swarmed with enemies—including an intact army that had not yet descended into Obann. That was what had convinced him to follow the Chariot instead.

He knew enough to dig up edible roots that would tide them over for a while, and he was lucky enough to snare a plump animal that was probably edible. It looked like a beaver without a beaver's tail.

The second night in the cottage was as bad as the first,

but the morning was worse. After a meager breakfast, Hlah said, "Well, friend, let's be on our way. It's a long journey to the Abnaks' country, and we want to be over the mountains before the snow falls."

"Mountains!" cried Orth. And then ensued a struggle. He sprang at Hlah, reaching for his throat. He was a big man, and out of his senses—no easy job subduing him. Hlah had to knock him down and wrestle him, tie his hands behind his back, and gag him.

"Behave yourself!" he said. "It's for your own good. You can't just stay here and die. As for your angel, and your curses—if an angel really wanted you, don't you think it could come after you here in the marshes? You might as well come with me and help me to serve God. My people will surely take you for a holy man."

Orth glared at him, but when Hlah yanked the rope, he had no choice but to go along with him.

Maybe it was right, he thought. After all, there was no escaping God's wrath. It didn't matter whether he crossed the mountains or not. He'd betrayed the Temple—how could he look for anything good to happen to him?

He surrendered to God's judgment.

CHAPTER 21

Lord Reesh's New Disciple

A few days after Tim and Osker left for Obann, the scouts brought dire news to Jocah's Creek.

Hamber, the town where the villagers used to go to services at the chamber house, had been taken, ravaged, and was in the hands of enemies. And it was only fifteen miles down the creek.

"Zamzu are there now," Shingis said, "big men, very strong. They eat man's flesh. We see maybe five, maybe six times our number. They make slaves of town people. Some they eat. They make the people dig deep ditch all around, so no one can get in or out. Maybe someday they come here."

"What are Zamzu?" Gurun asked.

"Men from south shores of Great Lakes. All peoples fear them. They had a giant, but we hear a man killed him. No giant in Hamber—just plenty big men. Thunder King likes Zamzu very much."

"If they do come here," asked Gurun, "can we defend ourselves?"

Shingis grinned. "Best defense—run away!" he said. "You pray Obann God to keep Zamzu away from here. If they come, I don't know."

It wasn't long before the entire village had the news. Old women wailed. Men gathered in small groups, nervously whispering.

"Counting some of the older men and bigger boys," Loyk said, "this village has forty-four able-bodied men, none of them warriors. Add to that the twenty Blays, and we have sixty-four. Not much good against at least a hundred fighting men! And no militia anywhere! What are we to do?"

He was asking Gurun, as if she were a hero in the Scriptures and not a girl who was a stranger in the country. "Just a year ago," she thought, "I was telling bedtime stories to my littlest brother. Now I am to be Elilah the Fox, whose strategy was better than an army! How would I know how to save this village?"

"Shingis says we ought to run away," Loyk went on, "but where could we go? Our farms are all we have. If we lose them, we'll never own anything again. And the old women and the little children—how far can they go? Such things have never happened in my time—or anybody else's."

Gurun wished her father and his friends were here: strong men, who would know just what to do. She didn't!

"We shall have to pray," she said. "Pray that God will fight for us, if it ever comes to that. Remember the story of Ishik the Old. In his day, three nations of the Heathen came up against the children of Geb, with an army of a thousand thousands. Ishik had two thousand men, no more. But the prophet told them to stand fast and see what the Lord would do for them."

Loyk nodded. "I know. The three nations turned on one another and slaughtered themselves to the last man. But that was in ancient times."

"God has not changed since ancient times," Gurun said.

God does not change, but the world does. Even as Gurun and Loyk made ready to pray, Lord Reesh was admiring one of those changes.

When they quit the fens along the Chariot, the First Prester and his escort made excellent time on a new road hewed out of the wilds by order of the Thunder King. Multitudes of slaves labored on it—including many of Reesh's own countrymen, pressed into servitude.

Down from the mountain pass it ran, through the forested foothills, on a course parallel to the river. Mardar Kyo said it would someday run all the way down to the junction of the Chariot and the Imperial; and its purpose was to speed Heathen armies into the heart of Obann.

"This is the kind of work that has long needed doing!" the First Prester said to his servant, Gallgoid, who now rode with him in the coach. "For centuries the people of Obann were content to let the river be their road; but it was not so in ancient times. The Empire had roads that went all the way out to the Great Lakes and were useable in every kind of weather."

"They've chewed up a lot of pretty countryside, though," Gallgoid said.

"Don't talk like a farmer. I tell you, whatever else he may be, the Thunder King has vision. This road should have been built two hundred years ago."

It was as yet but a raw swathe hacked through the landscape, with heaps of chopped-down trees on either side of it. Gangs of men toiled to smooth and harden it, rolling heavy logs back and forth upon its surface. In many places trees were piled for burning, and a haze of smoke lay over the land. The ashes would be mixed with water and used to harden the road's surface. Eventually it would be given a permanent surface of crushed stone mixed with lime, Kyo said.

"You must learn to reach back into the past to find the future of mankind," Reesh told his servant. "I know it will be hard for you: I had you trained as an assassin, not a scholar. But you've heard me speak of the great days of the Empire. Those days must come again! That's what I've been working for. That's the reason for everything I've done."

Gallgoid nodded. He'd seen his master's collection of relics from the Empire. He knew the mountains that dotted Obann's plains were the remains of great cities.

Reesh flayed himself for investing so much in Orth as his successor, a man whose nerve broke as soon as he was separated from the city. At least Gallgoid wouldn't lose his nerve. But was his mind agile enough, his vision broad enough, to become his lord's disciple—maybe even to become First Prester after him?

"The purpose of the Temple is to lead men to the future, Gallgoid. We must become again what once we were—the masters of the earth. We must be free to work out our own destiny—free from the constraints of hunger, weather, distances, and time. Free from the countless petty idiocies in which the human race muddles along from day to day, accomplishing nothing, getting nowhere."

Gallgoid made no reply. Reesh continued: "But to be free, we must have power. Power to feed ourselves, regardless of the vagaries of rain and drought and frost. Power to go where we wish to go, when we please, regardless of how far away the destination, regardless of the weather. Power to channel human labor, and direct it. The men of the Empire had such power. So must we."

Gallgoid nodded. Reesh didn't like his taciturnity.

"Talk to me!" Reesh said. "Tell me your thoughts. I can't teach you if you won't talk."

"I was only thinking," the assassin answered slowly, "that if we had that kind of power, we'd have no need of God. We'd be kind of like gods ourselves."

"Yes. We would." Reesh sighed. "Do you believe in God, Gallgoid?"

He shrugged his bony shoulders. "Never gave it much thought, my lord. But I suppose I do."

"How do you reconcile your belief in God with your work as an assassin?"

After a long pause, Gallgoid said, "I never let it trouble me. You're the First Prester, God's servant. I obey your commands. You would know better than I would what was right or wrong. I really never had to think about it much."

"When I die," said Reesh, "and you take my place in the new Temple, you'd better be able to think—long and hard and cleverly! It'd be well for you to get into the habit of it now."

CHAPTER 22

Cold Wind

Ellayne felt the pull of Ninneburky, of home—her father and mother, and her brothers, her own bed, her books. It pulled on her with every step they took through Oziah's Wood. When they came out of the forest, they would be almost within sight of the town.

One day it rained. It was just a gentle rain at first, but then it came down harder, and after a while there was nothing for it but to stop and put up a shelter. The rangers had given them a sheet of waterproofed canvas for a roof, and Martis soon had a fire going. Wytt came out from behind some bushes and nestled in Ellayne's arms.

"Wish we had some ale," Jack said.

"What rot!" Ellayne answered. "You're too young to drink ale. I've had wine, though—lovely golden wine, shipped all the way up the river from Durmurot, where it's sunny all the time. Sunshine in a bottle, my father calls it—"

"Peace!" said Martis. "What's the use of wishing for things we can't get? Be happy we have a little tea left over and some of that venison jerky. Would you like a sip of tea, Chillith?"

Chillith didn't answer. He sat staring into the distance, where there was nothing to see but rain-soaked tree trunks. He showed no sign that he heard anything that anyone said.

"Obst gets like that sometimes, when he's praying." Jack spoke in a whisper. "But Obst's lips move when he prays. And he says God speaks to him, but not in words."

"How could he be praying? He's a heathen," Ellayne said. "He wouldn't know how to pray. He doesn't believe in God."

"Let him be," said Martis.

Three of them had tea, while Chillith never stirred. He sat there like a rock. Rain pattered on the canvas. Ham and Dulayl stood tethered to a tree, bearing the weather patiently. Chillith's silence put a damper on conversation.

How long they sat like that, Jack didn't know. But at last Chillith sighed and shifted his position.

"Are you all right?" Jack said.

"We are not going to go to the Temple, after all," Chillith said. "We shall see the Thunder King's face, but not at Kara Karram. He will not stay there, for God has called him west, and he must come."

"What are you talking about?" Ellayne said; but Wytt leaped out of her arms and chattered loudly. He snatched up his little sharp stick and brandished it over his head and started prancing all around.

"It's a war dance—he's doing a war dance!" Jack said. "He's all excited, but he isn't saying why. He's all keyed up."

Martis shook Chillith's shoulder. "What did you mean, just now?" he said. "Can you explain it?"

"Maybe," Chillith said. You would swear he saw something, something big, pushing aside the trees just a few yards from their shelter; and yet they knew he couldn't see at all. "The Thunder King swore he would take Obann, but he failed. Soon all the peoples of the East will know it.

"Now he will have to come in person and make good his oath, or everyone will know he was defeated by the God of Obann. He cannot allow it. He has never been defeated anywhere, by anyone, but has always conquered. He must conquer Obann and destroy the city. Your God has put it in his mind. He must go to Obann."

"I knew it!" Jack said. "I knew the war couldn't be over yet."

"So if we're not going out to that Temple at wherever-it-is," Ellayne said, "where do we go? And why is Wytt doing a war dance? There's no fighting in Oziah's Wood."

"No—not yet," Martis said. "But there may be, and maybe sooner than we'd think."

"The Thunder King knew it when his armies failed before the city," Chillith said. "He will have seen it through his mardars' eyes."

"I don't believe he can do that," Jack said. "That'd be magic, and there's no such thing as magic."

"Nevertheless, he does it," Chillith said. "I was a mardar. Someday, had I proved worthy, I would have been presented to the Thunder King, and he would have given me power to be his eyes and ears, and to hear his voice from a thousand miles away. Our own Griff gods could never do that, but he does."

"Maybe he's doing it with you now," Martis suggested; but Chillith shook his head.

"It is your God who speaks," he said; and then Jack noticed the Griff was shivering from head to foot.

As it rained on Oziah's Wood and on the slopes of the mountains, very strange weather indeed poured out of the north—across the River Winter, down into the lands west of Obann City. Over warm and sunny lands, it snowed.

It snowed on Jocah's Creek, too. It was unheard-of, so early in the season. Villagers stood outside and watched. Their children ran up and down, playing in it.

Gurun looked up into the pearl-grey heavens. Snowflakes melted on her cheeks.

"Distraction," said Loyk. "It's good for the soul."

"This is a gentle snow," Gurun said. "In my country the snow usually comes down sideways, driven by a howling wind."

"This snow comes a month too early," Loyk said.

The Blays' scouts were out, along with most of the young men of the village. They had need to be. The day before, they'd surprised a lone Zamzu scout not fives miles from the village. They killed him and concealed the body; but as Shingis said, the man would be missed and others would come looking for him. "They come, big trouble for us," he said. So they were scouting energetically. If they could spot the Zamzu early, Shingis hoped to stage an ambush some distance from the village. But what twenty or thirty men could do against a hundred, Gurun didn't know. Not much, she supposed.

Meanwhile Tim and Osker were overdue: they should have been back from Obann two days ago. That was another thing to worry about.

"Soon the creek will freeze," Loyk said. "It'll be a hard winter. The bandits will be hungry, and we have food. If we beat them one day, they'll be back the next."

"At home we sometimes have bandits," Gurun said, "but they don't live too long. They raid two or three times.

Then men like my father exert themselves, and raise the district, and soon the raiders are put down. They are outlaws, so they may be killed on sight. That's what happens to them. Can't the villages work together to do the same?"

"Our people don't know how to fight," Loyk said. "In all my life, there's never been a need for it."

"There is need now," Gurun said. Beyond that, there was nothing to be said. The girl and the old man stood side by side and watched it snow.

There was no snow south of the Imperial River—just a cold north wind that combed the yellowed grasses of the plains.

Here and there, few and far between, huge birds stalked in search of prey. Too big to fly, they ran as fast as horses and took down sheep and cattle with their great, hooked beaks. They were a new thing in the country. No one knew where they came from and no human language had a name for them.

There were other creatures, too, that had no proper names. Along the fringe of Lintum Forest lived the hulking knuckle-bears, who grazed on the plain by night and melted back into the forest in the morning, walking on their knuckles to protect their long, sharp claws. Because the land was sparsely inhabited, few people had ever seen them.

But everyone in Obann knew there were creatures stirring in the world that didn't belong there, some great, some small. The cities were full of prophets, but no one understood their prophecies. As word spread of the destruction of the Temple, congregations drifted away from the chamber houses, and reciters had no one to recite to.

King Ryons, maybe ten years old, maybe eleven, lay awake in his bed, listening to the wind. It was the first real bed he'd ever slept in, and there was a Ghol slumped against the door of the bedchamber, snoring; but the slightest movement of the door would have him on his feet in an instant, dagger drawn, ready to defend the boy he called his father.

Ryons had crossed the great plain from Lintum Forest to Obann, all alone but for Cavall. He knew the spirit of God had walked beside him all the way, and that the great beast that had no name had watched over him from afar, patiently following him until the time came for it to set him on its back and save the city. Ryons had seen the great birds from a distance, and something even more fearsome up close. It was a giant, striped, huge-headed predator—a death-dog—that would have eaten both him and Cavall in just a few gulps. But when the great beast bellowed, the death-dog turned and fled.

Ryons knew—better than most grown men and women knew—that in these days God had set His mighty hand upon the world and was doing things that no one understood. What would be the end of it? Why had God plucked him out of slavery and set him on a throne? Why was He bringing forth strange beasts out of the earth? Why had He brought ruin upon this city of Obann, and then miraculously saved it—and yet allowed His Temple to be burned to ashes?

Who in all this world knew what to do? Ryons didn't! But did Obst, or any of the chieftains?

Ryons listened to the wind, and prayed, and after just a few minutes of praying silently, fell asleep. And his sleep was troubled.

Born into slavery without even a name to call his own, with no memory of mother or father, Ryons had never had a home. But in his dream he was passionately homesick, although in waking life he didn't know the word "homesick." But that's what it was. His soul was torn. If he were a grown man who had learned to know the human heart, he would have recognized his pain as a kind of bereavement—a separation from someone, or someplace, deeply loved. But how could that be? In all his short life, up until just a little time ago, no one had loved him, and no place was any better than another. From whom could he be separated, that it should pain him so? What home could he long for, who had never had a home?

When he woke in the morning, he found his eyes and cheeks encrusted with dried tears, and he remembered the dream: the pain of it still throbbed. Yet more than the pain, a wild thought gripped him.

"It was God speaking to me—that's why I didn't understand it!" That was what he thought, and he just accepted it: he was only ten years old. "God was telling me something, and I didn't understand."

If he'd known enough to think of all the holy men and scholars and presters who'd never heard God speak to them, and so believed God never spoke to anyone, Ryons might have been even more confused than he was. But then the Ghol who was guarding his door yawned noisily, stretched, got up, and grinned at Ryons in his bed.

"I hope my father had propitious dreams!" he said in Gholish. Ryons, who still struggled with that language, understood enough to answer, "Thank you—is it time for breakfast?"

CHAPTER 23

How Tim Met the King

Trapper Tim had heard of Obann City all his life. The laws came out of Obann; taxes flowed into it. The Temple was there: every prester for every chamber house had to be ordained there. Obann was the seat of oligarchy, the heart of government, and so on.

Hearing of it was one thing, but being there was overwhelming. Tim had never dreamed so many people could be packed into one place. They made a noise that never stopped, just like a waterfall. The flow of people through the streets was like a river, never ceasing. And the city's walls were like the cliffs of mighty mountains.

Osker the plowman, who'd been there once before, tried to pretend he was used to it, but Tim more than once caught his eyes goggling. So many big buildings, everywhere you looked! The entire populace of Jocah's Creek could live in one of them.

Tim and Osker stood for a long time before the mountain of blackened rubble that used to be the Temple. Workmen picked away at it, filling carts and wheeling it away. Their efforts didn't seem to amount to anything. A crowd of men and women stood and watched. Tim didn't see a smile anywhere.

"I was never what you'd call a religious man," he

whispered to Osker, "but I've got to say, this was a terrible thing to happen! I don't like to look at it, and yet I can't stop looking."

"I don't see how we can get on without the Temple," said Osker.

They weren't in the city for an hour before Tim was satisfied that there was indeed a king in Obann now. Everybody said so.

"He saved the city," a sober, portly, grey-haired woman said. "He came down from Heaven on a giant horse and chased the enemy away. I saw it with my own eyes."

"I was on the walls when I saw it," a soldier said. "The waters of the river parted like a great gate, and the king came riding on a monstrous creature that was like a storm come to life. And before you could catch your breath, he slew ten thousand of the Heathen! They're still burying the bodies."

Everyone Tim spoke to saw something different, but they all saw the king; and the king was in the city now. The Oligarchs' Palace was now the King's Palace, and he lived there. He had an army of two thousand, or five thousand, or ten thousand Heathen who'd sworn blood oaths to him. He was attended by prophets and magicians. He had a champion who'd slain a giant, and special warriors who ate and slept and lived on horseback without ever coming down and spoke only the language of birds. He was of the lineage of King Ozias and had been raised by elves in Lintum Forest— or else by dwarfs in caverns under Bell Mountain, and he came out when King Ozias' bell was rung.

"I never heard such balderdash in all my days," Tim said, "but I guess the king is real, at least. The thing is, how do we get to see him?"

"I don't know if I want to see someone who's done all those things," said Osker. "It don't seem natural, to be raised by dwarfs. And how can it be that we have a king in Obann, but not the Temple?"

"You don't want to believe in dwarfs and fairies and the like," Tim said. "I've spent most of my life alone in some of the loneliest, wildest parts of the wilderness, and never yet saw hide nor hair of elf or dwarf or giant. But I'll be satisfied if I can see the king."

They took lodging in an inn. The rate charged was cheaper than usual, Osker said. The innkeeper said he was glad to have them. "So many people ran away from all the trouble," he said, "and of course no one was able to get into the city all summer, with the Heathen laying siege. But the king sure sent them packing!"

The next morning they went to the palace, where there were soldiers and guards, some of whom did not speak Obannese and could only stare at them. Tim asked to see the king, and kept on asking, and the next day came back and asked some more. Finally a man-at-arms took pity on him and ushered him into the building, made him sit down in a little room and told him to wait. "You may have a long wait," the warrior said, "but I'll see what I can do for you."

Tim waited all day long with nothing to eat or drink. He kept getting up to pace the room, to stretch, to mutter curses under his breath. But finally the man-at-arms came back, and not alone.

"This is General Hennen, trapper," he said. "He's a very important man, and you're lucky to be seeing him."

"Thank you, Sergeant," said the general. He was a sturdy man, dark-haired, blue-eyed, some good years short of middle-aged. He dismissed the sergeant and turned to Tim. "You've asked to see King Ryons. The king likes to meet his people, but he can't meet everybody. You told the sergeant you've come a long way—all the way down from the mouths of the River Winter. That is long! I've never been that far north, myself.

"Tell me why you wish to see the king—exactly why—and if I think it's worthwhile, I'll arrange an audience."

"Well, sir, this wasn't my idea," Tim said. After hemming and hawing a little, to collect his thoughts, he told the general about Gurun: how she'd come from some unheard-of country amidst the sea, how he'd met her, and that she knew there was a king in Obann when it wasn't possible that she could know. The general stopped him there and questioned him closely—especially as to what day of the year it was when the girl first spoke of the king. Tim answered as accurately as he could.

"That's something!" said the general. "At that time of the summer, the city was still surrounded by enemies and King Ryons had never yet set eyes on it."

General Hennen kept Tim answering questions until well into the evening, learning everything Tim could tell him about Gurun. The general took pity on him and had some bread brought, and ale. The ale was most welcome indeed.

"You shall see the king tomorrow morning, Tim," Hennen said, "that much I promise you. Come as early as you can; the sergeant will be waiting."

"The king will really see me?"

"Yes."

"Only thing is," Tim said, "I ain't got proper clothes for

meeting an important personage like that; nor proper manners, neither, if it comes to that."

"Never mind," the general said. "The king won't even notice such things."

———

Kings appeared in stories from the Scriptures, from long, long ago. Tim knew very little history; but he did know, as everybody knew, that Ozias was the last king of Obann, ages and ages ago. After him came long ages of wars and chaos, and then the Empire. All Tim knew about any empire was that God had destroyed that one, Obann's Empire. And then followed countless years of terrible times, and somehow during all of that, a new Temple got built in a new city of Obann—the ruined city across the river remained uninhabited forever—and after they had the Temple, men began to get things back in order. They set up the oligarchy, no king, and that's how it was. And it was good enough, Tim supposed. No one ever thought of having a king again.

But here and now stood Tim in the presence of a king: and he wanted to laugh because it was just a scrawny little kid. He didn't dare laugh, though, because General Hennen was there, and a tall old man who looked like he, too, might've just stepped out of the Scriptures, and also some fearsome barbarian with a shaved head and blue tattoos on his face. Behind the king stood a couple of small, slant-eyed men who might have come from Elf-land. "What is this world coming to?" Tim wondered.

"I've told His Majesty everything you told me yesterday," the general said. "This is the king's teacher and counselor, Obst"—that was the tall, old man—"and this is subchief Uduqu, the king's friend."

They wanted Tim to tell his story again, the story of Gurun, in his own words. The old man, Obst, was full of questions. The boy king said nothing at all, but he listened most intently. Tim found himself speaking mostly to him, although it wasn't the king who was asking the questions.

"She came over the sea, out of the North!" Obst said, pondering Tim's words. "The Old Books do speak of countries far across the sea, but ..." he shook his head. "No one sails the seas anymore. Not for centuries! And yet you say this maiden prays to God—our God—and knows the Scriptures—our Scriptures?"

"Yes sir, the very same—and she knows them like a prester," Tim answered. "In her country, she says, they all do their own praying, and they all learn bits of Scripture by heart, and they have their own books. It's on account of their being so far away from the Temple, so they couldn't do the proper religious things."

Obst actually laughed at that, and the boy king smiled, although Tim didn't see what was so funny. And then came another several dozen questions: the old man wanted to know everything. Meanwhile the barbarian chief seemed to be asleep on his feet; and the men behind the king's chair just stood there, not taking in a word of it. But at last the king himself spoke—in Obannese, with a thick Wallekki accent.

"Please, Obst," he said, "I want to see Gurun! Can't we have her brought here? Or I could go where she is."

"I think you should see her, Sire," Obst said. "I'd like to see her, too! God's hand is in this, depend on it. How else could she have gotten here from across the sea? And to think there are people living so far away that no one's ever heard of them or their country, and yet they know the same Scriptures we know and pray to the true God—it makes my head swim. By all means, we must have her here."

"We can send cavalry for her," Hennen said.

"Begging your pardon, sir," Tim interrupted, "but it won't be as easy as all that. Those Blays won't let Gurun leave, and she wouldn't want any harm to come to them. But they're afraid to come to Obann. And then there's the village—"

"I want to go to her myself," said the king. "My Ghols will ride with me, and they'll keep me safe. I want to go!"

The general frowned. "It might not be so easy for the king to get back into Obann, once he leaves it," he said.

"Hah! Then back we'll all go to Lintum Forest, and the fools in this city can look after themselves from now on." That was the barbarian chief, speaking for the first time. His Obannese was better than the king's. "It won't hurt His Majesty to take a little ride, and we might as well find out where we stand with these people. If they won't want him for their king, he shouldn't have to be their king. It'll be their loss."

"Peace, Uduqu!" Obst said. "Ryons is king of Obann by the will of God."

"Someone will have to govern the city in the king's name while he's gone," Hennen said.

"The council of chiefs can govern," Obst said. "It'll only be for a few days."

So everything was arranged, and King Ryons was delighted. "He does blossom when he smiles," Tim thought. "But what will Gurun think of him? She'll be expecting a big, tall, mighty man."

CHAPTER 24

Men Like Gods

The Griffs led Helki straight back to where they'd left Jack, Ellayne, and Martis, and their blinded chief; but of course they were gone by then. The Griffs expected to find their mardar left behind, dead. But they could read the ground almost as well as Helki and could see the others took Chillith with them when they left the camp.

"What do they want with him?" wondered Tiliqua, the son of Thurr. He could think of no reason why Martis wouldn't have killed Chillith.

"You boys are going to have to learn some new ways of thinking," Helki said. "It's wrong to kill a man because he's helpless, and most of all to do wrong just because you can. Martis and the children will protect that blind man and feed him."

"That is a very strange way to behave!" said Shalamoc, the son of Thilmoc.

"The true God is merciful, and He wants us to be like Him," Helki said. "I know it sounds peculiar; but that's what Obst says, and he's our teacher, and I reckon he would know."

"But Chillith was their enemy," Shalamoc said. "They could have easily killed him, now that he's blind."

The Griffs marveled over this lesson in mercy, and

Helki marveled over them. Griffs weren't a savage people; they had no name for cruelty. But then how many Obannese understood mercy, as Obst taught mercy? Helki knew many men in Lintum Forest who didn't. Meanwhile the Griffs fanned out in all directions, trying to pick up the trail. But Cavall found it first, and before the end of the day, it led to a ford across the Chariot River.

"They've gone into King Oziah's Wood," Helki said. "Martis must know they'll be safe there. The rangers will take care of them. The question is, should we go in after them?"

"We can't!" Tiliqua said. "Everybody knows it's death to enter that wood. There are ghosts in there who drink men's blood."

"Oh, faw! That's twaddle," Helki said. "I could go in alone, and it'd be perfectly safe for me. But Oziah's Wood has never been a hospitable place for Heathen."

The Griffs begged him to take them back to Obann and present them to the king, so they could receive amnesty and enter the king's service. It was hard to turn them down. They were frightened of many things, although they would be brave in a fight, and Helki pitied them. There was just time to get back to Obann before the snows, if they hurried, he thought. And Martis and the children would be safe in Oziah's Wood, as safe as they could be anywhere in the world.

"I promised the king I'd bring his hound back to him," Helki said, "so I guess we might as well go to Obann. I can't bring you men into Oziah's Wood with me: the rangers might fill you full of arrows before they knew they shouldn't. We might as well stick together."

The Griffs cheered; but if they'd known what lay in store for them, they probably wouldn't have.

Lord Reesh anticipated great things from the future, always provided he lived long enough to see them. Thanks to the road that the Thunder King's slaves had hacked through the woodlands, Reesh began to think he might last to the end of the journey, after all.

Everything was superbly organized, he thought. When Kyo and his men needed fresh horses, the horses were provided. Food, drink, shelter—all were available at regularly spaced outposts along the way. Whatever the mardar needed was his for the asking.

"Men like gods," Reesh meditated: for the men of the Empire were like gods, and what men were once, they could be again. "A road through the mountains is a very good start indeed!" For they were on the mountains' skirts now, and climbing, steadily climbing.

"I hadn't known the road was so far advanced," Kyo said. "Now I'm sure we'll be across the mountains before it snows enough to stop us. Someday there will be one road all the way from Kara Karram to Obann—maybe even to the sea."

"Someday there will be many roads like that," Reesh said.

When Kyo had spurred his horse ahead of the coach, Reesh caught Gallgoid looking pensive. "Speak your mind!" the First Prester said. "Hide none of your thoughts from me. I can't teach you if we don't talk."

"I was just thinking," the assassin said slowly, "that

things are going to get dicey when the Thunder King dies. Do they really think he won't? Can they truly believe he's a god? And what's going to happen when they find out that he isn't?"

"What do you think will happen?" Reesh said.

"I think they'll stop building roads. I think everything the Thunder King built will be torn down."

Reesh nodded. "So do I! That's why the new Temple must be firmly established as soon as possible," he said. "The Temple must do for East and West what it always did for Obann—hold it together. Be the center: the one thing that never changes, even when everything else changes. Only the Temple can keep man moving toward his destiny."

The cussetest thing about Gallgoid was that you knew he was thinking his own thoughts—and not the thoughts you wanted him to think!—but you couldn't pry them out of him. Lord Reesh knew that, and it taxed his patience. It made him miss Orth. There was a man who had no secrets—but burn him for a weakling!

"I have to keep on living," Reesh thought. "There has to be someone who can understand the mission of the Temple, and believe in it, and live for it. I can't be the only one!"

Fool that he was! Internally, Reesh sighed. Orth wasn't just a weakling. He was a parrot. He said what he thought the First Prester wanted to hear. He hadn't believed in the Temple. His vision was of First Prester Orth, the master of the Temple—that was the only future that had ever interested him. And this Gallgoid—Reesh ground his teeth. If Reesh had to guess—and with this fellow, everything could only be a guess—he would say the thing that most interested Gallgoid was waking up alive tomorrow. If he had to choose between his own skin and the Temple, the Temple would lose every time.

"I'll have to find true and trusty servants of the Temple among the servants of the Thunder King—no easy task!" Reesh thought. "Maybe there are mardars who might understand. Perhaps the Thunder King himself—"

He didn't dare put the rest of the thought into words.

CHAPTER 25

Hlah and the Rangers

Getting over the mountains was going to be harder than Hlah had expected. The upper reaches of the Imperial were thick with enemy camps; but now he learned he couldn't journey up the Chariot River, either. The Heathen were building a road, and there were armies waiting to use it.

He learned those things by talking to refugees. There weren't many of them. Most of the people had either fled months earlier or else been taken into slavery. The few refugees Hlah encountered had to be chased and cornered before they would talk to an Abnak. Hlah didn't blame them for that.

"There's only one way left for us to go," he told the madman, whom he had to drag along with him. "We can work our way around Oziah's Wood, and hope the rangers don't come out and kill me on sight, then struggle up the foothills and climb the mountains where there's no pass. I could do it, but I'm afraid you can't. You'll have to try, though."

Orth only showed his teeth. He hadn't told the Abnak his name yet, and he wasn't going to. He wasn't interested in getting across the mountain. All he wanted was to escape from himself, and that was impossible.

"You don't say much, do you?" Hlah said. "I wonder why God moves me to feed you every day. You wouldn't survive two days on your own. Come on!"

So Hlah passed under the eaves of Oziah's Wood, along the northern edge of the forest, where none of the Thunder King's scouts would see him. But he wasn't there for long before the rangers found him.

An arrow whistled past his ear and slammed into a tree. He knew it would have hit him between the eyes, had the archer been aiming for him. He stopped in his tracks and threw up his hands.

"Don't shoot—I come in peace!" he cried. "I know my looks are against me, but I'm King Ryons' man. Come out and talk to me before you kill me."

The rangers might have answered him with arrows, and he wouldn't have been surprised. Instead, four men with bows came out of hiding. They wore clothes dyed green and grey and brown, and deerskin moccasins that made no noise.

"Here's an Abnak who speaks our language and dares to come into King Oziah's Wood. Unusual!" said one. "And who's this with you? He's no Abnak."

Hlah shrugged. "I don't know what he is. I found him starving in the fens. He's lost his wits. I took him with me so he wouldn't die."

"Even more unusual!" said the ranger.

Hlah explained who he was and where he was going and why. The rangers questioned him closely.

"It's not likely anyone would make up a story like yours," said another. "Besides, we've heard something of these matters: that they have a king in Obann now, and that he came there with a Heathen army that fought for Obann. And we've heard the Temple is no more, although the city itself is safe."

Orth let out a sharp cry that startled everyone. He beat his breast with a fist and groaned. He clenched his eyes shut, but tears flowed out of them.

"What's the matter with him?" asked a ranger.

"I don't know. He's told me nothing."

"We won't kill a man who's on God's business," said the leader of the rangers. "Still, you can't stay here with us. We'll guide you through the wood and put you on your way to the hills. After that, let God preserve you if He will."

Two days they were with the rangers, during which they were conducted swiftly through the wood, to emerge facing the mountains. Orth hardly spoke a single word the whole time. The rangers could see he was a city man: "Tender feet and weak legs," they said.

Now under grey skies that maybe carried snow, they came out of the wood and looked up at the mountains, a purple rampart stretched across the sky.

"No one ever crosses by this route," a ranger said.

"That's why it's the only way that might be safe," Hlah answered.

"Do you know why they call this King Oziah's Wood?"

"I've heard the name of King Ozias," Hlah said, "and that he was the last of Obann's rightful kings. But I haven't been taught much of his history."

"He stopped here on his way out of Obann," the ranger said, "when they drove him out for the last time. It was here he wrote the last of the Songs. Here he spoke with Penda the prophet, and with the angel of the Lord. His enemies never came in after him: they were afraid. God's spirit rested on this forest. It kept them out.

"Now the Heathen mass along both rivers. They know we're here. Someday they might come in and hunt us down—maybe soon, we fear. But so far they haven't."

Hlah nodded. "Abnaks have never raided here," he said. "I never heard the reason why. Maybe God's spirit is still here."

The ranger grinned. "Our lives depend on it! There aren't enough of us to hold back even a small invasion. We pray the angel of the Lord is never far away."

Orth's teeth chattered. He shivered from head to toe, but wouldn't say what troubled him.

With his madman in tow, Hlah bade farewell to the rangers and left the wood. A few miles of withered grassland separated it from the forest that clothed the ankles of the mountains. Whether they could get up beyond the forests, and over the bare rock on the peaks, was all in God's hands, Hlah thought.

Before they reached the forest and the hills, it began to snow.

CHAPTER 26

How Gurun Met the King

The Blays scouted as close to the town of Hamber as they dared, practically venturing into its streets, to see when the Zamzu would come out in force. Shingis confided to Gurun, "My men fear Zamzu—afraid of being eaten! A hard thing, to stand and fight Zamzu. Much better run away."

"The whole village can't run away," Gurun answered. "What would you do if it was your own village, back home?"

He shrugged. The Blays' country had never been raided by the Zamzu. But Shingis was an honest man. "Can't let wives be eaten," he said. "Better to die fighting."

Before the Zamzu ever marched out of Hamber, two scouts—a Blay and a young farmer—came running one morning with evil tidings.

"Horsemen, many horsemen, coming from the east!" was their report. "And men on foot, too—too many to count. But they're not our own militia!"

At this hour of the morning, most of the Blays were off spying on the Zamzu, leaving just five behind to defend the village, along with the villagers themselves. Shingis was at Hamber, and none of the five Blays left spoke Obannese. One of them was Ghichmi, the expert marksman. Gurun sent a man to wake him. As soon as he saw the villagers' faces, he set about trying to organize a defense, manhandling villagers into position behind their flimsy fence. Loyk helped him round up able-bodied men—and women, too—and see that they all had some kind of weapon in their hands.

"I suppose this is the end!" he said to Gurun. "Even if all the Blays were here, what could we do against a horde of enemies?"

"That is no question to be asking me!" Gurun said. "We do the best we can—what else?—and pray that God will fight for us."

"And if He doesn't?"

"It's a shame to say a thing like that," said Gurun.

It didn't take long to get the defenders mustered to their posts; there weren't that many of them. Nor did they have long to wait for the first of the horsemen to appear atop the nearest hill.

Gurun took a stand in the middle of the village, where everyone could see her. If they thought she knew how to command them in a battle, they were wrong. But at least she wouldn't hide.

"They're coming!" cried a farmer. Some of the defenders put stones in their slings—but how many riders could they hope to stop? Loyk's knuckles went white as he gripped his scythe and waited. The old man had courage, Gurun thought.

And then Ghichmi yelled something at his fellow Blays, and shoved a villager who was about to let fly with a stone. What could he be doing?

"It's Osker!" someone shouted. "Osker and that trapper, come back from Obann!"

Gurun moved up to the fence for a closer look. It was

true: Tim and the plowman rode out before the other horsemen, and Tim was waving. Gurun went outside the fence to let him see her.

"It's all right," he called to her. "The king has come to see you!"

So it was the king, and those were the king's horsemen and the king's foot soldiers; and Gurun nearly fainted on the spot. Who was she that a king would come to her? She felt like a child caught in an outrageous lie, for which the punishment would be severe. It was worse than the time she'd told her uncle that her father said she could take the skiff out on the bay alone—when he hadn't.

She tried to spot the king among his men. He would be tall, and dressed in shining armor, with a gold crown on his head. But there was no one like that anywhere in view.

Nor were the king's men as she imagined them. Some of the riders were wiry little men with bows and arrows. Others were tall and lean with feathers in their hair. Most of the footmen had shaved heads and tattoos; a few wore wolf's heads for helmets. What kind of Obannese troops were these?

The villagers dropped their weapons and gathered round her, staring hard. "These are no men of Obann!" Loyk said. Nevertheless, there were Tim and Osker, and they seemed perfectly happy in that company.

"You were right, Gurun—there was a king in Obann," Tim said. He reined his horse to a halt in front of her. Beside him, Osker the plowman dismounted and stretched like a man still not used to riding.

"Who are all those men, Osker?" Loyk asked.

"They're some of the Heathen men the king brought with him when he saved the city," Osker said. "They look like Heathen, but everybody says they aren't anymore, that they serve God the same as we do. It's quite a story, if you can find someone to tell it."

"But where is the king?" said Gurun, still looking for him.

"Why, he's right there—riding with those little fellows with the bows and arrows," Tim said. "I guess you can't see him from here."

"Well, then, take me out to meet him!" Gurun wouldn't let the king come to her; it wouldn't be good manners. She made Tim turn his horse and lead her toward the advancing riders. When they saw her coming, they all stopped.

"Here she is, Your Majesty!" Tim called.

The mounted bowmen parted ranks; and there on a small horse that was still too big for him, Gurun saw not a man, not a mighty warrior, but a boy—a scrawny little boy with a headdress of black feathers (the headdress of a Wallekki chief, if she but knew it). Beside him on his left, on a bigger horse, sat a tall man with a taller headdress, and on his right, one of the little archers.

Was this the king the filgya meant for her to see—this boy? It was as if her littlest brother, runny nose and all, were called a king. And yet Gurun found herself curtseying, island-fashion, as a girl would curtsey to a chief of men, or to her father on her wedding day. What made her do it? She didn't know. But she said, in spite of her surprise, "Your Highness does me greater honor than I deserve. Welcome, King of Obann!"

Ryons enjoyed getting out of Obann, out from other roofs and walls. At the insistence of the chiefs he went with five hundred picked men—all of the Ghols, who would never leave his side, plus some Wallekki riders under a trusted subchief, a few of the most valiant among the Fazzan, and two hundred Abnaks on foot led by Uduqu. "I've never seen the sea," Uduqu said, "and I'm not even sure there is such a thing. But to see this girl who came over the sea would be the next best thing."

And now here she was, tall and fair and dressed in a white homespun dress (Loyk's wife had made it for her), and Ryons had never seen anyone like her before. It was easy to believe she'd come from across the sea. It was almost as if she shone. Ryons didn't even know what the sea was, not really. Maybe it was something like the stars in heaven. Maybe this girl had come down from a star.

"You wished to see me," he said, "and I wanted to see you! Now here we are."

"Sire, this is Gurun, who came here from certain islands on the sea—a place that no one ever heard of before," said Tim. "Gurun, this is His Majesty King Ryons, King of Obann. And that's all I know how to say!"

Ryons tried to remember the advice Obst had given him. "Surely God's hand is in this," Obst had said. "No one sails the sea. It's been a thousand years since any man of Obann did so. How a girl could do it is more than I know! But you can be sure that she was sent to you for a reason. She spoke of a king in Obann before you came here—at the very least, she is a prophet. Treat her with respect and honor, and bring her back to the city with you, if you can."

Some of the villagers had crept after Gurun, close enough to whisper to her. This they were now doing with some urgency. She listened to them for a moment, then turned back to the king.

"Sire," she said—because that was how Tim had addressed him, and it must be right, "you find us in danger. Not far from here, there are a hundred bandits in a town called Hamber. They are eaters of men. They were once in the Heathen army that was driven from Obann. Zamzu, they are called."

"Did you say Zamzu?" Out from the ranks of the footmen stepped Uduqu, brandishing the sword of Shogg. "Do you see this sword, maiden? It used to belong to a Zamzu champion, a giant. Now its purpose is to chop down Zamzu wherever they may be. King Ryons is here to protect his people from the likes of them."

His Obannese was good enough for the villagers to understand him, and they cheered his words.

"Another thing, Sire!" said Gurun. "I have with me twenty men from the country of the Blays. They, too, were in the Heathen army. Now they live here in Jocah's Creek, in peace. But when they see you, they'll be afraid."

"Tell them they have nothing to fear," Uduqu said. "There's a pardon for anyone who swears peace to the king of Obann. Thousands of men have been so pardoned. Some of them have gone home, but most have taken service with the king."

Gurun curtseyed again. Ryons couldn't take his eyes off her.

"Let's get the tent pitched, Father," said Chagadai, the

captain of the Ghols. "Then you can eat and drink and have a proper talk with this unusually tall young woman." He spoke to Ryons in Wallekki, which they both understood: few of the countries in the East were unvisited by Wallekki traders. Ghols complained the Obannese language was too barbarous for ordinary men to learn. "I know Teacher Obst thinks she's a person of great importance. So let's serve her a nice supper, eh?"

CHAPTER 27

What Angel Saw, But Could Not Tell

This was the day they would emerge from King Oziah's Wood, Martis said; and he had decided to go to Ninneburky. "It'll be good for you to be home again," he told the children. Ellayne rejoiced, but Jack sulked.

He wasn't allowed to sulk for long. They hadn't seen Wytt all morning. Now, as they approached the forest's edge, he suddenly burst out on them, chattering excitedly.

"We can't go on!" Ellayne said: she and Jack understood the Omah's message. "There are a lot of men out there between the forest and the river, more men than Wytt can count—not that he can count very high. But he thinks it looks bad."

"Are they like the men who are here in the forest?" Jack asked. Wytt chirped and whistled. "He says they're different," Jack explained. "He doesn't like what he sees."

"Can I get close enough to see for myself?" Martis asked. "Would he go with me, to show me?" Wytt agreed, and Martis went off with him. Jack wanted to go, too, but Martis said, "Easier for them to spot two of us than one. And if I get captured, maybe the three of you can help me."

"Two kids and a blind man—some help!" Ellayne said after he was gone. "It'll be Heathen out there, of course. Right between us and home!"

"They must be planning to come into Oziah's Wood, after all," Jack said.

Chillith stood quietly, peering, peering ahead as if he expected to see something, when he could see nothing at all. It got on Jack's nerves.

"They will come into this forest, and soon," the Griff said. "The Thunder King desires it. I can feel his desire like a hot breath on the back of my neck."

"He'll be sorry if he tries it," Ellayne said. "God put a blessing on this place. The Thunder King's men can't come in."

"But they will," said Chillith. "He will defy the God of Obann, to prove himself the stronger god. Stronger than the God who took away my sight." And he fell silent after saying that.

Martis soon returned. "There's a fortified camp between the forest and the river," he said. "I climbed a tree and had a good look. I saw Zephites—easy to recognize them by the horns they wear. They must have been part of the army that tried to capture Ninneburky, but failed. I saw horses with Wallekki riders. There are several hundred men, and it looks to me like more will be coming to join them."

"We ought to tell the rangers," Jack said.

"I'm sure they know already—at least the rangers in this part of the wood," Martis said. "We're going to have to change our course. We can't come out of the forest anywhere near here."

"Chillith says they're going to come in," Ellayne said.

"We don't want to be here when they do," said Martis.

Angel the hawk saw more than any man could see.

She saw the new road inching its way down from the mountains along the north bank of the Chariot, the masses of slaves toiling over it, the armies poised to march—and some already marching. She saw Heathen hosts camped in forts along the west slope of the mountains, slowly working their way down the Imperial River into the heart of Obann. She saw several camps made north of the Imperial, where men mustered for the invasion of King Oziah's Wood.

She flew sometimes as high as the mountains themselves, and higher still—high enough to see what was on the other side. High up in a pass, where the new road began, she saw fresh snow on the mountains and a vast army of warriors and slaves feverishly working.

Across the pass, facing Obann, they were constructing a stone wall, with great gates bound in iron. Behind the gates they had enclosed a wide area within a palisade, occupying nearly the whole pass itself; and inside the palisade were staked out the shapes of many buildings yet to rise. An endless procession of teams of oxen transported lumber up the east side of the mountains to the site. Men toiled day and night, hammering, sawing, digging.

Angel was a man's hawk, hand-raised, not a wild bird: she looked on wild birds with disdain. The man who had raised her from an egg was gone now, killed by enemies. For a time Angel hadn't cared whether she herself lived or died. But there was a new man for her now, a man who knew how to look into a hawk's eye, and how to let her see into his. They couldn't speak to one another, and yet their minds met. So Angel was content; and no matter how high she soared, nor how far, she always came back to Helki.

When she did, she tried to tell him what she'd seen, because he was a man and he would want to know. But of course no hawk has ever learned quite how to do that.

"I wish I could fly up there with you, baby-girl," Helki said. "You must know where everything is—if only you could tell me!" He tickled a special spot at the base of her neck that she couldn't get to with her beak. The twelve Griffs watched him uneasily. They were convinced Helki and Angel spoke to one another without words, by some kind of magic.

They'd turned back and were following the Chariot down to what was left of Cardigal Town, where the Chariot flowed into the Imperial. From there it would be an easy trip back to Obann City.

But now Helki didn't feel like turning back. "Something's up," he muttered. Today the hawk had stayed aloft for a long time, flown clear out of sight, and had come back tense and fidgety. She was seeing things that made her so. And Cavall kept pricking up his ears and prancing around in circles; something had his nerves on edge.

"What's bothering the animals?" asked one of the Griffs.

"I don't know," Helki said. "Maybe they sense bad weather coming." And maybe, he thought, they feared worse.

They were passing many parties going down the mountains into Obann, Lord Reesh noted, as the coach and its escort carried him up into the foothills.

"I have told you my master the Thunder King cannot be defeated," said Mardar Kyo. They had stopped at an outpost on the road for a change of horses. "Even now his thought speaks to me, as he speaks to all his mardars.

"He is stretching forth his hand. Before this country sees another summer, he will have seized all Obann. He will pull down that great city and build a greater city in its place, one that will bear his name forever. He will not stop for the winter, as a mortal man would do."

When they were on their way again, Gallgoid said, "I wonder what he meant. I wonder what they're going to do."

"The Thunder King is going to finish what he's started," Reesh said. "It's obvious he's moving new armies into Obann. They'll be poised to strike as soon as spring begins. His resources must be inexhaustible."

"Unless he dies," said Gallgoid. "I'm surprised he's lived this long. They mustn't have very good assassins out there in the East."

Reesh then answered, very slowly, "And what if he were not to die?"

Gallgoid looked at him, leaving the question to lie unanswered for a minute.

"I'm a plain man, my lord," he said. "I can't make out what your lordship means."

Reesh suddenly knew exactly what he meant. The idea had been a-birthing in some dark cellar of his mind where he didn't have to look at it, or acknowledge it was there. For a time there were only faint stirrings of it, easily repressed.

But now here it was, fully formed and right out in the open: his own words, just now, had let it out of the dark. It was an appalling thing to see—to know that a thing like that had come out of your own mind.

"My lord?" said Gallgoid.

Reesh shook him off. What he had in his mind was for the Thunder King alone. Not for Gallgoid, not even for a mardar—this was a thing to be kept secret.

And it was rapidly revealing itself as a thing that had to be. It would be wrong, and foolish, to shy away from it. If you begin by admitting that there is no God, Reesh reasoned—

"My lord!" Gallgoid was staring at him. "Are you going to be sick, my lord? You've gone all pale."

"It was just a little spasm," Lord Reesh said. "I'm all right now." At least he would be, he thought, if this new burden didn't crush him.

CHAPTER 28

How the King Saved Hamber

The chiefs who were with Ryons decided to clear the Zamzu out of Hamber right away. Growing up as a slave among the Wallekki, Ryons had heard of the Zamzus' taste for human flesh. For this all the peoples of the East despised and loathed them. But they feared them, too.

"We'll hit them before they even know we're here," Uduqu said. And so it was that they marched out that very night, and Shingis and the Blays marched with them, overjoyed that the king would have them for his friends.

Gurun rode with Ryons in the rear. She'd never been on a horse before and was trying very hard not to look like a clumsy fool.

"It's hard, isn't it?" Ryons said. "I've had a lot of practice, and I'm still afraid I might fall off. And then my Ghols would be ashamed."

"We don't have many horses, where I live," she said.

"Did you really come here over the sea?" Ryons asked.

"Yes—and it wasn't easy," Gurun said.

"What is the sea?"

To someone who has lived on an island all her life, that

is a rather difficult question to answer. But before she could get halfway into an answer, the chief of the Ghols bade them to be quiet from now on. They were approaching Hamber and mustn't be heard.

It was just midnight. Because the Blays had already scouted the approaches to the town, the chiefs had been able to devise a plan. Part of it was for the king and Gurun to stay out of the fighting, with a few Ghols to watch over them. Ryons had already been in battles and had no wish to be in any more of them.

The Zamzu had dug a ditch around the town but not yet flooded it with water, nor erected a stockade. The Blays knew where all the sentries were. Abnaks crept up and silenced them before they could raise an alarm. The rest of the king's men, most of them dismounted, rushed over the ditch and into the town. Abnak war-whoops, Wallekki battle songs, and the weird and wolfish howling of the Fazzan shattered the silence of the night.

Taken in their sleep, the Zamzu had but little chance. Some fought their way out of the town, only to be shot down by Ghol horse-archers and Blay slingers. The rest fell to Abnak tomahawks, Wallekki swords, and the short spears of the Fazzan. The Zamzu were big men and strong, but badly outnumbered and surprised. Three or four of them broke through and charged straight for Ryons and Gurun, but they didn't get far. Ryons couldn't help admiring how Gurun sat straight up in her saddle and didn't turn a hair, when it was all he could do not to jump to the ground and run away. If he had known more about such things, he would have thought her every inch a queen. But he did think she was very fine indeed.

"Now hear this, you people of Hamber!" That was Uduqu, whose barbarously accented Obannese was better than anyone else's in the king's company. He stood on a barrel in the middle of the town, with a crowd of pale-faced, wide-eyed townsfolk gathered round him. "We've saved you from your enemies at the command of Ryons, King of Obann by the grace of God whose mercy endureth forever.

"There is a king in Obann now because God wills it. We who fight for him were Heathen once, but we aren't anymore. Don't be afraid of us! When the sun comes up again, you'll find yourselves safe and free, with all your enemies destroyed. Praise God and honor your king."

There was some cheering, but most of the people didn't yet understand what had happened and were still afraid of the Zamzu. They were probably afraid of Uduqu, too.

"Let the Zamzu lie where they've fallen," said the Wallekki chief. "When the people find them in the morning and have to bury them, then they'll understand." The other chiefs agreed; and before there was a hint of dawn in the sky, they were on their way back to Jocah's Creek. Shingis came running up to salute Gurun with his spear.

"Good to see Zamzu all killed—very nice!" he said. "You pray good and strong, Gurun, and Obann God hears you. He sends a king. A king for everybody—eh?"

"Yes," said Gurun, looking at Ryons and not knowing exactly what it was she saw, or what she said. "Yes—I think a king for everybody." And she believed it as she said it.

There was resting and feasting at Jocah's Creek all the

next day, but the king's men wouldn't stay a second day. They understood it would deplete the village's stores if they did.

Gurun tried to explain to Ryons the nature of the sea. He wasn't the only one who'd never seen it. Only a few of the Wallekki in his company had ever been that far west.

"There is the earth, and heaven, and the sea," she said. "The sea is water. I think there must be more of the sea than there is of the earth. Once upon a time there was nothing but the water, until God made the dry land to rise up from the deep and placed the heavens over all. That was in the very beginning, as Holy Scripture tells us."

"But how can people live in the sea?" Ryons wondered.

"They don't! They live on islands, which are dry land in the middle of the sea. My home is on an island. A great storm blew me all the way across the sea to Obann."

It amazed Gurun that men could know so little of the sea. Tim told her that no one in Obann ever ventured out on the sea, not ever. They had boats of all kinds for going up and down the rivers, and there were the ruins of cities by the sea—cities that must have once been ports. But there were no live cities, with people living in them, within miles of the coast. Why this was, Tim didn't know.

Ryons pleaded with Gurun to come back to Obann with him. Now that they had amnesty, the Blays were happy to go there with her. "Where you go, we go," Shingis said.

"All of us here in Jocah's Creek will miss the Blays," Loyk said. But at least the Zamzu were put down, and the king's chiefs had promised to send officers to raise a militia in the country. "We'll miss you, too, Gurun. But maybe you'll come back to us someday. Maybe in the spring, God willing."

"I've never seen a great city," Gurun said. "We have none, on our islands—not even villages like this. I will be the first of all our people ever to see a city."

Yes, the idea of it excited her; but it was more than just the lure of the city. The filgya had told her she must see the king, and now she had. There had to be more to it than that, she thought: "No filgya speaks without good reason. There must be something about this little king, something very important. But I must wait to find out what it is."

They said he saved the city just as the enemy was about to destroy it. They said prophets of God had named him king. There were prophets in the Scriptures, but those were tales of ancient times. Who, wondered Gurun, would have thought there could be kings and prophets in the present day?

So it was that Gurun rode beside the king when he returned to Obann, and her Blays marched around her, among the king's Ghols on horseback. It was funny to see them try to talk to one another. As for the king himself, he sat a little taller in the saddle, thinking about the sea, and how it had brought this marvelous creature of a girl to Obann—and to him.

CHAPTER 29

How the Animals Fled

Ordinarily it would be a day's hard hiking from Oziah's Wood to the edges of the forests on the foothills. But with his madman in tow, Hlah thought, they would do well to make the trip in two days, maybe three.

He soon began to doubt that estimate, too. The snow didn't come down hard, but it didn't let up, either. Not a ray of sunlight peeped through the clouded sky.

There were movements in the grey grass. Ever on the lookout for edible game that he might bring down, Hlah found a few stones suitable for throwing. Sooner or later an animal would show itself. When they came to a place where there were some bare spots in the grass, he stopped.

"Be quiet now, and be still," he said. "Something tasty might come our way." Orth made no answer, but he did keep quiet.

First Hlah saw a few birds running, birds with long tails and dirty purple plumage. There was something about them that looked wrong, but he only glimpsed them for a moment, and when he threw a stone, he missed. They vanished back into the grass in the blink of an eye. He wondered if they were like the bird Jandra had—that hissing horror with teeth in its beak and claws on its wings.

Just out of sight, always out of sight, small creatures

darted here and there. And then Hlah saw an animal he couldn't name, although he'd been a hunter all his life. If he had ever seen an alligator, he might have described this as a small alligator covered with untidy black fur and running very fast indeed with a peculiar scuttling motion. But he'd never seen anything remotely like it, and he wouldn't mind if he never saw it again.

Then, of all things, a fat groundhog burst out of the grass and Hlah had the good luck to knock it over with a stone. He killed it with his tomahawk before it could recover, and held it up triumphantly.

"Look! A fine supper for us tonight!" he said. "We could have asked for nothing better."

Even a madman would be pleased, he thought; but Orth only stood and stared. He stared so hard that Hlah turned around.

Coming straight at them at a high speed was a bird the size of a horse, with a massive hooked beak gaping open like the gulf of doom. And there was absolutely no chance of escape and nothing to hide behind.

Hlah had heard of these great birds, even seen some at a distance, and he knew that they were lethal. There was nothing he could do but stand his ground, tomahawk in one hand, knife in the other. "So dies Hlah, the son of Spider!" he thought.

But he didn't die. The bird veered a little and charged right past them, turning only its head to glare and hiss at them as it passed, not even breaking stride. And behind it came a stag and several does. These passed, too, following the giant bird. Hlah turned and watched them go.

"What do you think of that?" he said. "If you asked me,

I'd say they were all headed for Oziah's Wood. Does something chase them there? But I don't see anything."

"The prophets said it was the end of days, the day of the Lord's wrath—but I hanged the prophets. The Lord sent His prophets to us, and we hanged them!" The madman threw back his head and laughed. "The beasts run from the wrath of God. Someone must have told them Oziah's Wood has a blessing on it. But all blessings are revoked, revoked—hah!"

It was the longest speech Hlah had ever heard him make, but he couldn't get him to explain it. It took some doing to get Orth moving forward again. All around them, running past them, fled animals and birds in the opposite direction. It kept on snowing. You could now see it on the ground.

"We'll have to stop early to set up any kind of decent shelter," Hlah thought. "If it turns into a heavy snow, then God help me"—he meant it as a prayer.

Cavall faced the East and howled. None of Helki's men saw anything for a dog to howl at, so Cavall's performance made them all uneasy. Cavall didn't care about them, and paid them no attention. Snow blew into his face, and he howled. Great evil lay in that direction. It lay heavy on his heart.

Helki knelt beside him.

"You know something we don't know, don't you? There's a good dog—you'd tell me all about it, if you could." The man ruffled the thick fur between the great hound's shoulders. Cavall realized the man understood as much as any man could understand. Cavall inched a little closer to him and howled again.

With a harsh cry, Angel flew down and landed on Helki's shoulder. She hunched up her wings and scrunched her head between them, glaring fiercely. She, too, had things to say, if only she could, Helki thought. Then he noticed the Griffs staring at him.

"Don't be so superstitious, boys—there's no witchcraft here," he said. "These animals are upset. If you look around, you'll see they're not the only ones. Birds have been flying east-to-west all day—and when was the last time you saw a squirrel? You can hear them chattering at someone, but not at us. Use your eyes and ears."

"Our eyes and ears are not like yours, Giant-killer," said Tiliqua. "You understand the speech of birds and beasts. The soles of your feet see and study the ground even as you walk on it. Probably the snow is speaking to you, too."

Helki shook his head. "Not today it doesn't." He stood up. "But I don't need the snow to tell me there's something nasty brewing in the East, and not so far away. We'd better go see what it is."

That was not at all what the Griffs wanted to do, but they would follow Helki. Angel dug her claws into his shoulder and made an odd purring noise when she saw he meant to turn back the way they'd come. Few men had ever heard that noise—the strongest protest that a hawk could make, short of biting. But she did nip him when he reached up to pet her.

"Don't want to go that way, do you?" he said. "Well, you're probably right about it; but stick close to me, and Cavall will protect the both of us." Helki knew the hawk understood him much better than he could understand her. She settled down into a quiet sulk.

Jack liked snow and snowball fights and sliding downhill on stiffened cowhides. That's what all the children in Ninneburky would be looking forward to today. But here there was nothing to do but to trudge back into the depths of the forest, away from the edge where the Heathen were encamped. Martis set a brisk pace for the party; it was cold, and no one talked.

Just past noon, three rangers met them.

"We were looking for you," said their leader.

"And we were looking for you," Martis said. "There's an enemy camp by the south edge of the wood, with several hundred warriors in it. Zephites, mostly."

"We know," said the ranger. "There's a bigger camp up on the northern edge. They've crossed both the rivers. They mean to come in here and flush us out, but they're building up their numbers first. Women and children have to move to the center of the wood. That's why we were looking for you: we were told about these two kids and the blind man. We'll take them to a safer place. If you want to stay with us and lend a hand in the fighting, when it comes, we'd appreciate it."

"I'm under a vow to protect these children," Martis said.

"There are other children in Oziah's Wood," said a younger ranger. "Some of us have brought our families here."

"How many fighting men do you have?"

"In the whole forest, maybe a thousand of us, all told. Not enough!"

The youngest of the three rangers, hardly more than a boy, shook his head. "Why would they go to so much trouble to drive us out of here?" he said. "There's nothing here for them to take, except our hides. What do they need to do it for?"

Wytt never showed himself to strangers—so Ellayne yelped when he suddenly leaped on top of the pack on Ham's back and startled everyone with a series of ear-piercing shrieks. The rangers jumped. The leader actually dropped his bow. But he was quick to snatch it up again.

"Stop! It's all right, he's with us!" Ellayne held up her hands, terrified that these men would kill Wytt.

"What is that critter?" growled the leader. He'd been scared and he didn't like it.

"He's our friend," Jack said, stepping up beside Ellayne. "Don't hurt him! He's telling you to fight—fight hard."

"But what is he?" the second ranger cried.

"He's one of the Hairy Ones mentioned in the Scriptures," Martis said. "Mostly people never see them."

"He's an Omah," Ellayne said, "and he's telling us that there are Omah in this forest and that they'll fight for us. He's already spoken with them, and they're ready." And Wytt chattered loudly, brandishing his sharpened stick.

"You mean it speaks?"

"He speaks to us," Jack said, "and we understand him when he does."

"You have to believe us!" Ellayne said.

"Why have we never seen anything like him before?" demanded the young ranger. But the eldest put a hand on his shoulder and said, "No one has ever seen everything that's in the forest, son. Any man who says he has, hasn't been here very long."

"Well, they do say God put a blessing on King Oziah's Wood," the second ranger said. "Funny kind of blessing, though!"

Chillith nodded, and for the first time spoke.

"He has put a blessing here," the blind man said. "That is why the Thunder King must send his army here—to defy the God of Obann. He must show himself to be the greater god."

"Then," said the eldest ranger with a grin, "this ought to be a fight worth having!"

CHAPTER 30

The Golden Pass

The new road wound its way up the mountain, turning a journey of weeks into one of days. On either side of the road marched dense, dark forest. Lord Reesh could not imagine the labor required to hack a passage through that forest. It was an achievement worthy of the ancient Empire. "Whatever else he may be," Reesh thought, "the Thunder King is a man who gets great things done."

"Do you smell that, my lord?"

Gallgoid startled him by speaking. Between the monotony of trees everywhere you looked, and the rocking motion of the coach, the First Prester had been lulled into something like a trance.

"What are you talking about?" he snapped.

"That smell, my lord."

Now Reesh noticed it. Quite a nasty smell it was—sweetish, cloying: just a little more, and it would be downright sickening.

"I don't like it," he said. "I wonder what it is."

"Dead bodies," Gallgoid said, "the people who died building the road. No telling how many. It smells like they tried to burn most of them—probably too many at once."

"You're a fine one to be getting squeamish over some dead bodies!"

"Can't help minding the smell. I hope it's gone, once we get above the tree line."

"You have tender sensibilities, for an assassin," Lord Reesh said. "Do you think we can turn back from the course we've chosen? Do you think God will reach down from Heaven and pluck us out of the Thunder King's hand?"

"He'd hardly do that for us," Gallgoid muttered.

Reesh pretended not to hear it. "I am unlucky in my allies," he thought, pitying himself. He spent some moments silently cursing Orth. Mardar Kyo interrupted him, spurring his horse up beside the window of the coach.

"By this time two days from now, we will have reached the pass, First Prester," he said. "I am told it used to be called Bear Pass, and was only good enough for trading men and Abnak raiding parties. No good for an army! But this road has changed everything—even the name of the pass. Now it shall be called the Golden Pass."

"Why golden?" asked Reesh.

The mardar grinned at him. "Soon you will see for yourself!" he said.

Angel the hawk had already seen. Flying up as high as the bottom of the clouds, her eye caught a far-off glint of gold. No human eye would have seen it at that distance. Because it was something that should not have been there, she swooped eastward for a closer look. Many miles that would have wearied man or beast to trek slipped away under her wings. Riding the air currents, she hardly had to flap her wings. In moments she was out of Helki's sight, far down below. His eyes followed her as far as they could, and his thought, much farther.

Where before she'd seen a wall flung across the pass and a stockade, she now saw swarms of men within the stockade working like ants. It unsettled her to see so many.

They were building a hall, a very great hall, and had already set up the strong timbers that proclaimed its size and shape. Wherever the sun peeked through the clouds, its rays struck sheets of gold. These were laid out on the ground: a human would have been hard-put to count them, and the hawk didn't try. But a human would have guessed that the gold was meant for the walls and for the roof so that the whole building would be golden.

Angel felt a strong compulsion to keep her distance from the place. She was a brave bird, with little experience of fear; but this new thing in the mountains made her uneasy. Had she been able to speak, she couldn't have told you why. It was a fear that had no name. It was like black water seeping up inside her. With a shrill cry of defiance, she turned away from it.

When she returned to Helki, he looked into her eyes and knew she'd seen something evil. He held her in his arms to comfort her. Cavall looked up at them anxiously.

"Boys," he said to the Griffs who followed him, "people who've got any sense don't make war in the winter; but something tells me war is coming. The question is, where do we want to be when it comes, and how much time have we got to get there? We ought to have an army, and there are only thirteen of us—fourteen, counting Cavall."

A Griff named Shalla said, "If we keep on going east, we'll find the war soon enough. It's going to pour down from the mountains." The others nodded. "But we have put our lives in your hands, Giant-slayer. Lead us where you will."

"If I had any sense, I'd go back to Lintum Forest where I belong," said Helki.

"If we stretch our legs, and if we can cross the rivers, we can get to Lintum Forest in seven days," Tiliqua said. "Maybe we can find an army there."

Maybe we could, at that, Helki thought. There were the settlers. There were the robber bands he'd conquered. Maybe he could scare up a hundred good men.

"Lintum's where I come from," he said. He wished Obst were here, or Jandra, to advise him. "And God is there, as He is everywhere. Maybe back in Lintum Forest, God will speak to me."

CHAPTER 31

How the King Returned to Obann

Chief Shaffur and a hundred of his riders met the king before his party came in sight of Obann. The tall Wallekki was without his feathered headdress. Instead, he wore a bandage round his forehead, and some blood had seeped through. He seemed to take no notice of Gurun riding beside the king.

"What news, Chieftain?" asked the subchief who rode with Ryons.

"Your Majesty," Shaffur said, "the city has risen against us and you are locked out. Except for me and these few warriors, the rest of your people are locked in. We were lucky to fight our way out before it was too late."

It took Ryons a moment to grasp what Shaffur was saying. Locked out of his city? But Uduqu understood at once.

"What of our people in the city?" he said. "Do they live? Can they be rescued?"

"I don't know. We got out yesterday. It was necessary for us to escape so we could warn you. When we left, our people held the palace, with Chief Spider and General

Hennen in command."

"How much fighting?" Uduqu asked.

Shaffur flashed a grin at him. "Once they saw your Abnaks waiting for them with stone tomahawks, the rebels kept their distance. Most of the fighting was at the gate: they tried to keep us in. There would have been much more, but Obst restrained the chiefs. It took some doing to hold back Zekelesh and his Fazzan. They longed to wash their spears!"

Ryons found his voice. "But what happened?" he cried. "How did it get started?"

"It was those young men who started it—the ones who say we burned their Temple." Shaffur frowned. "Hennen warned us they'd make trouble."

Gurun spoke no tribe-talk, but she could see that something bad had happened.

"But Obst is safe?" said Ryons. "And Nanny?"

"Sire, none of your people have been killed," Shaffur said, "although a few were hurt when the rebels pelted us with stones. Obst is safe in the palace. I don't know about Nanny; but Zekelesh is guarding her, so she should be safe enough.

"But the rebels have manned the walls and blocked the gates, and throngs of them surround the palace, ready to stone anyone who shows his face. Before long the chiefs must drive them back, and then there will be killing. Maybe, now that you've returned, we're strong enough to fight our way back into the city."

"I don't doubt we are," Uduqu said, "but I wonder what Obst would say. I don't think he'd like it."

Ryons didn't know what Obst would say, but he did

know what God had said—it seemed a lifetime ago, but it was only this just-past summer—when He spoke through Jandra. Ryons heard it again in his mind: "Wherever you go, I am with you; whatever you do, I shall protect you."

"Chief Shaffur," he said, "take me to my city. I want to talk to the people."

Gurun couldn't understand what Ryons said, but the warrior with the bandaged forehead stared hard at him. This was a boy speaking to a seasoned man of war: and in the man's eyes was something that saw not a boy, but a king. Maybe even more than a king—Gurun thought there was awe in his expression. And all the men around the king fell silent and still—grown men doing honor to a boy.

Shaffur pressed his fingertips to his lips and bowed his head. That was how the Wallekki saluted a great lord. "As Your Highness commands!" he said.

"There's trouble in the city," Ryons explained to Gurun, as they rode toward Obann. "Some of the people think we burned down the Temple. It isn't true. The fire was already burning when I first saw the city, and our men hadn't got there yet."

"But you saved the city, didn't you?" Gurun asked.

"God did it all. I just tried to hold on!" He told her how the great beast followed him across the plains, then picked him up and set him on its back and scattered the Heathen. "But now the people have locked us out of the city, and most of our men are trapped inside."

"What are you going to do?" Gurun wondered.

He shrugged. "Ask them to open the gate and let us

in," he said. "Or else let my people out—and then we'll go away."

He didn't know how to tell her that God had made him a king, who was a slave, and given him Obann. Not that he didn't believe it. After everything that had happened, he had to believe it. But he didn't know how to talk about it.

Gurun looked down from the hills upon the city of Obann, where there were more people than on all the northern islands put together, and great buildings like mountains, and a vast wall all around it. South of the wall stretched the silver ribbon of the river; and across the river she saw the wilderness of stone and rubble that was the ruins of Old Obann.

"Is this a dream?" she marveled. But it was too fantastic for a dream: no one born on Fogo Island could ever dream a thing like this. Besides, there were people all around her, and the sun shining, and a nip of winter in the air, plus the horse she was riding and the smell of horses all around her. This was no dream. They were up on a hill, and the road before them led straight down to the city, just a mile or two away. She hardly knew what to make of it.

Then she saw a man out in front of the king's company, marching alone. He hadn't been there an eyeblink ago.

At that moment he turned and looked at her, and smiled—a fine, tall man, young, with flowing golden hair and beard, eyes of icy blue, clad in gorgeously dyed and patterned woolen clothes, with sealskin boots on his feet and a short sword thrust into his sealskin belt: a man of the North, an islander.

"Filgya!" she gasped.

"Stay close to the king, Gurun," he called to her—and no one else heard him, although he spoke up loud and clear and in the language of the islands. "Don't leave his side."

Gurun couldn't help turning to look at the boy king. He was staring straight at the filgya, leaning forward in his saddle like someone keenly listening. Great heavens! Did Ryons see it, too? But when Gurun turned again, the filgya wasn't there anymore.

"Your Majesty!" she said. "Did you see that man?"

"Yes!" Ryons answered. "And I saw him once before, when I was on my way to Obann. He said he was a servant of the Lord. He told me I would cross the river. Obst said he might have been an angel. He said God was pleased with me, and that someday he would speak to me again—and he just has."

What had Ryons seen? That was not the filgya, Gurun thought. A filgya was never visible to but one person at a time. But could there be two of them in the same place at once?

"What did he say to you just now?" she asked.

"Only that I should go down to the city and that God is with me." His eyes widened. "You didn't see him, too! Did you?"

"What did he look like?" Gurun said.

"Just an old man with a white beard."

They'd each seen someone different—and no one else saw anything at all. Or had they? "Ask one of those riders if he saw anyone," she said.

Ryons asked Chagadai, the captain of the Ghols. Chagadai looked at him quizzically. "What do you mean,

Father?" he said. "There was no one out in front of us. Are you all right?"

"Yes—I just thought I saw someone." Ryons didn't try to tell Chagadai any more than that—not now, at least. He turned back to Gurun. "They didn't see him. Only you and I did. What does it mean?"

"It means that God is with us, like the old man said," Gurun answered. "I will go with you to the city." How could she tell him she'd seen a different personage and received a different message? "Maybe that's just how it is with filgyas," she thought. It wasn't as if there was anyone alive who understood the ways of filgyas.

The way to the city was all downhill. The wall loomed like a cliff. Shaffur arrayed the company so that the king and Gurun rode out in front where all the people on the wall could see them.

The gate that lay before them, broken during the siege, had not yet been repaired. People in the city had dragged carts into the gap and turned them over on their sides, creating a barrier. Above it, on the wall, there was a throng. It looked to Gurun, from a distance, like a swarm of bees.

What if they were enraged enough to stone their king? Chagadai's horse-archers had their bows in hand, with arrows on the strings.

The people saw them coming and started to shout, cursing them, warning them to stay away. But when Ryons was close enough for them to recognize him, they subsided and were quiet.

Now they were within bowshot of the walls. Gurun

could see the people clearly. They were just plain people, like the villagers of Jocah's Creek: not warriors. The wrath in their faces had given way to puzzlement. Quite a few of them were pointing at her. She heard a confused murmur; again they reminded her of bees. And it was not wise to stir up bees. These bees had stones in their hands, but as yet no one had thrown one.

"Father God," she prayed silently, "protect this boy whom you have made a king. And give me courage, so that no one can see that I'm afraid." She'd never in her life seen walls like these, nor such a crowd of people. What if the walls fell down? What if all those people let fly with stones? Gurun let out her breath slowly. Her hands on the reins trembled, but she hid all other signs of fear. She hoped she hid it well.

Ryons reined in, and all his riders and foot soldiers came to a halt behind him.

"Sire," said Chief Shaffur, "you are already too close to these walls, and it is not safe to venture any closer. Let us attack suddenly and clear the way."

"Attack my own city?" Ryons shook his head. "No—I have to talk to them," he said. And he dismounted from his horse. Seeing that, Gurun came down, too—with just enough grace so as not to fall.

The little men the king called Ghols sucked air through their teeth. "Father," said Chagadai, "you mustn't do this! At least let us stand before you, as your shield."

"No. I can't," said Ryons. "You have to wait here. I command it."

Chagadai stiffened in his saddle, then grinned. "When you command, we must obey," he said. He turned and shouted something to the others, then turned back to Ryons. "Father, you're growing up so fast!"

Gurun understood none of those exchanges. She was resolved to stay beside the king, as the filgya had told her she must.

Their hands found each other, and together they advanced toward the gate. Ryons stopped just short of it and looked up at the people on the wall. "So many faces looking back!" Gurun thought. More than she'd ever seen in one place before. But now they looked more curious than angry. "That's something."

"Good people of Obann," Ryons said, "why have you locked me out of the city and locked my people in? What have we done to make you angry? But if you don't want us here, we'll go. Only let my men come out, and we will go in peace."

Gurun didn't know how it was possible, but it seemed that all the people in and above the gate could hear him. Men crouched behind the toppled wagons, armed with sticks and stones. There wasn't room for one more person on the wall. Yet silence reigned over them all—until someone called out, "Who's the girl?"

"Her name is Gurun," Ryons said. "She came from over the sea, from a faraway country in the North. God sent her to us. I wanted to show her the city."

"What do you mean, 'over the sea'? No one crosses the sea!"

Gurun couldn't help answering, "I did—and it was not easy! A great storm blew me south, and I landed on the coast of your country. My people live on islands far away from here. Long, long ago they came there from a southern land, seeking refuge from God's wrath. We believe it was Obann that our forefathers came from. Our language sounds very much like yours, and our Holy Scriptures are the same.

"I do not know why God sent me here. But I do know that He sent you a king and saved you from your enemies."

A young man climbed onto the parapet and shouted down at them: "We want our Temple! Ask this king—who burned God's holy Temple?" Behind him, other young men grumbled their assent.

"In my country," Gurun said, "we've never had a temple. But we do have God's Scripture, and we know our God. He hears our prayers and cares for us, and that is all the temple that we need."

The young man on the parapet was going to answer, but angry voices drowned him out.

"Get down, get down!"

"Shut up, you!"

"Everybody knows the king and his people weren't in the city when the fire started!"

"He saved us! He rode the great beast and crushed the Heathen!"

"Let him in, let him in! Long live King Ryons!"

And someone else cried out, "Long live the Queen!" Gurun blushed and held her tongue.

Hands reached up and dragged the young man off the parapet, and he was never seen again. More hands tipped the carts right-side up and started pulling them out of the way.

Up on the wall, the crowd began to cheer. Behind the king and Gurun, the king's men broke out singing—barbarously, in several languages all at once, tunelessly, and joyously. It was their battle anthem: "His mercy endureth forever!" The men who sang had once been Heathen and knew whereof they sang. God's mercy had saved their lives many times over.

"What made them change their minds?" Gurun cried into Ryons' ear.

He shook his head. "I don't know!" he shouted: it was the only way he could be heard above the din. "Maybe they'll tell us later." But he thought, in his heart of hearts, that this girl's bravery had shamed the people of Obann and brought them to their senses.

CHAPTER 32

How Orth Received a New Name

The rangers in Oziah's Wood could only watch and wait as Heathen swarmed along both rivers and set up camps around the forest. Hundreds more came over every day—thousands. There were too many of them to attack.

As the Heathen marched down from the mountains, along the Imperial River in the south and upon their newly built road in the north, slaves managed to escape and unwilling warriors, pressed into service, to desert. The mardars had no time to send troops after them. These persons fled into the foothills east of Oziah's Wood, where they had to struggle mightily to stay alive. The land was full of them.

Hlah met a group of them almost as soon as he set foot in the hills. Men of Obann and a few women—maybe thirty of them, all told—huddled under the fir trees around a few poor campfires, hungry and cold. The path Hlah was following, with Orth in tow, led straight up to their campsite.

"Away with you! We kill!"

A few half-frozen men stood in the way, brandishing sticks.

"We come in peace, in God's name," Hlah answered.

"I come from Obann City, where my lord King Ryons has crushed the Heathen host. But who are you? We came this way because I thought this country would be empty."

A hollow-cheeked man in ragged clothes answered, "You're not from Obann—I know an Abnak when I see one. Accursed Heathen!"

Hlah was not afraid. These men looked barely strong enough to stand on their feet. But he was moved to pity.

"Abnak I am," he said, "but heathen I am not. I serve the living God. My companion is Obannese, but he's out of his wits and I make neither head nor tail of him. Maybe you can! But first you'll need hotter fires and food and better quarters than those flimsy lean-tos that I see. Who are you, and how came you here?"

Before anyone could answer, Orth gave a great cry and sank down to the ground. He sat in the snow with his legs spread like a child's, wailing. But then, suddenly, he spoke.

"Hear, O my people, hear the word of the Lord. If you will humble your proud hearts, my people, and turn to me, and call upon my name; then I the Lord will hear you, and remember you, and deliver you out of your distress.

"O my people, why will you walk in darkness, and dwell in the shadow of death? Remember your God, whom you have forgotten, and I will turn to you. Cry out to me, you who have been silent, and I will hear you as a father hears the crying of his children. Why have you forgotten me so long? Return to me, return!"

Orth fell silent then and sat as a man in a daze. His words went echoing off among the trees.

"That's something from the Scriptures," someone said. "I'm sure I've heard it before, in the chamber house."

"Prophet Ika, Fifth Fascicle, eleventh verse," Orth said. "Will someone help me up? I seem to have fallen, and there's a weakness in my legs."

Hlah helped him, and after a moment's shakiness, he was able to stand.

"Who are you, mister?" a man asked.

That struck Orth as a very good question; and he didn't know the answer. When he searched for it, it wasn't there. His name, his career in the Temple, Lord Reesh, the city—it was all gone from his memory, without a trace.

"It's a very strange thing," he said, "but I truly don't know who or what I am, or what I've been. Even stranger, I don't care! I feel as though I've been sick, gravely ill, for a long time; and now I'm well again.

"But I do know all the Scriptures. And I know that you are persons who've been evilly used by the Heathen and only just escaped. There are many like you in these hills, aren't there?"

They all stared at him, and Hlah stared harder than anyone. Was the fellow talking sense, all of a sudden, or was this just another kind of madness?

"Don't be afraid!" Orth said. "You're starving and you're cold, but God has not forgotten you. This young man—" he clapped Hlah on the shoulder and made him jump—"is wise and strong. Something tells me that I owe my life to him, although I don't remember how. But he knows how to find food in any kind of country and how to build warm shelters and fires that don't easily go out. And he is a servant of God. He'll be a great help to you."

"How can someone not know who he is?" a woman asked.

Orth shrugged. "The Lord has taken away such knowledge from me. Someone will have to give me a new name, for I've forgotten my old one. But I made no jest when I said that I was sick and now I'm well. I do feel very strongly—indeed, I know—that I have received God's mercy. Why I stood in such dire need of it, He has caused me to forget. For that I give thanks!"

He turned to Hlah. He looked perfectly sane now. Whatever had been haunting him was gone. There was no denying the change in him. It went clear through him.

"Friend," Orth said, "I know you have been good to me, even as you'll be good to these poor people here. But I've forgotten your name, too."

"I'm Hlah, the son of Spider."

"Hlah, these folk need a hotter fire, and they're hungry. And I think that after needful things are seen to, as you order them, there will be time for prayer."

"How can we pray?" someone said. "Are you a prester?"

"I don't know that I am or ever have been," Orth said, "but I do know that nowhere in the Scriptures, nowhere at all, does it say God's people need a prester if they wish to pray. I know the whole body of Scripture. The Lord has taken away everything else—and I don't want it back. I'm well now and have no desire to be sick again."

Enough of this, Hlah thought. The day was moving on, and it would be cold and dark tonight. He clapped his hands, startling the refugees.

"First thing, let's build a big fire that'll make everybody

warm!" he said. "I see plenty of wood available. And then we'll have to build some better shelters; those lean-tos are no good for a winter night. There's just enough time to get it done, if we start now."

"Show us what to do," a man said; and Hlah did. By nightfall they had a bonfire in the middle of their clearing and several Abnak wigwams arranged around it—conical frames of saplings, held together by leafy branches woven among them, insulated by many, many armfuls of dead leaves. These would do, Hlah thought, until they could build something better.

There had been no time to find food. That would have to wait until tomorrow. No one would die of hunger overnight. It would be crowded in the wigwams, but that would only make them warmer.

Standing before the fire after sundown, when it had grown too dark to do any more work, Orth recited several of Ozias' Sacred Songs, then raised his arms and spoke a prayer. It was the noblest and most moving prayer that Hlah had ever heard. Obst himself could not have done better. The refugees, doubtful at first, eventually closed their eyes and bowed their heads and crossed their hands on their chests; and not a few of them wept silently. When Orth at last said "Amen," they all echoed him.

"You must have been a prester, to know how to pray like that," a man said. "If not, you should have been."

"I don't know," said Orth. "It doesn't matter."

"But what'll we call you?" asked a woman.

"You may call me whatever you please."

Someone said to Hlah, "You know him best. Give him a name."

Hlah was young and had never named a human being before. Abnaks often take new names—when they married, or took an enemy's scalp, when there was a death in the family—to mark occasions in their lives. Hlah as a little boy had been named Salamander.

"I name you Sunfish," he said. "It's a good name to start out with, a very popular name. It brings good luck."

"Sunfish I am, then," said Orth, beaming. If this was madness, Hlah thought, then it was a new kind that no one had ever heard of. But some of the refugees around the fire, maybe for the first time in a long time, had smiles on their lips.

CHAPTER 33

To See Without Seeing

Except for the end facing the mountains in the East, Oziah's Wood was now surrounded. Heathen camps had sprung up everywhere. Wallekki riders patrolled the gaps between them, watching the eaves of the forest against any sortie by the rangers.

The children and Martis had been taken to a camp some miles from the edge of the forest. Farther in, the rangers were gathering their women and children at another camp with food supplies to last the winter. Scouts came in every day, constantly reporting on the movements of the enemy. A white-haired man named Huell was in command.

"There's at least four thousand of them out there now," he told Martis. "Worse news—they have about half a thousand Abnaks, maybe more. We're not afraid of the Wallekki or the Zeph, but Abnaks are as good as rangers in a forest. And murdering devils, to boot! They'll know what to do, once they're in here."

It was a cold morning with a light snow on the ground. Outside the forest it would be colder. "They won't want to sit out there in the wind much longer," Huell said. "They'll be coming in soon."

"Your archers will be ready," Martis said.

"They'll pay a price to come in here," the ranger agreed.

"But I don't think we can make it high enough to keep them out."

Chillith, standing nearby with Jack and Ellayne, shook his head. None of the men noticed, but Ellayne said, "What is it, Chillith?"

"Hear me, Martis, and all you others," said the Griff. "The Heathen gather to invade Oziah's Wood, but they will not come in. They cannot enter."

Huell laughed, not merrily. "Tell it to the Heathen, blind man! They sure as sunshine are fixing to come in, and there's no way we can stop them."

"Someday I will speak to them," Chillith said, ignoring Huell. "They'll see my face and hear my voice. But they will not come into this forest."

"How the devil do you know that?" Huell said. "I hate loose talk!"

"You'd better listen to him," Ellayne said. "He's a prophet."

"He's an extra mouth to feed and no use in a fight."

"There will be a fight very soon," said Chillith, "but it will not be yours.

"You ask me how I know this thing. I cannot answer. Your God took away the sight of my eyes, so that in my darkness I would know that He is God. It is He who will keep the Heathen out."

"What—does God whisper secrets to you, a Griff?" The ranger's scowl was lost on Chillith, who only shrugged.

"No," he answered. "I don't think your God would speak to me. Not in words. Nevertheless, I say what I know to be true. God has made me to see without seeing."

Huell spat and turned away. "We'll have our archers

ready, anyhow," he said, "just in case you're daft as well as blind. Don't tell me you believe him, Martis."

"I was there when God took away his sight," Martis said. "He went to sleep a seeing man, like you or me, and woke up blind. Yes, I believe him. But if the Heathen do come in, I'll kill as many as I can."

They hadn't seen Wytt in two days. But tonight, after everyone had bedded down to sleep, he came for them.

In this camp the rangers slept in low, domed huts. You couldn't stand up in them or prepare a meal, but they were just right for keeping warm while sleeping. Jack and Ellayne had a hut of their own—a ranger built it for them in less than an hour—and Wytt came in and woke Ellayne, nuzzling her cheek and chattering softly in her ear. Ellayne shook Jack awake.

"Wytt wants us to come with him, right now," she whispered. "He wants us to see something."

"See what?"

"He just says come and see."

They knew Wytt's ways and trusted him. They knew he couldn't say everything he thought. He'd led them across the plains to Lintum Forest and saved their lives more than once. If he said "come," they would come.

It didn't occur to the Omah to explain. His mind didn't work that way. He never thought of trying to tell the children what he'd been doing for two days. He wasn't like a human being, with the ability to lay things out in his mind and analyze them in an orderly way. Where his thoughts came from, no human being could know. Jack and Ellayne communicated with him, but didn't know how: it just happened. Obst told them it was a gift from God.

The camp was not a proper camp with a fence, birch-bark cabins you could stand up in, or sentries. Some of the rangers patrolled the woods by night. The rest slept.

Ellayne and Jack crawled out of their shelter, following Wytt. They were fully dressed, but they missed the winter clothes they had when they first set out from Ninneburky. Ellayne's teeth soon began to chatter. "Cold!" thought Jack. Winter was early this year.

They crawled out of camp; Wytt put them on a path, and they stood up.

"I can't see a thing!" Ellayne said. Anyone who has ever tried to make his way through a forest in the dead of night, without a light, knows what darkness really is. She groped for Jack's hand, found it, and held on. A few steps in front of them Wytt chirped, urging them on. They couldn't see him, but they could follow the sounds he made. By and by their eyes adjusted and they could see well enough to avoid blundering into trees.

"Where are we going?" Jack asked. To see Omah, was the answer that he got. "What'll we say to any ranger who finds us here in the middle of the night?" he wondered. Wytt didn't tell him that there were Omah in the woods distracting rangers from this path. Not that he didn't want Jack to know; but all he could think of at the moment was to lead the children to the edge of the forest as quickly and quietly as possible.

They had miles to go, and it seemed even farther in the cold and dark. Wytt's path was more direct and much shorter than any used by the rangers, and in most places too narrow for the children to go side-by-side. Had it not been so much shorter, they never would have reached the forest's edge by midnight. But it was, and they did, and they were both exhausted.

"Stay here. Watch and see," were Wytt's instructions.

"I couldn't go another step, anyhow!" Ellayne gasped.

They were in an evergreen thicket, looking out on one of the Heathen camps. It was close enough so that they could see a fence of sharp stakes all around it and campfires and lanterns inside the fence. Jack thought it was a good bit too close.

They were still panting when the underbrush began to rustle and Omah came out all around them. These were Forest Omah, dark-furred, almost invisible at night. They chattered, chirped, and purred, and Wytt went back and forth among them. He was telling them not to be afraid—here was the girl with hair like the rays of the sun. He reminded them that many of them had already seen her from hiding and knew he spoke the truth.

"What is it about your hair?" Jack whispered. "Every Omah in the world gets all excited over it!"

Ellayne didn't know. When they'd first set out on their journey, they had camped for a night among some ancient ruins and Jack had cut her hair to disguise her as a boy. That was how they had met Wytt. He and all the other Omah in that ruined city had gathered up her hair and made a celebration with it, dancing and waving it about. It was something that Wytt had never explained to them because he didn't know how—something secret, they had come to believe, between the Omah and God, that no human being would ever understand.

The Forest Omah milled around the children's ankles like a thousand cats—always clockwise, round and round, like a dance. There might have been a dozen of them, there might have been a thousand: it was too dark to tell. Maybe it went on for an hour; maybe it only seemed like an hour. But at a sudden squeal from Wytt, the Omah all went rushing out onto the plain.

"What are they going to do?" Ellayne said. "Attack the camp?" Wytt was leading the Omah, so she couldn't ask him.

They'd seen Wytt, all by himself, kill a sleeping man, and knew a swarm of Omah could kill many sleeping men. Was that what they were going to do? Even if the camp had sentries, they wouldn't see the little hairy men crouched down in the tall grass. No fence would keep them out. But how many warriors, out of hundreds, could they possibly kill?

"I wouldn't want to be sleeping there tonight," Jack said.

Ellayne wished she were sleeping in her own bed in her father's house under a heap of blankets. The fires flickering in the Heathen camp seemed to taunt her: there was warmth for her freezing hands and feet, but she couldn't get at it. She could only blow on her hands and stamp her feet. And she didn't dare make noise doing it. In the stillness of this wintry night, she was afraid the slightest noise would carry to the enemy.

What were the Omah doing? They'd been gone for hours—minutes really, but it felt like hours—and nothing was happening.

Jack muffled a sneeze. She glared at him. "If you don't mind!" she hissed.

"Sorry. My feet are going numb."

"Mine are already gone."

"We don't know the way back to the camp," he said. "I just thought of that."

"Please try to think of something else."

Before he could answer her, there was noise—an explosive burst of deep and angry voices in the camp, a mob of men alarmed, enraged. And then the ringing clash of steel on steel and screams: it froze the children in their tracks. It was a noise of battle.

It was time to go, but neither Jack nor Ellayne had the slightest idea which way to go.

Then they heard a high-pitched riot of squealing and chirping in the grass, and the host of the Omah came flooding back into the forest. Ellayne yelped when Wytt suddenly jumped into her arms.

"We kill some," he reported, "and now they kill each other. They see us, think they see devils." He made a squeaking noise that was Omah-laughter.

"They're killing each other out there?" Jack asked, pointing to the camp. A few of the shelters were on fire now and burning brightly. He thought he could see dark shapes moving in front of the light.

"Wytt, can you take us back to our camp now?" Ellayne said. "We're cold."

They had to wait. Omah were milling all around them. You could hear a rhythm in their chattering, as if they were rejoicing. It was too dark to see, but Jack supposed each of the little hairy men was brandishing a pointed stick—with blood on it. The eyes and throats of sleeping men—he didn't like to think of it.

"Now we go," Wytt said. Out on the plain, more of the Heathen camp was burning. Horses screamed now, too. At any moment, Jack thought, men would be fleeing from the camp—"straight at us."

Wytt guided them. After a time, the celebration of the Forest Omah died away as one by one or two by two they stole back to their nests and burrows. The sky was grey with dawn when Jack and Ellayne laid eyes on the rangers' camp again. Wytt vanished into the underbrush.

Everyone was already up and about. Martis saw the children and came running to meet them.

"Where were you?" he cried. "I was about to beg the rangers to track you down—and I would've had to beg because just now they have more important things to do!"

"Why is everybody so excited?" Jack asked.

"Because the Abnaks are fighting with the Wallekki and the Zeph. They burned down one of their own camps during the night—we've just had word. More scouts are going out to try to find out why that happened."

Naturally the rangers had been watching all the Heathen camps, day and night. They would have seen the battle in the camp. But they would've been too far away to see the Omah.

"It was the Omah who did it," Ellayne said. "We were there; we saw. Wytt led them, and they snuck into the camp. They started the battle somehow. Next thing we knew, the Heathen were killing each other."

"They had to see Ellayne before they did it," Jack said.

"That's why we had to be there. Wytt came and got us. You know how he is."

Martis sighed and ground his teeth. "All I know is I've had a very bad half-hour worrying about you two! I'll have more to say about that later. But let's find Huell and tell him what you saw."

"We didn't see it very well," Ellayne said. "It was mighty dark out there."

"We saw like Chillith sees: we saw without seeing," Jack said.

"There are different kinds of darkness," Martis said. "I think the kind I used to live in was the worst." But he said no more about that, for the time being.

CHAPTER 34

Helki and the Town

What happened was this.

Wytt understood much of what he heard men say, and he knew how to make the Forest Omah understand it. He met with the fathers of the Omah, and together they planned to attack the invaders as they slept.

It would be hard to explain why they so decided. Wytt would not have known how to explain it. But it had to do with Ellayne, and whatever she meant to them—a meaning that was written on their hearts where no words understood by human beings could find it.

Wytt had overheard the rangers talking about the Abnaks and their woodcraft: so the Omah sought out sleeping Abnaks and killed some of them. It wasn't long before the camp awoke; and knowing nothing of the Omah, the Abnaks could only believe the dead men had been murdered by the other Heathen. Those who saw the little hairy Omah scampering away thought they were devils. To avenge their fellows, the Abnaks attacked the Wallekki and the Zeph, and a general fight broke out. The end of it was a burned-out camp, a hundred men killed outright, and the surviving Abnaks marching on to the next camp to bring the battle there. "Treason and witchcraft!" was their cry.

By mid-morning the rangers knew it was the Abnaks

fighting with the other Heathen. This was all on the north side of the forest, but there were already Wallekki riders speeding to bring the tidings to the south-side camps. They would have to ride around the forest. Inside, runners brought the news to all the ranger camps.

"Are we saved?" Huell wondered. "There's no love lost between Abnaks and Wallekki. Maybe the whole Heathen army will tear itself apart."

Chillith heard him say it and replied, "The heaviest strokes have yet to fall."

Helki and his Griffs had crossed to the south bank of the Imperial River and were moving east toward Caristun—or rather, what was left of it. Early in the summer the Heathen attacked it on their way to Obann. The town survived, but much of it had been burnt and ruined. Now refugees had returned to Caristun, trying to rebuild it. They weren't happy to see Griffs.

"Peace, peace—we come in the king's name and in God's." Helki stepped out in front of his men to confront a throng of fifty refugees armed with clubs and stones and makeshift spears.

"Who are you?" their leader demanded.

"My name is Helki. I come from Lintum Forest."

"Helki? Is that Helki the Rod?" a woman cried. "The one they call the Flail of the Lord? Praise God you've come in time!"

Flail of the Lord—he'd first heard that from Jandra's lips, in the prophetic voice. He didn't like the name: it made him out to be something grander than he was.

"If you're Helki the Rod, what are you doing with those Griffs?" a man said.

"These men have surrendered to me. They serve King Ryons, as I do," Helki said. "But what do you mean, I've come in time? In time for what?"

The townspeople stopped brandishing their weapons and gathered around Helki. He didn't like the way they marveled at him, as if he were an angel come to earth. They muttered about him killing the giant, stared wide-eyed at him. Their tattered clothes and hollow cheeks testified to poverty and hardship. They all tried to speak at once, until the biggest man among them got them to be quiet.

"It's like this, sir," he said. "We're trying to make this town livable again before the winter comes; but now we see Heathen camps across the river. They're all over the country between the north bank and Oziah's Wood. They could cross over any day and burn us out again. And this time, that'd be the finish of us."

"But now you're here—the Giant-killer! Our prayers are answered," said somebody else. "You won't let them drive us out."

"Oh, fry me!" Helki thought. "A dozen men and a dog—what are we? Maybe in the forest I could do something, but not out here." But how could he say that to these people?

"Do you have any stock of food?" he asked.

An old man grinned at him. "It's short rations," he said, "but we aren't going to starve. Believe it or not, there are a lot of nice, big fish in the river hereabouts, and we catch enough to keep us alive. And we have some onions and turnips stored in the cellars. There aren't that many of us here—see?"

"How many?"

"Two hundred, counting children," said the leader. "Fifty more or less able-bodied men. Some of the women will fight, if it comes to that. But the town has neither wall nor ditch. If the Heathen come, we don't know how to keep them off."

"And do you think I know?" Helki thought. But he said, "We'll see what can be done. It's all in God's hands."

The refugees had repaired some of the least-damaged barns and houses with lumber salvaged from the ruins. Much of Caristun was a forest of charred timbers pitched at crazy angles, but the living quarters seemed adequate. About half of the people now lived in the town hall, and the rest in half a dozen houses and a livery stable.

They took Helki to the ruins of the docks and bade him look across the Imperial. That country teemed with Heathen warriors, they said.

"A few of us have been across on boats," said the leader. "We've seen the camps."

"Do the Heathen have boats?" Helki asked.

"We haven't seen any. They must have crossed over far upriver, where it's not so wide. But they can always build rafts. If they want to come across, they'll find a way to do it."

"This is a bad place, Giant-slayer," said Tiliqua—in Griffish, so that the townspeople wouldn't understand him. "If we stay to help these people, all we can do is die with them."

"I reckon it might come to that," Helki answered. "But let's try a few other things first."

CHAPTER 35

Gurun and Obst

Gurun was given her own room in the palace, with a Ghol to stand outside her door to guard her, and a maid to come in and wake her up in the morning and bring her breakfast. The Ghol didn't speak a word of Obannese and only grinned at her when she tried to speak to him. His name was Kutchuk. The maid was a girl of her own age; Bronna was her name. She lived with her father and mother in the city. The first time she came into the room with a tray, she amazed Gurun by curtseying to her and calling her "my lady."

"Why do you call me that, and why do you curtsey?" Gurun said, sitting up in bed—by far the most luxurious bed she'd ever slept in, or even imagined.

"Why, because the people call you Queen, my lady," Bronna said.

"What people? Who says I'm a queen?"

"Everyone, my lady."

"Well, that must come to an end right away," Gurun said. "I am a plain girl, just like you. In my country there has never been a king or queen."

"They said you came across the sea, my lady. No plain girl could do that!"

Gurun ate her breakfast hurriedly, eager to find someone in authority who would understand—and make it clear to everybody else—that she was nothing more than King Ryons' guest. All this talk about her being a queen must stop! She was sure God would punish her if she ever started to believe it.

When she was ready, the maid and the Ghol took her to another room within this enormous building called a palace. There a tall, old man was waiting for her. This was Obst, the king's teacher. She'd met him last night at supper.

"Sit down, sit down, be comfortable," he said. "I was awake all night, looking forward to this meeting. Tell me all about your country, and how you came to Obann."

"Where is King Ryons?" Gurun asked.

"Visiting various places in the city: letting his people see him."

"I want to see him, too. I am told the people are calling me a queen, and I am not a queen."

The old man smiled. She'd thought him grim, the first time she saw him. But when he smiled, he was warm and wise and sweet.

"No one knows how that got started," he said. "People will take notions—who can account for it? Perhaps they think you look like a queen.

"But to cross the sea! There were seagoing men in ancient times, but there aren't anymore. It's been a thousand years since any man of Obann dared to put to sea."

"Why is that?" said Gurun. She could hardly imagine anything stranger. "My people live on islands. The sea is how we travel. We couldn't live without it. Fish, sealskins, seal meat, whales, and whale blubber for fuel in the winter—by God's providence, our living is the sea. Why should Obann's people fear it?"

Obst shook his head. "No one knows," he said. "It happened in the days of Obann's ruin, when God's wrath fell on us. We have no writings from that time: everything was destroyed. It is said that God's wrath came down from Heaven—and up from the sea. All our ships and all our ports were suddenly destroyed. Since then our people have feared the sea and will not live in sight of it."

They had a long talk. It was pleasant for Gurun to talk about her island, although it made her homesick, too. Obst was most interested in the way the islanders had preserved the Scriptures, and studied them, and knew them—and all without the guidance of the Temple and its presters.

"I believe that in these days, God wants His people in all lands to do as your people have done," he said. "I believe that God Himself ordained the destruction of the Temple, because instead of bringing the people into communion with their Lord, it became a separating wall between them and Him. But don't speak of these things in the streets of this city! Having lost the Temple, the people are afraid."

"I have noticed that they will not pray unless somebody leads them," Gurun said. "In the village where I stopped, they asked me to lead them in their prayers. It wasn't proper, but I did it. I hope I did no wrong."

"Of course not," Obst said.

He was also greatly interested in the filgya. He believed it must have been an angel, but Gurun didn't know about that. She wanted to know how Ryons became king, and Obst told her: how a prophet of the Lord proclaimed him king while he was still a slave, how the power of God converted a Heathen army and made it Ryons' army, and how lost Scriptures were found. "We believe," he said, "that Ryons is of the seed of King Ozias himself, miraculously preserved in fulfillment of prophecy."

"King Ozias? But he lived so long ago!" Gurun cried.

"Nevertheless, we believe King Ryons is his descendant in the flesh."

Gurun knew that God had promised Ozias that his seed would never fail: that the throne would be reserved for his bloodline forever. But Ryons? It made her head reel to think she'd ridden side by side, and stood hand in hand, with a descendant of that same King Ozias who wrote the Sacred Songs. How could such things be?

"I know—it's hard to believe," Obst said. "But most of the people of this city believe it. They saw Ryons come riding on the shoulders of a beast that was like a mountain walking, and he saved the city when it surely was about to be destroyed."

"And yet they locked him out," Gurun said.

"They couldn't bring themselves to keep him out, when he came back. They couldn't look him in the face and be against him. The troublemakers who blame us for the burning of the Temple are silent now. The people are ashamed they ever listened to them."

Gurun shook her head. "Did not this city also turn against Ozias—and more than once?"

"You do know the Scriptures, don't you?" Obst said. "Well, we've only followed where the Lord has led us. Left to myself, I would have stayed in Lintum Forest. But God wouldn't let me."

Each story Obst told her was more wonderful than the last. He climbed Bell Mountain, where he should have died.

And maybe he had: he wasn't sure. Two children went on to the summit to ring Ozias' bell; but Obst came down alone with new life and the gift of tongues.

"I've been brought to a country of marvels," she thought. They were God's marvels, the work of His hand. And she was more than just a little bit afraid.

CHAPTER 36

How Lord Reesh Met the Thunder King

At last, the Golden Pass: but the first thing Lord Reesh saw was a stone wall stretched across it, with three massive wooden gates. The wall, a good twelve feet high, spanned the gap between two mountain peaks. Above each gate rose a fighting tower, where a catapult might be installed. Men with spears marched back and forth along the top of the wall. A deep-voiced horn sounded, and the middle gate swung open.

"A nice piece of fortification," Gallgoid said. "Not that anyone in Obann would dream of sending an army across the mountains. I wonder why they took the trouble to build that wall."

"It proclaims their master's power," Reesh said.

Behind Mardar Kyo on his horse, the coach passed through the gate; and then the passengers saw something worth seeing.

"Behold! This is greatness!" Reesh said.

It was a golden hall—walls sheathed in pure gold, golden roof, a pair of golden doors. And on the doors were raised figures of fabulous animals, monsters, and winged men with crowns. Had the sky not been totally overcast, the hall would have dazzled the eye. It was every bit as big as the Oligarchs' Hall in Obann, but infinitely grander because of all the gold. Lord Reesh in his long life had never seen anything like it. Could there really be so much gold in all the world?

The coach stopped, and Kyo rode up to the window.

"Welcome to the Golden Pass, First Prester!"

"What is this glorious hall?" Reesh cried. "The top of a mountain pass seems a strange place for it."

Kyo dismounted, stood closer to the window, and lowered his voice. "Can't you guess, First Prester?" he said. "Wherever our master the Thunder King stops, there must be splendor."

"He's here?" Reesh whispered.

"He will spend the winter here, feasting and reveling, until the snows melt and he can lead an army down the mountain into Obann. He arrived here just two days ago, as soon as the golden hall was made ready for him. After you have rested from your journey and refreshed yourself, you will be privileged to meet him. He has a desire to look upon your face."

Reesh's heart fluttered. How could the Thunder King have known he would be here? How could Kyo have known what his master desired? "It was things like this that the ancients used to do," he thought. "They spoke to one another over vast distances." Could the Thunder King have rediscovered how that was done? Had he acquired the lost powers of the ancients? Reesh himself had dreamed of that very thing for years, dreamed fervently. But to think that dream might have now come true—it made him short of breath.

"Come, my lord," said Kyo. "Quarters have been prepared for you, and hot food and wine. We will be stopping here some days."

They didn't stay in the hall itself, but in one of the many log cabins clustered around the hall. It had a fireplace with a fire in it, a bathtub with hot water in it, and clean clothes laid out on a pair of perfectly acceptable beds. One of Kyo's men brought food and wine.

"Try to sleep, First Prester," the mardar said, when he took his leave. "Our master the Thunder King understands that you've had a long, hard journey. He will send for you after you've had ample time to rest."

But sleep eluded Reesh. Gallgoid had hardly finished eating when he stretched out on one of the beds and fell asleep. Lord Reesh soaked in the tub until the water was lukewarm, ate and drank his fill, and tried to enjoy the luxury of a warm bed with a feather mattress. His old bones appreciated it, but his mind could find no rest.

In truth, Reesh had never expected an audience with the Thunder King—certainly not until he'd been installed as First Prester in the New Temple. He was not prepared. He was old and weary, all alone, and out of his element. He missed his robes of office, the elegant appointments of the Temple, and his flock of servants. He felt more like a wandering hermit with a begging bowl than a prester: let alone First Prester.

What should he say to a man who claimed to be a god? What would such a man want to hear? Would he, Reesh, have to pretend he believed in this man's divinity? How could he do that?

Finally he did fall asleep, after all, without even knowing it until Gallgoid shook him awake.

"Kyo is waiting, my lord—wake up. The Thunder King has sent for you."

———

Their shoes crunched on frozen snow. Reesh was surprised to discover he'd slept through the night and much of the next day. It was now going on noon, and the cold air crackled in his nostrils. But he was dressed in clean furs, with a hot breakfast in his belly. It was only his spirit that was unready for this meeting.

The decorated doors of the hall swung open, and Mardar Kyo ushered him through. The hall's interior blazed with the light of a hundred lamps, and more lamps hung on long, golden chains from the high ceiling.

This portion of the hall was partitioned off from the rest by hardwood walls polished to a high gloss, with brass-bound doors giving entrance to the other precincts. The floor here was slate covered with woven reed mats brightly dyed in red and yellow.

Two long, sturdy, hardwood tables stretched across the space: for this, Reesh saw, was a banqueting hall. Around the tables were arranged high seats like thrones, some of them occupied by mardars wearing furs—men of many nations, with wide gold collars around their necks, golden bracelets on their wrists, and golden cups before them filled with wine.

But none of this was what captured Reesh's attention.

There was an aisle between the two tables with a rich

red carpet on it, leading up to the six stone steps on a raised dais. Chained securely to this elevated dais was a creature the like of which Lord Reesh had never seen or heard of. A heavy collar and stout chains restrained it: a nightmare held in chains, Reesh thought.

He could liken it only to an enormous cat. Lord Reesh had never seen a lion in the flesh, although there were some in the Southern Wilds and Scripture recorded their presence, long ago in Obann itself; but he'd seen old woodcuts of them. The lion was the king of beasts, tradition said; but compared to this cat, a lion would seem like a kitten. This creature had massive shoulders like a bison's, eyes that were like green fire—and a pair of fangs like long, curved knives or drawn swords protruding from its upper jaw. Whatever was the name of such a monster? There was nothing like it in Scripture, or even in the most lurid medieval fairy tale. Reesh's heart clenched at the sight of it.

But on top of the dais was a throne, and on the throne a man—a man with a mask of gold over his face. He wore a shimmering robe of many colors that seemed to ripple into other colors as the eye ran over it. In his right hand he held a rod of ivory, tipped with a blood-red ruby the size of a dove's egg.

Laboring to breathe, Lord Reesh followed Kyo onto the rug, onto the aisle between the tables; and then he stopped, behind Kyo, when the mardar halted before the throne. The chained cat glared at them.

Kyo spread his arms and bowed his head, dropped down on one knee.

"My master and my god," he said, "I have brought you Lord Reesh, the First Prester of the Temple, from Obann.

He has been obedient to your will and has come to you of his own free will."

"Rise, Kyo." The voice that issued from behind the mask had no particular character. Reesh wondered if it were a mask at all. "I will receive Lord Reesh in my chamber and grant him private audience."

"As you wish, O Master."

Without a sound, the Thunder King rose from his throne and descended the stone steps. The great cat shied from him, but he paid it no heed. A mardar sprang up from the table and opened one of the brass doors, and bowed his head as the man in gold glided past him and vanished into the interior. The mardar shut the door after him.

"You are being shown great favor!" Kyo said. "Wait until the door is opened to you, then go in. Have courage. Our master must be greatly pleased with you."

After a wait that seemed excruciatingly long, Lord Reesh was admitted to the Thunder King's own chamber. He had to grope his way along a shadowy corridor, with his legs threatening to fail him. At the end of it he found a door lit by a single lamp; and from behind the door a soft voice said, "Come."

With trembling hands he opened the door, shut it behind him. He found himself in a small, windowless room, gently lit, walls hung with woolen curtains dyed red and gold, black and white, and soft rugs covering the floor.

"Sit, Lord Reesh. Don't tax your strength."

The words were in perfect Obannese. The Thunder King sat on a carved, high-backed chair with his mask set on a little table beside it. He had the face of a man—just a man.

Reesh felt for the nearest chair and gratefully lowered himself into it. His heart was playing him up. He hoped he wouldn't faint.

But it was only a man who sat across the little room from him: a bearded man with fine but swarthy skin, glittering dark eyes. It was hard to guess his age. He looked like a man still some years shy of forty—but that was impossible, Reesh thought.

"Be at ease, First Prester. I know all about you. I have seen you through Mardar Kyo's eyes and heard you through his ears. You sacrificed your own Temple to me, and I have accepted your offering. I welcome you into my service."

Reesh nodded. His tongue stuck to the roof of his mouth. How could the Thunder King be so young? Given his long career of conquering the East, he should have been at least sixty. But there wasn't a grey hair on his head.

"Yes, Lord Reesh, I was very pleased that you offered up your Temple to me. You were prepared to sacrifice your city, too. I don't hold it against you that the city still stands."

"What does he want me to say?" Reesh wondered. "He'll have me killed if I say the wrong thing."

"Even a god," said the Thunder King, "must be patient. By this time next year, the city of Obann will no longer exist. You do believe I am a god, don't you? Be honest!"

Now he had to answer—and what answer could he make?

"My lord," he said, "I am an old man, and many years out of the habit of believing. In God, that is—the God of Obann's Scriptures.

"But I do believe in man—in his glorious past and in his future. I believe that you hold the key to that future. I am willing to serve you. I hope I've proved that."

The Thunder King studied him. His expression was not unkindly, but even so, Lord Reesh began to sweat under his clothes. He was old, but not so old that he was ready to be killed. He felt like a mouse being studied by a snake.

"Whether or not you believe I'm a god, I am," the Thunder King said. "I have put down and enslaved all the gods of the East. The God of Obann is the last that still resists me. In time he, too, will be my prisoner.

"For he is real, Lord Reesh: you were wrong not to believe in him. They're all real, the gods. I have spoken with them. But I don't wish to frighten you. I understand your weaknesses. In time you'll come to believe in me, as all my people do. For now, I'm satisfied you wish to serve me, and I accept you as my servant. You will be First Prester at my New Temple at Kara Karram."

Reesh bowed his head, which had begun to pound. "I am honored, my lord!" he said.

"And now you may return to the banquet hall. I don't want to weary you," said the Thunder King. "We'll talk again before you resume your journey east. For I am pleased with you."

CHAPTER 37

How Some Abnaks Were Tamed

All around Oziah's Wood, the Heathen fought among themselves. Some of the camps on the north side were burned down and deserted. The camps on the south side still stood, but their Abnaks were lost. Receiving the news from the north, the Wallekki, the Zeph, and others struck first, believing they were stifling an Abnak mutiny. Those Abnaks who were not killed broke loose and fled. Some of them escaped to the hills where they were most at home, after killing their own mardars.

Twenty-six of them stumbled upon the camp where Hlah and Orth had stopped. By now the people had bark shelters and were eating better. Hlah had put several of the men to hunting and trapping every day and taught them how to do it better. They didn't do badly, for town-dwellers who had suddenly found themselves living in a forest. Winter notwithstanding, the woods were full of game. And Orth, now called Sunfish, led the people in prayer every night and expounded the Scriptures to them. Now they believed they were in God's hands, and it gave them hope.

Even so, they might have been massacred, late one

afternoon, had Hlah himself not been in camp when the Abnaks came.

"I am Hlah, the son of Spider, who is a chieftain of the Turtle Clan. Who are you men, and why do you come here as in war?"

When they heard him challenge them in their own language, they lowered their tomahawks. Besides, they could see the speaker was an Abnak like themselves.

"What does a Turtle warrior here, with slaves and castaways?" answered a barrel-chested, middle-aged man who had two Wallekki scalps dangling from his belt. "I am Ootoo, son of Beetle, of the Sparrowhawks. I met Chief Spider once, many years ago, when you were but a child. He was a famous man. Does he still live?"

"He lives," said Hlah. "He is held in great honor in the city of Obann. Sheathe your knives, warriors, and rest here for a while. These are poor people who have nothing worth taking; nor are they fighters. No honor or glory in killing them! They don't even have any extra food they can offer you as their guests."

Hlah fully expected to be killed. There was no good reason for twenty-six Abnaks to be here. They could only be here for a bad one.

"We've had enough fighting to suit us for a while," a warrior said. "Let's hear Hlah's story, Ootoo, and see if it's more interesting than ours."

Of course the people in the camp were afraid. But the Abnaks stoked up the bonfire, sat down by it, and showed no sign of harming anyone. So after an hour or two, they began to come out of their shelters to see what they could see and hear.

Orth called them out. "Don't be afraid! These men won't hurt you. I think they've been sent here for our good."

"Who's that?" demanded Ootoo.

"His name is Sunfish. He's lost his memory," Hlah said. "He's a servant of the God of Obann—the true God, who calls all nations to Himself. Chief Spider is His servant, too, and so am I."

Hlah told them how God struck down the mardar who commanded the Heathen army in which Chief Spider served; how the Thunder King sent armies to destroy them; and how God saved them every time; how they became His people; and how by a greater miracle God saved the city of Obann and made a slave-boy king of Obann.

"Huh!" Ootoo snorted. "We didn't do a thing, and yet our allies turned on us. We thought we were going to go into Oziah's Wood to flush out some rangers. Next thing we knew, we were accused of being rebels. We had to kill our mardar and make tracks! Most of us didn't get away; at least they died fighting. As for us, the Thunder King will hunt us down—but we'll make it hard for whoever tries to do it." The other twenty-five men clapped their hands and cried, "Ho! So!"

"Your story is better than ours, Hlah," Ootoo said, "but not so different—eh? We'll both be lucky if we ever see the other side of the mountains again. Burn the cusset Thunder King! He should have left us alone."

"He turns on those who serve him," Hlah said. "But Chief Spider and his people serve the living God, who is faithful and merciful. And in the end, God will destroy the

Thunder King."

"I hope he does it soon," said Ootoo, "and everything can go back the way it was."

Ootoo and his men carried their own rations: the rich, fatty trail-meat that Abnaks made for winter journeys and an ample supply of venison jerky. Toward the end of the day, Ootoo said they would sleep by the fire that night in their bags and move on early in the morning.

"You are now the Thunder King's enemies and may never be his friends again," Hlah reminded them, when morning came and they were about to leave. "If you meet more people in these hills, like these poor people here, do them no harm. If you hurt them, you'll be doing the Thunder King's work for him."

"They ran away from building his road," said Ootoo. "Probably they'll all die in the winter—no need for us to kill them."

Orth didn't speak Abnak, but he could see the twenty-six men were about to leave. He stepped up to Hlah and tapped his elbow.

"Please tell these good men," he said, "that God is merciful to them that show mercy. This country is full of poor refugees. These Abnaks could save many lives, if they cared to. And then I think God will save them."

"Sunfish, these men don't know God," Hlah said. "They worship little gods, which they think inhabit trees and ponds."

"So did you, not so long ago," Orth said. Hlah couldn't deny it.

"Ootoo," he said, "my friend here says that God will favor you if you stop and take care of any refugees you meet, so that they don't starve or freeze to death. The favor of this God is worth more than you can imagine. He can protect you from the Thunder King. As I've told you, He saved us many times."

Even as he spoke, Hlah thought, "What foolishness!" Defenseless Obannese were Abnak raiders' natural prey. It was like asking wolves to protect the sheep.

Ootoo puffed out his tattooed cheeks and blew. "Whew! Ever since the Thunder King's mardars first came to our country and took away our gods, everything has been out of joint.

"When I was young, if a few men wanted to go over the mountains and lift some scalps, they did—nothing more to it. No one could tell them not to go, nor could anyone make a man go if he didn't want to. We fished and hunted when and where we pleased. And in the winter we slept in furs among our wives and children. Life was good.

"Now they marshal us into great armies full of foreigners; and if a man wants to go back home, they kill him if he tries. The hunting and fishing are poor because they took away our gods. They promised us the spoils of Obann, but all we got is toil and trouble."

His men nodded vigorously and grunted their agreement.

"I can only speak for myself, as one man among twenty-six free men," Ootoo said, "but it seems to me, Hlah, that if I help the Thunder King's runaway slaves, I hurt the Thunder King. That appeals to me! And if your new God can do anything for me, so much the better. I doubt we'll ever get across the mountains, anyhow."

"I'll stick with you, Ootoo," one of his men spoke up.

"Maybe we can raid the Thunder King's new road. Arm some of these wretched slaves, teach them to fight, and help them to avenge themselves—the mardars won't like that, eh?"

No, they wouldn't like it at all: everyone agreed.

After the Abnaks departed, Hlah turned to Orth. "What have you done, Sunfish?" he said. "Ootoo's heart is changed."

"I haven't done anything," Orth said; "but I think that maybe God has."

CHAPTER 38

Helki Picks a Fight

Not all of the Abnaks around King Oziah's Wood fled to the hills. Some of the fugitives from the westernmost camps managed to get across the river. In sight of the town of Caristun, some two hundred of them crossed the Imperial, assembling on the south bank of the river.

"As soon as they can organize themselves," Helki told the townsfolk, "they'll come running to take everything you have. There's no way to keep them out of this town. The only thing to do is to attack them first—right now."

"Look at them all!" a man objected. "We'll all be killed."

"We'll all be killed if we wait for them to come to us," Helki answered. "If you think you can get away during the fighting, God speed you. Take the children with you! But I'm going out there now."

He spun his staff over his head and set off toward the Abnaks. "Might as well," he thought. The townspeople couldn't get away. Even if they could, the winter would kill them as surely as the Abnaks.

Cavall trotted beside him, barking. Angel flew overhead. He spoke to the hound.

"Better stay out of this fight, little brother. It's likely to have a bad end." But Cavall only barked louder.

Helki didn't turn to see whether anyone had followed him. If somehow the children in Caristun could be saved, he would be content. He wondered how many Abnaks he could fell with his staff before they killed him. Knowing Abnaks, he thought a good fight would satisfy them. If they could take his scalp, and the fight was worth remembering, they might be moved to spare the townspeople.

"Helki the Rod!" It was the Griffs, all dozen of them, following close behind him, making noise enough for several dozen. "Giant-slayer!" they cried. "The Flail of the Lord!"

The Abnaks, wet and weary after crossing the Imperial on logs and rafts, could hardly believe their eyes. Most of them just stood and stared; but a few came running to meet Helki and his men, brandishing their tomahawks.

In no time at all the clash came. Helki was used to fighting alone against a group. He kept the rod moving, whirling, striking whom it would and moving on to strike again. Out of the corner of his eye he saw Cavall pull down an Abnak and savage his arm, then leap nimbly aside to dodge a tomahawk. He didn't see Angel swoop down and rake a man's face with her talons, although he did hear her shrill cry of attack and a harsh scream answer it. Nor did he see the thirty or forty townsmen who snatched up rakes and clubs and rushed into the fray. He had no time to fix his eyes on anything. Spin, stride, lunge—keep the staff in motion, keep himself in motion for as long as he could: don't stop moving and become a target. His rod would crack skulls and shatter shoulders, and keep on doing it until a stone tomahawk finally found him.

But suddenly there was no fight. Suddenly the Abnaks were all down on one knee, with their weapons on the ground before them and empty hands raised high—even the ones by the river who hadn't joined the battle.

"Respite, respite!" they all cried. Helki knew this was what Abnaks said when they meant not to surrender, but to declare they had no wish to fight. It was an Abnak truce, which no man of honor would violate.

Helki stopped moving and rested, panting, on his staff. Angel came down and settled on his shoulder. Cavall, unwounded, sat beside him.

"I agree to the respite," Helki said, which was the proper thing to say.

"Why do you attack us, Flail of the Lord?" an Abnak chief demanded.

"To protect the people in that town," said Helki. They could all see Caristun from where they were.

"If you are Helki the Rod, we will not fight with you," said the chief. "Our fight is with the Zephites and the Wallekki and all the servants of the Thunder King who turned against us. We want their scalps, not yours! We will not harm any of your people."

Now for the first time Helki surveyed the battlefield. All his Griffs were still alive, and all the townsmen who'd come after them. A few Abnaks lay on the cold ground, but no one seemed to have been killed: the men who were hurt were gasping and groaning, but still alive. The fight must not have lasted even a minute, Helki reckoned.

So he did what was proper, according to the manners of the Abnaks. He took the chief's hand and raised him to his feet, which meant that he and they would be at peace from then on.

"I am Santay, son of Bug, a chieftain of the Marmot

Clan," the man said. "We have all heard of you, Helki the Rod. You have a famous name—and no man but a great chief would a hawk follow into battle. No man would go up against two hundred men unless the gods favored him."

"Not gods," Helki said, "but the one God whom I serve."

Santay nodded. "The God of Obann shows His might, these days. What man has not seen it?

"Helki, Flail of the Lord lead us, that we might be revenged on the men who betrayed us—who accuse us, the Marmot Clan, of witchcraft! Lead us, and we shall follow. I have spoken."

Leading these men back across the river and carrying the fight to the Thunder King's troops around Oziah's Wood ought to keep the Heathen too busy to prey on Caristun, Helki thought. They might recruit more Abnaks and get help from the rangers in the forest. He might yet meet up with Jack and Ellayne and Martis.

"If you give your oath to fight against the Thunder King from now on," Helki answered, "then I'll do my best to lead you. And maybe God will make us prosper, after all."

It took all afternoon, but one by one, each in his own name, all those Marmot men swore to follow Helki.

"I'll never get back to Lintum Forest," he thought. It seemed that he, who'd never wanted any more than to be left alone, would die an Abnak war chief. "That, at least, is funny!" he thought.

CHAPTER 39

Lord Reesh Says a Prayer

In the golden hall there was a banquet every night for all the mardars. The Thunder King sat on his throne, behind his golden mask, and neither ate nor drank, nor spoke a word, nor moved. It was uncanny, Lord Reesh thought.

Before they sat down to eat, the mardars turned to the Thunder King, bowed their heads and spoke a prayer: "O god over all gods, master of the universe, hail! We pledge our service to you to the death—to you, all-powerful, who cannot die."

Reesh was expected to dine with the mardars every night and join them in the recitation of this prayer. "You must not keep silence," Kyo told him. "It would be taken as an act of rebellion and punished swiftly. The mardars would seize you and throw you to the great cat."

Reesh said the prayer. He didn't know what Kyo would do if he confessed he didn't believe the Thunder King to be a god.

"What does it matter, my lord?" Gallgoid said, when Reesh told him about it. "You never believed in God when you were First Prester in God's Temple, yet you led the prayers."

But it was a commandment of old, according to Scripture, that neither the Children of Geb nor their descendants were to worship any god but God. It was the first divine commandment given to them after the sons of men were cast out of Paradise. How many kings had been destroyed for disobedience? How many times had the people been afflicted with famine, war, or pestilence because they'd disobeyed and set up idols in Obann and honored the false gods of the Heathen?

The Scriptures were just stories that had survived from ancient times and probably not even true stories, at that. So Reesh believed. But it was necessary for the common people to believe in Scripture, and Reesh had spent many years seeing to it that the Temple fostered such belief. It was good for the nation, and his own unbelief had nothing to do with it.

Why, then, did it distress him to say prayers to the Thunder King?

"It'd trouble me," said Gallgoid, "but I'm only an assassin, not a scholar. Besides which, my lord, they'll kill you if you refuse to say the prayers."

So Reesh said prayers to the Thunder King and feasted with the mardars every night and shuddered whenever the great cat's green eyes chanced to fall on him.

"No one knows what kind of beast it is, nor whence it came," Kyo said. "Some men captured it one day, up in the hills north of Kara Karram, and presented it to the Thunder King. Our master feeds it on the flesh of slaves and rebels. You will see that done, if we stay here long enough. It is said that our master himself called the beast up, out of the depths of the earth. Certainly no man has ever seen another of its kind."

Around the walls of the banquet chamber, behind the

high chairs, stood massive wooden posts with rudimentary, rather sad-looking faces carved into them near the top and barbarous runes inscribed below the faces.

"Those contain the spirits of the gods whom our master has imprisoned," Kyo explained. "Here they must stand, powerless, to witness his greatness and his continuing victories. They groan and wail most piteously, but only our master the Thunder King can hear them. Once he has conquered all the nations of the world, then he will devour their gods."

Superstitious tripe, thought Reesh, fit only for overawing primitive pagans. Nevertheless, he said prayers to the Thunder King while Gallgoid every night had his suppers in a wooden hall with the mardars' servants, who merely caroused and otherwise enjoyed themselves.

"But we do have to watch what we say, my lord," he said. "They all believe the Thunder King's a god. Those who don't, get fed to the cat. Those who do, might wind up in Hell when all is said and done. But that at least comes later."

In King Oziah's Wood, the rangers watched intently as the Thunder King's army clawed itself to pieces. The Abnaks tried to escape; the Zeph and the Wallekki tried to wipe them out. "They won't be invading the forest anytime soon," Huell said. A few of the Abnaks had tried, but the rangers' arrows had accounted for them all. "But we'll have to be ready in case they try to come in without the Abnaks."

Huell didn't know that the Omah were coming out of the forest every night to kill as many Heathen as they could. They couldn't kill many, but they were destroying the courage of the army. The Heathen thought they were imps and devils, summoned by witchcraft, and feared them inordinately. Huell didn't know because there was no one to tell him. Wytt hadn't told Jack and Ellayne that the attacks were continuing: it wasn't in his nature to give reports. He came and went as he pleased. Wherever the rangers made camp, Wytt found them. He liked to come late at night and snuggle up in Ellayne's arms. He would leave early in the morning, and none of Huell's rangers ever saw him.

But somehow Chillith knew of Wytt's comings and goings. One night, he drew Jack aside to speak to him alone—a little distance out of the camp, under the stars.

"I know what the little hairy men are doing," he said. "You remember how my men and I thought your Wytt was a kind of devil, and how we feared him. The men on the plain are more afraid than we were! Their fear cries out to me, even in my sleep. Those men fear witchcraft. At first they thought it was the Abnaks' witchcraft; but they have driven away or killed the Abnaks and still the little devils afflict them by night."

"Yes, well, Ellayne and I saw it, the first time they did it," Jack said. "There's no need to tell me."

"That's not what I want to tell you," Chillith said. He lowered his voice. "Your God has spoken to me. I must confront the Thunder King. God has shown him to me in a dream, sitting in a golden hall atop the mountains. He feasts with his mardars. In the spring he intends to come down and destroy Obann. But before that happens, I must stand before him and denounce him. And then God will destroy him."

Jack shivered. "Why are you telling me this, Chillith?

What do you mean, 'denounce him'?"

"That will be seen when I do it. Only then."

"But what do you want from me?"

"Your little hairy man, to guide me up the mountains: to protect me. He'll do it, if you ask him."

"They say the mountains are crawling with warriors," Jack said. "Even with Wytt to help, you'll never get past them."

"If they capture me, well and good—they'll take me to the Thunder King," Chillith said. "If your friend can keep me from stepping off a cliff, it'll be enough. But I must start soon."

Jack didn't like any of this, not a bit. "I can't just tell Wytt to go," he said. "It'd have to be both me and Ellayne. You should ask her, too."

Chillith smiled. "She would say no."

"If I send Wytt away without asking her," Jack said, "she'd kill me. And then she'd follow after him, and Martis and I would have to follow her, and the next thing you know, it'd be a cuss't parade—and we'd all get caught."

"That's what I'm trying to avoid," Chillith said. "There is no need for anyone but me to stand before the Thunder King: I only have been called. Let it be a secret from Ellayne. Wytt can return to you after I'm captured."

Jack shook his head, forgetting Chillith couldn't see him. "She'd find out. I won't do it. You'll have to ask her."

"I'll go alone, if I have to," Chillith said. "It is the will of God."

"What are you two doing?"

Jack startled. It was Ellayne; they hadn't heard her coming. "What's the will of God?" she said. "What are you talking about?"

"You might as well know," Jack said, and so they told her.

"You must be crazy," she said to Chillith. "They'll kill you."

"I know," he said. "But when God called you to climb Bell Mountain, did you not go? If He can take away my sight, He can take away my life at any time. So I will obey!

"I was a mardar. One day I would have been presented to the Thunder King, and I would have sworn to serve him as my god. He would have taught me secrets and invested me with powers. For this, the true God blinded me. He put me in the dark so I could see. Only then did I see my own wickedness."

"We should all go with you," said Ellayne, "Jack and Martis and me."

"I forbid it. You have not been called."

Ellayne didn't answer right away. "What's she thinking?" Jack wondered. It was one thing to obey God, he thought—and quite another to do something foolhardy because you wanted to do it. He wished Obst were there. Obst would know what to do.

And then Ellayne said, "All right. When Wytt comes again, I'll ask him to guide you up the mountains. I don't know that he'll do it, but I'll ask."

———

Wytt didn't come that night. The children lay awake in their shelter, waiting for him, but he didn't come. After an hour or two of thinking, Jack whispered to Ellayne, "I know you—and you're up to something. You'd never let Wytt go without us, so what's your plan?"

"To do what God wants: to help Chillith," she said. "Wytt won't leave us. It wouldn't matter how I asked him. But God wants Chillith to go—I do believe him, you know!—and Chillith can't go without Wytt, and Wytt won't go without us. So we'll go. We'll follow along behind, and Wytt will know we're there, but Chillith won't."

Jack snorted. "And what about Martis?" he said. "The last time we snuck off without him, it was nothing but trouble. You know he'll follow us."

"He won't have to, this time," Ellayne said. "This time we'll ask him to come along with us."

Right on up to see the Thunder King! It was daft, Jack thought. "He'll kill us all." And he was pretty sure that if God didn't call you to do a foolish thing like that, it was better not to do it.

CHAPTER 40

A Message from the Thunder King

Shingis and the Blays didn't know what to do with themselves. They were treated as Gurun's personal retainers, so no one gave them any work to do. They ate and slept in a building next door to the palace along with many of King Ryons' warriors. Those men were Wallekki, Abnaks, Fazzan, and Griffs, none of whom spoke the Blays' language: so they had no one to talk to. Time hung heavily on their hands. After a few days of this, Shingis finally got into the palace to see Gurun.

They took him to a little room with pictures painted on the walls and ceiling, and a window looking out over the rooftops of the city. Never in his life had he seen anything like it. On the ceiling were painted clouds and the sun. He couldn't see the point of that. And Gurun was in a bright yellow dress that made her look like a flower. He shook his head.

"What's the matter?" she asked.

"We go back soon to Jocah Creek?" he said. "Nice place, nice people—not so different from Blays' country. Not like this city."

"I liked Jocah's Creek, too," Gurun said. "But I don't know when I can go back. My filgya told me to stay with the king. You and your men can go back to Jocah's Creek, if you like."

"No, no! We stay with you. Who else will pray for us?"

"You don't need me to pray for you, Shingis. You can pray for yourselves. Just talk to God, and He will hear you."

But that idea unsettled him. She could see it in his face. The Blays had been Heathen, worshipping idols. These had to be offered food before they could be prayed to. And then the Thunder King took them away, and the Blays had no gods. Gurun wondered if they would ever get over it. Would they ever understand that they belonged to the real God now? But then, she thought, the people of Obann didn't seem to grasp that any better than the Blays. What good had their Temple done them?

"It is strange, to be in such a city as this," she said, "as strange for me as it is for you. Look at this dress they gave me! It's beautiful, but it's much more than I need. In all the islands of my homeland there is no dress like this. Everything in Obann is so grand! It's like being in a dream."

"Some of us, we are afraid of this place," Shingis said. "Everything too big: it might all fall down, someday."

"I know," Gurun said, thinking of her home and family. "Tell the men, Shingis, that I will come and see them tonight after supper. We will all pray together. I would like that."

"I, too," he said.

While she was talking with Shingis in the palace, Gurun missed something that happened just outside the city, under the walls.

Three horsemen rode up to the East Gate. It was still being repaired, and there were guards on duty, but the horsemen didn't try to enter the city. They stopped before the gate, and one of them produced a brass bugle and blew a challenge on it. The workmen stopped working, and the sergeant of the guard came out to confront the horsemen.

"Our business is with the King of Obann," said the rider in the middle, a tall man in a black cloak, on a black horse. "Let him come and hear a message from our master the Thunder King."

"Maybe you'd like to hear a message from my archers," said the sergeant.

"We are heralds. It is not lawful to harm us."

Ryons was at his lessons when Obst came for him. One look at Obst's face told him that he brought bad news.

"It'll be necessary for Your Majesty to be brave," he said. "Three men are at the East Gate, claiming to be heralds of the Thunder King. I've seen them and spoken with them; I believe them. They will speak their message to no one but you. I'll go with you, and I've sent for Hennen, Uduqu, and Shaffur. You won't be alone."

Ryons shuddered. Once before, in Lintum Forest, he'd faced one of the Thunder King's messengers. Then the message was that the Thunder King would put out Ryons' eyes and cast him into a prison for the rest of his life.

Obst remembered that. "Be brave, my king," he said. "You have brave men all around you to protect you—and better than that, you have God's protection."

Ryons stood up. "At least I'll get some fresh air!" he said. "I'll listen to the message, Obst. But will I have to answer it?"

"Who knows? But you are king in this city—no one can force you to say anything."

For the first time in a long time, Ryons took Obst's hand, and they walked out of the palace hand in hand. Obst was the teacher: he would know what to say, Ryons thought, even if no one else did.

"God won't let them put my eyes out," he said to himself. Aloud he asked, "Where's Gurun?"

"I don't know, Sire."

"I want someone to ask her to come to the gate with us."

"As you wish, King Ryons." Obst bade a servant to find Gurun and bring her to the king; but they couldn't stop to wait for her.

Standing on the wall over the gate, with Obst at his right hand and Uduqu, Hennen, and Shaffur at his left, Ryons looked down on the three messengers. Two of them he recognized as Wallekki; but the tall man in black looked Obannese. How could that be?

By now the whole wall was lined with people, all of them waiting to hear the message from the Thunder King. Ryons wondered how far the messengers had had to come. Much of Obann, especially to the east of the city, still swarmed with invaders.

"So this is the king of Obann—the boy king!" said the man in black. "What kind of nation has a boy for a king? Couldn't you find a man?"

"He was man enough to shatter your king's army," said Uduqu. "It took us a long time to bury all the dead."

"Since when do Abnaks speak from Obann's city walls? Why don't you let the boy king speak for himself, Abnak?"

Ryons knew he had to answer, with so many of his people watching him. For a moment he forgot he was a king, and answered as Ryons the slave-boy would have answered, when he was under Obst's protection.

"They told me you had a message for me," he said, "but I haven't heard you say anything yet. Why so bashful?"

"Then hear this—king!" The herald raised himself straighter in the saddle and pulled a roll of parchment from under his cloak. From this he read:

"To Ryons, who is called the king of Obann, from the god, the Thunder King, master of the nations—

"Come East, little king, to the foothills of the mountains, to the headwaters of the River Chariot. Come East, with whatever following you can raise, and we shall look upon one another face to face.

"Let the city of Obann know that if you will come to me, I will break down the city of Obann and burn it with fire; but the people of the city I will remove alive, and settle them in other cities, and let them live.

"But if you will not come to me, little king, then I shall come to you; and I shall destroy the people of this city, man, woman, and child. I will come with my full power and leave no soul living in this place.

"Trust not in the God of Obann, for I am a god who conquers gods; and your God shall join all the other gods in my captivity."

The herald rolled up the parchment. "Those are the words of my master and yours, the Thunder King," he said. "Do as he bids you. Why should all the people die because of you?"

The crowd along the wall was silent. They remembered the vast armies that the Thunder King had sent against them in the summer. But General Hennen spoke up sharply, his words shattering the stillness like the crack of a whip.

"What is your name, fellow? Unless my eyes and ears deceive me, you're a man of Obann, the same as any man within these walls."

"I am," the herald answered. "I was at Silvertown when the Thunder King destroyed it. I made my submission to him, and he took me into his service. Goryk Gillow is my name."

"And in addition to being a traitor to your country," Hennen said, "do you believe this mere Heathen man to be a god? That would make you both an apostate and a fool."

"Do you think so?" Goryk said. "It's not my god's temple that lies in ruins, is it?"

"Enough!"

Obst's roar was like the sound of a mountain splitting in two. "You have delivered your foolish and abominable message, and now you may go."

"And what about my answer, greybeard?"

At that moment a soldier helped Gurun up onto the ramparts, and she stood there in her yellow dress, and the rays of the sun were like a golden fire on her hair. Goryk looked up at her and turned pale. Without another word, he wheeled his black horse sharply and spurred off into the east. His two Wallekki comrades were hard-put to catch up to him.

Ryons stared at Gurun. "He was afraid of you!" he said.

"Was that the messenger?" she asked. "What did he say?"

"Never mind that now," said Obst. "Come, we must call the chiefs together. Rumor is a fire that burns quickly in this city! You come, too, Gurun." He smiled at her. "He truly was afraid of you. I saw it, too."

Before the chiefs could meet together, a vast crowd gathered around the palace. Many had heard the herald's message, and spread it in the blink of an eye and the flap of a lip, from one end of the city to another. You could hear them through the thick stone walls, a sound like a swarm of bees buzzing.

"Why are they so fearful?" Gurun said. She sat beside Ryons at a table, where they were waiting for the rest of the chiefs. Hennen, Uduqu, and Shaffur were already there. At the head of the table sat Obst, with his eyes closed and his lips moving silently. "And what is Obst doing?"

"That's how he prays," Ryons said; he'd seen it many times before. "Two men could jump on the table right now and have a sword fight, and he wouldn't know it. He's talking to God, and God speaks to him. He is a very holy man."

"The people are afraid because they don't want to die," Hennen said. "This summer, it took a miracle to save them. I don't suppose they can expect another miracle."

Chief Zekelesh of the Fazzan came in, and a man named Hawk whose skin was dark, almost black. Chiefs of Griffs and Attakotts and other peoples Gurun had never heard of: they came in and took seats at the table.

"The question's a simple one," said Hennen. "Do we

stay, or do we go?"

"Stay!" Shaffur growled. "Do they think we're simpletons? It's a trick to get us out into the open, so they can destroy us."

"But it's a subtle trick," Hennen said. "If we stay, it may look like we value the king above the people. It will look like we're afraid."

Chief Zekelesh spoke some impassioned words in a language no one understood. Uduqu jogged his elbow and pointed to Obst. With the translator unavailable, so to speak, Zekelesh fell silent.

Ryons listened to the muffled noise of the crowd. It must have been very loud indeed, if they could hear it in here.

"It is shameful for a man to say he is a god," Gurun spoke up. "You may be sure God will destroy this Thunder King."

"It seems we have a new member of the council of chieftains!" Shaffur interrupted. "I don't remember when she was elected."

"Obst asked her to come—and I want her, too," Ryons said. "Please, Chief Shaffur—didn't you see that herald's face when he saw her?"

"And he fled like a berry-picker from a she-bear!" Uduqu added, grinning.

At that moment Obst's eyes opened and he slipped in his chair with a grunt. With another grunt he pulled himself up straight. All of the chiefs had seen him pray before.

"Did God answer you?" Uduqu asked.

"Not in the way I expected," Obst said. He looked at Ryons. "The Lord wishes to see what the king would do."

Shaffur shook his head. He would never get used to asking a boy for a decision—not that Ryons blamed him.

Gurun said, "Is it right to force him to decide?"

Obst shrugged. "He is God's chosen." He looked at Ryons. "Maybe tomorrow, Sire, after prayer and meditation, and a good night's sleep?"

But Ryons already knew what he should do, and what God wanted. Indeed, he'd known it as soon as he heard the herald speak.

"I'll go," he said. "Listen to those people outside! But it's not to please them. I don't know how to say it right, but we can't just wait here for the Thunder King. There won't be another great beast to chase away his army this time."

Uduqu nodded. "Yes—that would happen only once."

Ryons struggled to explain himself. It wasn't so long ago that he was a slave, an orphan, of less value than a goat. But then Obst came, speaking tongues, and God struck down a mardar just as he was about to study Ryons' entrails for omens of the future. Everything since then, Ryons thought, had been a miracle. Sometimes he imagined himself and his men as a herd driven by God with sure and certain wisdom. The herd didn't know where it was going, but the shepherd did. And sheep should trust their shepherd.

"I have God's promise to protect me," Ryons said. "I believe He will. He always has. And the Thunder King is not a god. I don't know what'll happen if I go to see him—but neither does he."

Chief Zekelesh stood up and slammed his wolf's-head hat on the table. He spoke passionately; and Obst translated.

"What can we accomplish sitting here?" he said. "How

are we ever to see our homes again—or make new homes—just by sitting here? I say that if any man is fool enough to offend the true God, we do ourselves dishonor if we don't go out to fight him! What is the point of talking and talking about it, when we all know what to do?"

The chiefs, all except Shaffur the Wallekki, pounded the table and growled their assent.

"He really is a king!" thought Gurun.

But Ryons thought, "How far will we get, I wonder? It's a long way back to the mountains."

CHAPTER 41

Of Gallgoid, and Helki

Up in the Golden Pass it was snowing steadily, day and night. A multitude of slaves kept clear all the area around the Thunder King's golden hall, the other halls and cabins, the great gates, and the new road down the mountain. But up above the hall, snow piled up on the shoulders of the mountains. Without the unending toil of the slaves, neither man nor beast could have used the pass until well into the spring.

In the great hall the mardars had a banquet every night, with the silent Thunder King presiding behind his mask of gold. Armies of slaves from forty nations labored night and day to keep supplies coming up the mountain from the East: the banqueters wanted for nothing. Roasted fowl and pork and beef, rich soups, sweet dainties, sparkling wine—all kept the mardars in a happy mood.

"Why so glum, First Prester?" Mardar Kyo asked Lord Reesh one night when they sat down to feast, after praying to the Thunder King. "We are warm, well-fed, and comfortable. Indeed, we occupy the center of the world."

"It's my age," said Reesh, which was a lie.

In truth he hated being in that hall. He hated the infernal cat chained to the Thunder King's throne, hated the way its green eyes always sought him out and watched him the whole time he feasted. Reesh had always had a cultivated palate. He appreciated good food and was a connoisseur of wines. But with that glaring monster contemplating him as a meal, even the fine fare tasted as bland as peasants' porridge.

He hated the unnatural silence of the Thunder King, who never said a word; but most of all he hated the fear that had settled over his own heart like a skin of ice. All the mardars said the Thunder King read their thoughts as plainly as if they spoke to him. Against his lifelong skepticism, Lord Reesh found himself beginning to believe it.

His servant Gallgoid certainly believed it. Gallgoid spent most of the day conversing with the mardars' servants. He spoke several Heathen languages and was quickly learning more. Reesh wondered what he got up to during the day. When he helped his master to bathe and dress for the banquet every evening, Gallgoid talked about the things he'd heard during the day—talked without really saying anything, Reesh thought.

"I don't know how it's done, the Thunder King getting into his mardars' heads, but everybody knows he does it," Gallgoid said. "Wherever a mardar is, he might as well be there, too. The Thunder King knows everything they know, and he knows as soon as they do. Everybody up here has seen it done a thousand times."

"Do you believe him to be a god?" Lord Reesh demanded, as he sat in a hot bath that couldn't seem to warm his bones and Gallgoid laid out his clothes—an assassin serving as a valet.

"Well, he can't be, can he?" Gallgoid said. "Not unless the Scriptures are all wrong. But he does things that no ordinary man can do. They all say so. But what about you, my lord? What do you think? You've seen him face to face, and I haven't."

"He's a man," said Reesh. That bordered on being a lie. There was a part of him that couldn't believe the Thunder King was just a man. "A god wouldn't sit on a chair."

"Well, my lord, you never believed in the real God," the assassin said.

"It's my age," Reesh grumbled. Maybe, he thought, this last year of his life had simply been too much for him, and his mind, tricked by the feebleness of his body, was playing tricks on him. He'd never been on top of a mountain before, and it had been many years since he'd traveled any distance from the Temple. Yes, that was it—too much stress and strain on an old man.

He wasn't sinking into a foolish belief in the Thunder King's divinity. And a cat, no matter the length of its fangs nor the width of its shoulders, was just a cat—just an animal. Neither it nor its master could eavesdrop on his thoughts.

And Gallgoid, he thought, never answered my question, did he? Burn the fellow! He never let you know what he was thinking: a desirable trait in an assassin, but an annoyance in a servant.

Farther west, below the mountains, it wasn't snowing anywhere near as hard. Between the Imperial River and King Oziah's Wood, Helki and his men were fighting.

Helki couldn't get into the forest, but the rangers could venture out and shower the Heathen with arrows. The rangers' scouts kept careful watch. They knew at all times where

Helki's little band of warriors was; they understood how badly outnumbered he was; and they did their best to help. And all the Abnaks still in the area flocked to him. Before three days were out, Helki had four hundred men.

Santay, the Abnak chief, was delighted.

"Very funny, Abnaks fighting for Obann!" he said. "The Thunder King's Wallekki won't dare enter the forest without us, and the mardars don't know what to do."

"I thought they always knew what to do," Helki said. "I heard they always know just what their master wants them to do, by some black magic that he does."

"That's what they told us," Santay said. "But if it were true, they wouldn't be in such trouble as they are today. They wouldn't have accused us of murder and witchcraft; they would have known what to do when the little devils plagued them—and they wouldn't be getting beaten by us in every fight!"

That afternoon they clashed with a hundred Wallekki horsemen and quickly routed them. The Abnaks scalped as many as they could lay hands on, but Helki was able to preserve a few, unharmed, as prisoners.

"If you boys talk to me, I might be able to save your skins," he told them. They knew what the Abnaks would do to them if they had the opportunity, so they were eager to cooperate with Helki.

"It's all gone bad!" said the man they picked to be their spokesman. "At night the devils come and kill us in our sleep. The mardars dance and sing spells, but they can't stop it. They said it was the Abnaks making witchcraft, but the Abnaks have left us and still the devils come.

"We know who you are—Helki the Rod, Helki Giant-killer. The mardars promised to make magic that would cause you to die: but here we are, your prisoners. And the bowmen shoot at us from the shelter of the wood, and we can't get at them! Nobody knows what to do."

"Why should we have made witchcraft?" Santay said. "That was a lie! Some of the men killed by the devils were Abnaks. And yet you Wallekki turned on us!"

"It was the mardars. It was the Thunder King. The mardars said he willed it," the prisoner said.

There were many Heathen camps between the forest and the river, Helki thought: if they ever came together under one commander, they'd wipe us out in two days. Aloud he asked, "Why haven't your people regrouped?"

"Because we can't! Our own chief was killed by an archer yesterday. The Zephites who were with us killed their own mardar and ran away. Nobody knows who's supposed to be in command."

Good news to us, Helki thought. Their morale was fading fast.

"Well, now," he said to the prisoners, "I want to help you men, but I reckon there's only one way to do it. If you swear an oath on the honor of your clan to ride with us and fight for us, I guess these Abnaks will let you live. We could use horsemen. There's already thousands of Wallekki fighting for the king of Obann, so you wouldn't be the first. What do you say?"

The prisoners looked at Santay and at the burly Abnaks around him, standing bare-chested in the snow because the battle had heated their blood. Steam rose from their skins: a daunting sight, thought Helki.

"We would be agreeable to that," the spokesman said,

"if we could trust the Abnaks—and if they can trust us."

"There's treason in the service of the Thunder King," Helki said, "but not in the service of the living God. In His service every man starts with an honorable name and is judged by what he does from then on."

"But what do the Abnaks say?" asked the prisoner.

Santay frowned. "You Wallekki turned on us when we were serving with you. Maybe the Thunder King's mardars led you into folly. If you swear to obey Helki the Rod, as we do, you'll have nothing to fear from us. We have already taken many scalps in payment for the wrong done to us, and we will take more. But not yours."

Helki ordered the prisoners cut from their bonds, re-armed, and given horses: the Abnaks had captured several dozen fine horses and didn't know what to do with them. These riders would make useful scouts, he thought, and maybe more Wallekki would join him later on. He would need every man he could get, to drive the Heathen out of this land between the forest and the river.

Angel flew down and settled on his shoulder. The Wallekki saw it and bowed their heads and kissed their fingertips, saluting him.

"Among our tribes," said one, "only the greatest and most noble chiefs have hawks."

"I'm not great and I'm not noble," Helki said. But Tiliqua the Griff, standing beside him, grinned and said, "He doesn't have to be great or noble—he's Helki the Rod, the Flail of the Lord!"

The men cheered, and Helki sighed.

CHAPTER 42

How Ellayne Carried Out Her Plan

Most of the rangers rushed to the southern fringe of King Oziah's Wood to harass the reeling Heathen army. They left a screen of bowmen in the north, but the hot fighting was all in the south. In the north, those Heathen who weren't still hunting Abnaks were trying to make their way around the forest to reinforce the units in the south.

Martis longed to join the fighting, but wouldn't leave Jack and Ellayne. They, with Chillith, remained some safe miles away from the forest's edge. Huell and most of his men had gone to battle, leaving only four men to guard their camp and run messages from north to south.

It was quiet in the forest now, Jack thought. He supposed most of the birds had flown south for the winter. The birds that remained had maybe gone to watch the fighting. Jack wished he could go. It'd be better than watching the light snow fall, on and off, every day.

Wytt was off somewhere in the woods, doing they knew not what. Chillith sat over his campfire day and night, brooding. Ellayne had not yet spoken to Martis about following Chillith up the mountain. "Not much point in doing that," she told Jack, "until we see Wytt again."

One night everyone in the camp went to sleep; and when Jack woke early the next morning, he found himself alone in the shelter.

Ellayne had gotten up first, he thought: nothing to that. When he crawled out of the shelter, he didn't see her anywhere around the camp. Chillith's fire was out. One of the rangers was up, engaged in restarting his own campfire.

"Have you seen Ellayne?" Jack asked him. The man said no. "How long have you been up?"

"An hour. I got up just before sunup."

"Now where the mischief is she?" Jack wondered. If she'd gone a little distance into the woods to do her morning business, she would've returned by now. The ranger would have seen her. It was mighty cold this morning to be just fatzing around in the woods.

Maybe he should worry. He went to the shelter where Martis and Chillith slept, and called for Martis to come out. Fortunately Martis was the kind of man whom it was easy to awaken.

"What's the matter, Jack?"

"I can't find Ellayne."

Martis had crawled out of the low shelter, but at those words he shot to his feet. He looked all around.

"Where's Chillith?" he said. "Have you seen him?" Jack shook his head. He'd thought Chillith must be in the shelter, sleeping. Martis gripped him by the shoulders. "Tell me what this is all about—quickly!"

"I don't know!" Jack said. "Chillith said he had to see the Thunder King. He had to go. He wanted Wytt to take him up the mountain, but Ellayne said Wytt would never leave us, so all three of us would have to follow Chillith without him knowing—" Jack stopped himself. Suddenly his stomach clenched. "Roast her hide! They've gone without us!"

Martis searched the powdery snow around the children's shelter. It didn't take him long to find what he was looking for: Wytt's tiny footprints. That made the story plain.

"She said she believed Chillith. I guess she really did," Jack said. "But why would she sneak off without us? I'll knock her down when we catch her!"

Martis shook his head. "She meant well, Jack," he said. "The fewer who go, the fewer who can get caught. Foolish, but it shows a noble spirit." Jack snorted, but Martis said, "Get something to eat and fill your pack. We've got to go after her."

Martis was right. For all three of them to go chasing after Chillith would be stupid, Ellayne thought. All along it had been her plan to be the only one to go.

When Wytt crept into the shelter that night, Ellayne had shushed him and crawled outside, careful not to wake Jack. After she told Wytt what she wanted to do, she sent him to wake Chillith. Everyone else in the camp remained asleep. Not a soul stirred, not even when Ellayne stepped on a piece of firewood and snapped it.

"Wytt won't go unless I go, too," she told the Griff. "So either take me with you or don't go at all. Tonight may be the only chance we have to give Jack and Martis the slip."

When they were out of earshot of the camp, following Wytt down a path he chose for them, Chillith pleaded with Ellayne. "It's a shame for a man to take a girl-child into danger," he said. "Why do you want to do this?"

"Because I believe you," Ellayne said, "because I want the Thunder King to be destroyed and for all of this war to be over and done with—so Jack and I and everyone else can go home."

"It's too dangerous."

"Dangerous? That's a laugh! Jack and I have been in more danger than you ever dreamed of. We climbed Bell Mountain. We went under the ruins of the Old Temple. And that's not even the half of it!" She sighed. "We've been in more dangers than Abombalbap himself—so don't worry about me!"

"Jack and Martis will follow us," Chillith said.

"I know. But as long as we can stay ahead of them, that's good. If we get into trouble, they might come along in time to save us. We mustn't get too far ahead of them. Anyhow, it's good for the four of us to be split up like this."

"If the rangers catch us, they'll make us go back."

"Don't be silly," Ellayne said. "The rangers are much too busy to bother about us."

Wytt led them along narrow paths. Maybe these belonged to the Forest Omah and the rangers didn't know them. Between the moonlight and the snow, it wasn't hard to see and they made good time, Ellayne leading Chillith by the hand. Except for when they spoke, the forest by night in winter was as quiet as a grave.

Ellayne thought she was following in the footsteps of Abombalbap. "Maybe someday there'll be books about our adventures," she thought. "How Ellayne and Jack climbed Bell Mountain and rang the bell—that'd make a story."

But at the same time she understood that this blind Heathen, whose hand she was holding, was a prophet answering a summons from the Lord—not even his own Lord, and a summons that would probably cost him his life. Then it seemed mighty childish to be thinking of Abombalbap.

It amused her to imagine how angry Jack would be when he discovered that she'd tricked him, but she was already missing him. She hoped he and Martis would never be very far behind.

CHAPTER 43

How Gurun Received a Gift

The maid, Bronna, knocked on Gurun's door, and the Ghol on guard, Kutchuk, opened it for her so she could bring in Gurun's breakfast tray.

"Wake up, my lady. It's going to be a beautiful day." She set down the tray and opened the curtains, letting the sun shine in. Gurun sat up in bed and rubbed her eyes. There was something about this bed that made her sleep longer than she usually did.

"Don't call me 'my lady,' Bronna. I am not a lady," she said.

Outside in the hallway, another Ghol came up and spoke to Kutchuk. "Our father wants to see the girl this morning. I think he wants her to ride East with us, but doesn't want to say so."

Gurun sat up straighter. She hadn't thought any of the Ghols could speak Obannese. But then Kutchuk startled her by answering in that language: "I don't think she'd like being left behind. She has a mind of her own, that one."

"Kutchuk!" she called. "When did you learn to speak Obannese?"

He stepped into the room and looked at her quizzically. "Obannese? Not me! But I didn't know you could speak the language of the Ghols. You speak it much, much better than our father does."

Bronna looked from one speaker to the other, thoroughly confused. Gurun and Kutchuk were conversing in mutually unintelligible languages.

"I hear you speaking Obannese, Kutchuk! Why do you deny it? As for me, I understand not a single word of Gholish."

His eyes widened, and then he grinned. "I see, I see!" he said. "You do what our teacher Obst can do. Every man can understand him when he speaks, and he understands whatever anybody says. You must be a prophet, like him."

She'd heard of Obst's God-given mastery of tongues: he, too, woke up with it one day.

"But how could it be?" she said. "I'm no prophet. I'm only sixteen years old!"

Kutchuk laughed. "The prophet who told us that Ryons was to be our king was just a little girl—only so high!" He held his palm just three feet from the floor. "And how old is our father, King Ryons? Not so old as you. No, honeysuckle—you're old enough."

"Honeysuckle?"

"Just a name we Ghols have for a good girl."

Gurun, who slept in a shift—another luxury that was new to her—threw aside her blanket. "Bronna, help me find my clothes. Kutchuk, take me to Obst right away."

"But your breakfast, my lady—"

"I'll wait outside," said Kutchuk.

Obst didn't want to go East with the army. There was more work for him to do here in the city than he'd ever dreamed of. But he would have to go—the council of chiefs couldn't function without him.

How he missed his cottage in the forest! What could be more perfect than a rainy day in the spring, and nothing to do but read the Scriptures and commune with the spirit of the Lord? The rain trickling down from the thatched roof, the robins and the redbirds singing in the trees, and sometimes a squirrel sitting on his windowsill—and prayer, uninterrupted prayer: Obst longed for it with all his heart. "But God has placed me here," he mused, and sighed.

This morning he was closeted with a seminary preceptor, pleading with him. The preceptor was a short, stocky, solid man who sat there like a rock.

"Don't you see?" Obst said. "Yes, the Temple is no more—but that only makes the chamber houses and the presters and the reciters more important than ever.

"We need your scholars to copy the Scriptures and render them into modern speech so the people can read them and be instructed in them in all the chamber houses everywhere. Don't you see? God wants the whole world now to be His Temple."

The preceptor listened, but his expression never changed. Obst felt like shaking him. Everything had changed! Why couldn't they understand?

"We aren't even sure your newfound books of Scripture are genuine," said the preceptor.

"Then study them!" Obst said. "Forsooth, they were found in sealed jars below the cellars of the ruined Temple in Old Obann. God Himself, through prophets, revealed their existence."

"Prophets!" the preceptor snorted. "They were hanging so-called prophets in this city, and the Temple never objected."

At that moment came a knock on the door. It was one of Ryons' Ghols, with Gurun.

"Your pardon, Teacher—but she says she has to see you. A very wonderful thing has happened to her!"

Gurun strode past him into the room. "Say something to me in a Heathen language!" she demanded.

"Allow me," said the preceptor. He rattled off something that very few people living would have understood.

"You have only recited one of Prophet Jarma's proverbs: 'He who wishes to be deceived will be deceived, and that out of his own mouth,'" Gurun said. "That was no foreign language."

The preceptor's eyebrows rose. "You are a scholar, maiden," he said. "But I rendered it into Old Wallekki."

"I know nothing of Wallekki, old or new," she said. "But when you spoke the verse, I heard it in the language of Obann. And I understand the Ghols' speech, too! When I went to bed last night, I couldn't. Now I can."

"What is this?" said the preceptor. But of course Obst knew what it was. He turned to the Ghol and told him to fetch Uduqu and Chief Zekelesh of the Fazzan: "And hurry, please!"

When the two chiefs arrived, Obst bade them speak to Gurun in their native languages. She understood what they said and translated perfectly.

"Now you see for yourself, preceptor," Obst said. "This

maiden has received the gift of tongues—even as I have, too. It's the gift of God."

"Or a trick, perhaps," said the preceptor.

"Oh, go to!" Gurun snapped. "I come from Fogo Island, far away across the sea. I never heard of the countries these chiefs come from, much less ever learned their languages." She turned to Zekelesh, who still hadn't learned a word of Obannese. "Chieftain, did you understand what I just said to this man?"

"Yes—you speak Fazzan very well indeed," said Zekelesh: but he meant that as a jest. He was used to seeing what Obst could do.

"Surely you can see the hand of God in this!" Obst said. "Surely you can see what great works God is doing in our time."

The preceptor sighed. "I have seen more changes in the past year than I've seen in all my life," he said. "I'm not a fool, hermit. I'm a scholar, with a scholar's caution. I will not abandon that caution now.

"But to this I'll agree, that seminary students should copy out the Scriptures to be disseminated to the chamber houses. They need something to keep them out of trouble, as you well know. And I myself will examine those scrolls from Old Obann."

"Thank you!" said Obst.

"We'll talk again soon," said the scholar.

So it was that Gurun rode out of Obann with King Ryons and his army, because Obst said God's hand was on her. "You can be sure she was sent here for a reason," he said to all the chieftains, "and someday we shall see what that reason was."

Obst went, too, although he had grave misgivings about leaving the city. They left it amply garrisoned with soldiers—most of the original garrison, after all, had survived the great siege—and governed by the city magistrates: the oligarchs having all fled or perished when the Heathen entered the city.

But Obst worried about what the former servants of the Temple would do. A host of them remained: presters, reciters, scholars, and students. Preceptor Constan, who now believed that Gurun's gift of tongues was no deception, but a miracle, tried to reassure him.

"The scholars are by no means as hostile as you seem to think," he said, "and neither are the presters—most of them, at least. They are eager to study the rediscovered Scriptures, and they know how important it is to get all the chamber houses functioning again throughout Obann. They understand the Temple can't be rebuilt—not now, and probably not for many years. As for the students, you can leave them to me."

Ryons concerned himself with none of this. He knew that trouble festered in the city, but what could he do about it? But he was happy to be out with his whole army again, riding with his Ghols all around him and Gurun beside him.

"Aren't you afraid?" she asked.

"The chiefs all think the Thunder King will try to kill us long before we get to the mountains," he said. "There's so much to be afraid of; I don't know where to start. I guess I'll be more afraid as time goes on."

In his heart he wished Helki were there, and Cavall. He missed the hound, and he had faith in Helki. But he didn't think it proper for a king to mention things like that, and so he held his peace.

The Ghols struck up a song that sounded like a swarm of giant insects droning. "Can you make it out?" Ryons asked Gurun.

"It's a kind of hymn," she said. "They are asking God to let you drink fermented mare's milk from the Thunder King's skull."

"That's probably what he plans to do to me," said Ryons.

CHAPTER 44

How Ootoo Practiced Charity

Orth thought the people ought to have a stout log building where they could meet for prayers and all crowd into if the weather got to be too much for them. In this project Hlah couldn't be much help: Abnaks make no permanent dwellings, nor do they grow crops or raise livestock. But three of the men were skilled in making cabins, and under their direction, the rest worked willingly. Hlah went out with the best hunters every day to keep the little community supplied with food. He was thinking they would need furs, too.

On one of their hunting trips they met some of the men of Chief Ootoo's following.

"We're living well!" a warrior said. "There are wagons going up and down the Thunder King's new road every day, and we take everything we want from them. When they send Abnaks into the woods to hunt us, we tell them what happened down by Oziah's Wood, and they make friends with us. This country's full of our people now, all getting fat on the Thunder King's supplies. Too bad there are more wagons than we can possibly capture—otherwise the Thunder King would be feeling it! But at least we can make him mad. Old Ootoo has two hundred warriors following him now. Not bad, eh?"

"Very well done indeed," said Hlah. "But what about the runaways?"

"Oh, we take more booty than we can use and give the rest away," the warrior said. "Those people aren't doing so badly, nowadays. Some of the younger men come out to raid with us. We're taking plenty of Wallekki scalps."

"My people need furs and blankets, if you've any to spare," Hlah said.

"I'll tell Ootoo. He'll have some sent over to you."

Orth, now known as Sunfish, rejoiced to hear the news. "Those who have preyed on the people have become their protectors," he said.

"They haven't changed so much," Hlah said. "Abnaks would always rather rob caravans than serve in an army with strangers telling them what to do."

"Nevertheless, the Lord makes use of them. They're serving Him now, whether they know it or not."

In truth, Hlah was surprised the next day when half a dozen Abnaks and ten refugees arrived with armloads of furs and blankets tied into bales. They also brought a few skins of southern wine, cheeses, a cured ham, and two steel saws. The women in the camp wept for joy to see so much abundance. It was much more than Hlah had asked for or ever expected to receive.

Sunfish laughed merrily and blessed the Abnaks.

"What's he doing?" one asked.

"He's commending you to the true God, for blessings," Hlah said. "He prays that God will keep you safe and make you prosper."

"Can the Obann God do that?"

"He can. He created you and all the world around you—everything you see and everything you don't see," Hlah answered. "He is not like our Abnak gods. It's an easy thing for Him to bless you, and He delights in doing it."

"It wouldn't hurt to have a god watching over us," another warrior said. "The Thunder King took away our little gods. He told us we would win glory, conquering Obann. He tricked us into serving in his armies and turned us into slaves. I hope this Obann God is big enough to bless us."

"He is," said Hlah. "Someday the Thunder King will see how big God is. But I doubt he'll profit from the lesson."

Down below, Helki took as many prisoners as possible; and soon Santay and the Abnaks saw the wisdom of it. Most of the prisoners quickly agreed to join them and fight against the Thunder King. The little army grew by the day. Some of the Heathen sought them out and joined without a fight.

"Soon the Thunder King will have no more men to fight for him on this bank of the river," Santay said.

Aided greatly by the Wallekki riders who had joined them, Helki's men won a prize that Helki had been coveting: they captured a mardar.

The mardar was in command of a body of Zeph, but he was not himself a Zephite. He belonged to some exotic nation who decorated their bodies with raised scars. His face was painted half-red, half-blue. But he spoke Wallekki, so Helki was able to question him.

"You will all be destroyed by my master the Thunder King," the mardar said, "when he comes down from the mountains in the spring."

There's something that I didn't know, thought Helki—that the Thunder King was up there. To the mardar he said, "Why doesn't he destroy us now? They say his mardars speak with his voice and carry his power in them and that he hears what his mardars hear. So he must hear me speaking to you. Ask him why you're our prisoner. Why didn't he give you the power to capture us?"

"All in good time!" answered the mardar.

"Things aren't going well for your side, are they?"

The mardar showed his teeth. "Did you capture me just to taunt me?"

Santay wanted to hang him by his heels until he learned some manners. "Mardars are the creatures of the Thunder King. It's dangerous to let one live," he said. "They do have power, Helki. They trapped our gods in wooden images and took them away."

"They turned our water bad, even as it flowed in the streams," spoke up Tiliqua the Griff.

"They caused our mares to foal prematurely, and our whole wealth in horses would have perished if we hadn't surrendered to the Thunder King," said a Wallekki.

"We've all seen these things with our own eyes," added another.

The mardar sat before them on the ground with his hands tied behind his back—and yet they feared him. Fear wouldn't stop them from killing this mardar, now that they had the chance, Helki thought: but fear had enslaved them to the Thunder King.

"Brothers," he said, "I don't believe in any of that mardar magic. If it was real, this man wouldn't be our prisoner. You should've seen what happened to the lovely big army they had before Obann! No one can find it anymore, and Obann still stands. There were hundreds of mardars with that army, all making magic. It didn't do them any good."

"But we have seen the magic!" Tiliqua said.

"Well, I haven't," answered Helki. "So here's what we'll do. We'll keep this fellow for a while, tied up good and tight. I don't want him killed or tortured. I just want to keep him uncomfortable until he shows me some mardar magic I can see.

"Don't anybody talk to him, and don't anybody listen if he talks—I don't want him to spook some poor fool into letting him go. Santay, can you see to that?"

"Huh! We killed our mardar," Santay said. "We'll kill this one if he can't hold his tongue. If he tries to put a spell on us, I'll cut out his tongue myself."

"If he can make some magic that I can see for myself, I'll let him go," Helki said. "But I don't think he will."

CHAPTER 45

A Valuable Piece of Rust and Dirt

In the morning Lord Reesh missed Gallgoid. He wasn't in their cabin, nor did he return when a slave brought their breakfast. He didn't come back to help Reesh dress, which was a cusset inconvenience. With some difficulty the First Prester struggled into his clothes, cursing under his breath. Once dressed, he opened the door and stood in the doorway, looking for his man; but not for long. It was too cold to be standing there, and snowing rather heavily. Reesh slammed the door and sat down to his breakfast.

He sat alone all morning. His thoughts were bad company. He used to dream he heard King Ozias' bell ringing from the top of Bell Mountain. He meditated on a verse in the Book of Prophet Ika: The least among you shall dream dreams: the boy and the maiden, the shepherd and the slave, the widow, the fatherless, and the old who are no more honored by the young. Reesh dreamed such a dream, and yet refused to believe in God. Now he wondered if perhaps he'd been wrong.

Early in the afternoon, Mardar Kyo came to him.

"Have you seen my servant?" Reesh said. "He wasn't here when I woke up, and I haven't seen him all day. It's a nuisance!"

"Never mind him, First Prester. I'll tell my servants to find him. But I came to tell you to get ready. Our master the Thunder King will speak with you again in private audience, this evening."

Words froze in Reesh's mouth. Kyo smiled at him.

"There's nothing to fear," he said. "Our master is pleased with you. I'll have servants come and help you bathe and dress if your man doesn't return."

"But what can the master wish to say to me?"

"I don't know," Kyo said. "He hasn't made it known to me. But you should be glad he holds you in esteem."

Reesh sat alone all afternoon. Gallgoid didn't come back. Outside, the snow muffled sound. It was easy to imagine there was nothing out there at all—that there were no people anywhere.

Gallgoid must have run away. But why? Reesh couldn't think of any reason. He'd put his trust in the man: "The more fool me!" he thought. First Orth, now Gallgoid. What would the Thunder King think of such poor judgment?

But no—he corrected himself. Before Orth or Gallgoid there was Martis. The best assassin in Obann: Reesh took him off the streets and trained him, raised him as a man would raise a fine hunting dog, practically hand-fed him. He sent Martis out to stop those accursed children from ringing the bell, and he failed. Reesh never saw him again, or ever heard what happened to him.

"The bell! It all started with that cusset bell!" Reesh's thoughts tormented him. He nearly fainted when Kyo knocked on the door to summon him into the presence of the Thunder King.

Once again he had to sidle past the monstrous cat as it glared at him. Once again he had to grope his way through the dark corridor, to be admitted into the Thunder King's private chamber. Again he found the Great Man seated with his golden mask on the little table beside him. This time there was a hint of an odd smell in the air, as if there were a butcher shop next door. But Reesh was given no time to wonder about it.

"I wished to see you again, Lord Reesh, before you continued on your way to Kara Karram. It will stop snowing soon, and my people will clear the road down the mountain. You should arrive at my Temple well before midsummer."

Reesh nodded, not knowing what to say.

"I regret to tell you that your servant is dead," the Thunder King said. "He tried to escape, tried to return to Obann, and he was slain."

"I didn't know. He never said anything about …" Reesh couldn't finish his answer. You never did know what that burn'd fool Gallgoid was thinking: well, now he wasn't thinking anything at all. "I never should've trusted him!" And now there was nobody else. All alone: Lord Reesh was all alone. He felt numb inside.

"Do you know how I make a man a mardar, Lord Reesh?" The Thunder King's question shook him back to full alertness. "He sacrifices his life to me, and I take it. And after a little while, I give it back—along with a little something of myself. They couldn't live without it, but with it they can live a long, long time. They might still die at men's hands or in some misadventure. True immortality belongs only to the gods. It wouldn't do for men. But each of those men whom you see in the banquet hall each night has been dead for a short time."

Reesh had never heard of such a thing. Was this mere madness? But how could a madman conquer all the East? What madman ever lived so long, or did so well? And yet who but a madman would say such things as this?

"You don't believe in me." The Thunder King's expression was kind and calm, but Lord Reesh was afraid. "He's too young!" the First Prester thought. "He sounds too sane!"

"Don't be afraid, Lord Reesh! I'm not about to take your life. You think you're going to die soon, but I tell you no—not until after you have served me in my Temple and taught the new presters, whom I shall give you, how the Temple ought to serve its god. I promise you all the time you'll need. Death cannot come near you until you have fulfilled your time."

Reesh bowed his head. "I am grateful, my lord," was all he could say.

"Nevertheless," said the Thunder King, "you are unwilling to believe in me, just as you were unwilling to believe in the God you served in Obann. But that didn't make your service less real, did it? Because you served something greater—something that you thought was real. Do you know what this is?"

He reached into the breast of his shimmering, multi-colored robe and produced a small object that he held up in his fingers. It might have been a mere chunk of dirt and rust. But it presented a more or less regular shape, oblong, with well-defined corners. Reesh took a long look at it, squinting in the lamplight.

"I would say it is an artifact, my lord," he said, "a manmade thing from ancient times."

"You have seen such things before."

"I have collected them, my lord. All kinds of things."

The Thunder King turned the object around and around, admiring it. "Ages ago," he said, "this little thing contained power. The power has all drained out of it, of course; you can see it's much decayed. But once there was power in it to move large objects, such as would require a team of horses today, and to give off heat and light."

"Yes, yes—the ancients had great powers!" Reesh said. His fear fell off him instantly. "I know; I've made a study of it. But those powers have been lost. They are forgotten. When the Empire was destroyed, its knowledge perished."

The Thunder King smiled. "In my country, far to the east of Kara Karram, there was the same knowledge. The same power. But it did not perish so utterly as it perished in the West. Some small scraps of it survived in hidden places—places that are known to me." He paused to turn the object in his fingers. "The ancients flew like birds, thanks to the power of such little things as this. Someday I shall fly from one end of my empire to the other, from Kara Karram to the Western Sea in just a single day. This I shall do, and you will see me do it."

Reesh gazed hungrily at the little piece of rust. "Mankind shall rise again!" he said. "Greatness, greatness—the progress of long ages, in just a single lifetime! For all my days I've dreamed of it!"

"But you," said the Thunder King, "must be the teacher of mankind. You must teach men how to believe in their god. How will you do that, who never believed in any god and don't believe in me?

"You taught the people of Obann to believe in God, but you did not believe in Him. You were really teaching them to believe in the Temple, weren't you?"

"It was for the best, my lord."

The Thunder King gently laid the artifact on the table, beside his golden mask. He leaned forward in his chair, lowering his voice.

"What you did was wise," he said. "Wrong, but wise. But I'll make you another promise, Lord Reesh.

"When I have conquered Obann and made captive the God of Obann, I'll allow you to speak with Him. Yes, just like you're speaking with me—and then you'll know that He was real all along. Then you'll believe in me, and your teaching will be much the better for it."

This was heaping blasphemy on top of blasphemy. Not so long ago, Reesh would have punished anyone who said such things. But now he could only think of what treasures of the ancient world might have been uncovered by the Thunder King. A man who owned such treasures, he thought, would be just like a god.

"You will believe in me," said the Thunder King, smiling, "and sooner than you think."

CHAPTER 46

The Road up the Mountain

They knew Ellayne and Chillith intended to go up the mountain, which was good, because with Wytt leading them, they left no trail for Jack and Martis to follow.

"They'll be lucky if they can get across the plain and reach the foothills," Martis said. It was the morning of their second day out from camp, and they had arrived at the northeast corner of King Oziah's Wood. "There are still Heathen out there: they haven't all gone south."

"Chillith doesn't mind if he gets caught, as long as they take him to the Thunder King," Jack said.

Looking outward from the trees, the plain was a white expanse of snow. You could just make out the forested hills in the east, under a low bank of dark grey clouds. Above the clouds, seeming to float on them, rose the mountains.

If they'd been on the southern fringe of the woods, they would have known from prisoners that the Thunder King had come out from the East and was now in his castle in the Golden Pass. But Jack and Martis hadn't heard this news.

"The question is, which way up the mountains would they go?" said Martis. "If Chillith really wants to be captured, he couldn't do better than to follow that new road they've built. They'd have to cross the Chariot to get there."

"It'd be funny if we got caught and they didn't!" Jack said. "We don't have Wytt to scout for us, and they do. I guess Ellayne never thought of that." He started to give her a good tongue-lashing, but Martis wouldn't let him finish.

"If we run into any Wallekki riders, I can probably talk us past them," Martis said.

"I wish you hadn't left Dulayl behind! And poor old Ham."

"A man and a boy can hide better than a man, a boy, a horse, and a donkey. Just remember that if we do meet any Wallekki, you're my servant and you don't understand their language."

"I don't see how anybody understands it," Jack said.

———

Ellayne and Chillith had already crossed the plain and were in the woods around the headwaters of the Chariot. The snow on the plain was crisscrossed with the tracks of men and horses. Wytt hurried them across as fast as they could go. It took all day, but they saw no one else. Ellayne could hardly believe it.

"We'll meet people on the road, once we find it," Chillith said. "And then you must leave me, if you can. There is no need for you to go to the Thunder King."

"Aren't you afraid, Chillith?"

"I am afraid of your God, who took away my sight so that He could give me understanding," he answered. "I've felt His power. I don't want to feel it again! What He calls me to do, I will do."

Their plan was for Wytt to go on a short distance ahead, to sniff out any danger and to warn them. If you looked at the tracks he made in the snow, they looked just like human footprints, only tinier than a baby's. Ellayne hoped the Heathen wouldn't be looking at tracks too closely.

"Are there Omah in these woods, Wytt?" she asked.

He chirped. Yes, a few—not many. The little hairy men didn't live in the mountains. They preferred the forest and the plain; and most of all, the ruins of ancient cities.

The next day Wytt led them across the Chariot, which at that place was frozen. They'd learned how cold it was at night, up here on the skirts of the mountains; and it didn't get much warmer by day. Wytt found places where they could huddle together, buried under fallen leaves and the blanket Chillith brought. Ellayne was cold all the time. "I'm going to get sick," she thought. But she didn't mention it; Chillith would only say she'd better turn back. She had a wolfskin wrap the rangers had given her—better than nothing, but not good enough.

The day after crossing the Chariot, they struck the road.

"Here it is—the road up the mountain," Ellayne said. They hadn't yet emerged from the woods. At the moment the road was deserted, but riders could come along at any minute.

"Here is what we ought to do," Chillith said. "As soon as someone comes who's going up, I'll ask to be taken to the Thunder King. I was a mardar; I know what words to say. But here we part, little maiden. The little hairy man will lead you back to safety."

"But you'll be all alone!"

"I'll be safe. No one will know I'm not a mardar anymore."

"You can tell them I'm your servant."

"I will not," said Chillith. "Where I'm going is no place for you."

Ellayne felt tears spring to her eyes. Who would have thought it possible? There was something about this blinded Heathen that she'd grown to love. And he was going to defy the Thunder King! She couldn't bear to think on what would happen to him then—and couldn't stop thinking about it, either.

He felt for her shoulder, found it, and embraced her gently. She did cry then, out loud, and didn't even spare a thought for what Jack would say if he could see her.

"It'll be all right," Chillith said. "We each have to do what God commands us."

"But I believe in you!" Ellayne said. "I hated you at first—and yes, I was glad when God made you blind; I thought it served you right. But I don't think so anymore! I don't want to let you go. At least let me lead you up the road until we meet someone. Anyhow, I'll just follow you if you don't!"

"You would, wouldn't you?" Chillith patted her head. "Let it be as you like, then. For just a little while longer."

They came out of the woods. Ellayne took Chillith's hand and began to lead him up the road. Wytt stayed hidden among the trees, but Ellayne knew he was nearby. But neither she nor Chillith knew that farther up the mountain it was snowing so heavily that hardly anyone tried to travel. The road stretched on ahead of them, empty. If Ellayne had paid more attention to the look of the sky, she might have guessed why.

Keeping Chillith on his feet took up most of her attention. There were ruts and icy patches everywhere. Finally they stopped so she could cut him a staff from a sapling. He said she might as well keep his knife. She'd just finished trimming the staff when Wytt came back, chittering.

"There's a cart coming," Ellayne said.

"Help me up, and I'll meet it. Hide yourself."

She had to obey. She ducked into the underbrush beside the road. Wytt huddled close to her, and Chillith used his staff to feel his way out onto the road. There he stood and waited, and moments later Ellayne heard the creaking of a wagon. Snow muffled any sound the horse's hooves might have made.

There were two men in the wagon, bundled up in furs. They yelled at Chillith in a foreign language, but he wouldn't get out of their way. He held up his staff and yelled back, and they stopped the cart. The two men got out and bowed to him. They spoke back and forth for a few minutes. Then Chillith made a certain gesture with his hand; the men climbed back into the cart and continued their journey down the mountain. Ellayne waited until she couldn't hear the cart anymore, then ran out to Chillith.

"What did they say?" she asked.

His face was stern. He didn't answer right away.

"My journey will be shorter than I expected," he said. "The Thunder King is at the top of the mountain at the end of this road. He has built a castle there."

Suddenly the top of the mountain seemed ominously close, although Ellayne couldn't see it for the clouds and trees.

"It's not very far to go, is it?" she said. "Did you tell those men you're a mardar?"

"I know the words of command. I spoke them. Had I

commanded them to turn their cart around and take me up the mountain, they would have done it."

"Why didn't you?"

"Because they were afraid," he said.

CHAPTER 47

The Toddling Prophet

Ryons and his army were a few days out of Obann City, marching eastward within sight of the great river ("That it might anchor our flank, should the need arise," General Hennen said), when they met a small company of archers waiting for them on the way. So far, the Heathen remnants in the country had avoided them; so they saw no menace in a few archers. But as they drew nearer, Obst cried out, "I know those men! They're from Lintum Forest. They were outlaws until Helki conquered them, and they swore allegiance to him. What are they doing here?"

"I think I know!" said Ryons, and he spurred his horse forward.

Just the mention of Lintum Forest raised his spirits. But he remembered that some weeks ago, he'd sent messengers to bring Jandra to Obann. It was her prophecy that had first proclaimed him king.

His Ghols rode with him. So did Gurun, who very seldom left his side. His troops made way for them. Obst dismounted and followed on foot. He was never comfortable on horseback.

The archers opened their ranks, and there Ryons saw Abgayle, holding Jandra's hand; and nestled in Jandra's other arm was that horrible bird of hers, with teeth in its beak and dirty purple plumage. The little girl, with her big blue eyes and her long fair hair, hadn't changed at all, thought Ryons—although it seemed years since he'd last seen her and not just months. The fierce warriors in his army fell silent at the sight of her: for they remembered her as a prophet.

Gurun had heard of Jandra and knew who she was. But she was such a little thing! Three years old, no more—and who ever heard of a toddling prophet?

The hideous bird squirmed loose from Jandra's embrace and flapped to the ground. Its feathers clanked like mail. It let out a harsh shriek that could be heard all over the plain.

And then out of the little girl's mouth issued a voice—a grown-up voice, almost as deep as a man's—that seemed to Gurun that men would be able to hear all the way back in Obann.

"Hail, King Ryons! Hail, Queen Gurun! The Lord is with you.

"For I the Lord have heard the bell of my servant King Ozias, and the prayers of all my saints in secret places: and you my servants shall go forth, and no enemy shall hurt you. And my Spirit shall go forth among the nations; no more shall it be fettered; and all men shall know me. My standard shall be raised among the Heathen, wherever men walk upon the earth which I have made; and all the tribes of men shall seek me."

Those words seemed to beat against the sky and fill it. Gurun shivered under her fur cloak. "It is Scripture that has not been written down," she thought. The sound of those words didn't fade away; rather, it was absorbed into the earth and into the hearts of them that heard it.

Then the little girl wrinkled up her face and wept.

She cried as if her heart would break. The woman who was her guardian, Abgayle, tried to comfort her but couldn't make her stop. The bird stood beside her and hissed at everyone. Finally the captain of the Ghols, old Chagadai, sprang lightly from his horse and picked up Jandra in his arms. He crooned something to her in the outlandish Gholish language, and in a few moments she stopped crying and fell asleep. He rocked her gently for a minute, than handed her to Abgayle. Ryons looked on in amazement.

"When did you learn how to do that?" he cried.

The old warrior grinned. "I've had many children of my own," he said. "And this little one has always liked me."

"Why does she cry?" Gurun asked.

"She does, sometimes, when God speaks through her," Abgayle said. "Usually she doesn't remember. But once or twice she's said something about being in a nice place with her mommy. We all think raiders must have killed her family; but she doesn't remember what happened to them. I suppose she cries because she doesn't want to leave her mother—wherever they are together."

"How did you know we left the city?" Ryons asked. "Nobody sent a message."

"Jandra knew."

"And now we ought to send her back to the city," Hennen said. "This is an army on the march. It's no place for a child."

Obst shook his head, hard. "Didn't you hear what she said, Hennen? No enemy shall hurt us. That was the Lord our God, speaking through a prophet. She couldn't be safer anywhere than she'll be with us." But Hennen had never seen Jandra before, and looked doubtful.

"Be assured she is a prophet," Chief Shaffur said. "We know."

"Where's Helki?" Abgayle asked. "Jandra was looking forward to seeing him again. She's missed him."

"He's off somewhere, trying to find Jack and Ellayne. Nobody knows where they are," Ryons said. "But now that Jandra's here, maybe she can tell us. Helki took my dog, and they haven't come back."

Obst patted his shoulder. "Prophets speak what God gives them to speak, Sire," he said. "We must all continue to pray for Helki—and pray he finds those children!" Then Ryons knew he'd spoken as a child speaks: but of course he couldn't help that. He was a king, but not a man. Not for a long time yet.

CHAPTER 48

How a Father Got News of His Daughter

In the teeth of a stiff snowstorm, the Ninneburky militia crossed the Imperial to join with Helki. It wasn't all the town's militia—just the hundred best and strongest spearmen, with the town's chief councilor, Roshay Bault, to lead them.

They came just in time. The next day Helki fought a battle, and the Ninneburky spearmen stood fast in the middle of it, holding the line while Helki's wild Abnaks and Wallekki riders swarmed around the flanks to crush the enemy. It was over by the middle of the afternoon.

"That was their last throw," Helki told his captains, after the prisoners were rounded up and it was finally time to rest. "A fair number of them got away, but I reckon they're scattered in a hundred different directions. From what the prisoners tell me, there's no one left in this country to fight against us.

"But it was a close shave today!" He turned to Roshay. "It would've gone hard for us if you hadn't shown up, Councilor. But they do breed tough birds in Ninneburky! Even the chicks are tough."

"What do you know of Ninneburky?" Roshay wondered. He couldn't take his eyes off Helki's clothes, which were all different patches sewn together, no two of the same color.

"I know a boy and a girl who come from Ninneburky. They've done some things that'll someday make them famous."

"A boy and a girl!" Roshay's knees almost buckled. He felt suddenly short of breath. "Their names—what are their names?"

"Why, Jack and—" Then Helki remembered. "You must be Ellayne's father, then. She said her father was the chief councilor, or something like that."

"Where is she? Is she well? Tell me, man!"

Helki had to find something for Roshay to sit on, before he fell over. A discarded saddle did the trick. This man, who'd been so strong and brave in battle, was about to faint for tidings of his daughter. A couple of his men gently lowered him onto the saddle, and Helki squatted before him.

"I wish I could tell you where Ellayne is. I've been looking for her," he said. "But she's still with Jack, and there's a man who travels with them to protect them. I think they're in King Oziah's Wood, but I couldn't get in. Now I guess we can."

Roshay took deep breaths. The day the bell on Bell Mountain rang, he and his wife ceased to mourn their daughter. "God is watching over her," they told each other. "She's all right." And they believed it with all their hearts. But now, to be told by this wild man that he knew her and had seen her and it was too much to take in, right after a battle.

"It's been so long since she ran away. She and that boy—" Roshay couldn't finish.

"Easy—I'll tell you all I know, once we're settled down," Helki said. "But first I've got a battle to clean up after. It's a long story, Ellayne and Jack's doings. You'll hardly believe it."

Roshay nodded. He probably wouldn't believe it. This was the first time in his life that unlooked-for good news hit him as hard as bad. At the moment it was hard to tell the difference. Maybe by the evening he might be able to understand whether or not he'd just received a blessing.

Helki stood up, patted Roshay on the shoulder, and strode off to see to his army.

Two more days went by, at the end of which Roshay knew that his daughter had stolen out of a ranger camp in the company of a blind Heathen medicine man. The camp belonged to a ranger captain named Huell; he'd left the children there and hurried to the south edge of the forest to harass the Heathen with his archers. Jack and Martis followed after Ellayne and the Griff, he said, and that was all any ranger knew about it.

"Exasperating!" Helki said. "But I reckon Cavall and I can track them down."

"I'll go with you," Roshay said.

"I can go a lot faster alone," said Helki.

The shelter in which the children slept was still there. Cavall crawled in and got their scent.

"So it seems they headed East," Helki said. "Why would they do that?" he asked Huell.

"Who can say? It's one way out of the forest. Then it's a short distance to the foothills and some more woods. And along the Chariot the Heathen have built a road that goes all the way up the mountains—all the way to the top."

"We'll find them," Helki said; and Cavall barked once.

"I can't go home without her," Roshay said.

Helki thought for a minute. "You can best help," he said, "by taking command of this army for me and leading it up the Heathens' road. It'll be a hard slog in all this snow, but that'll probably mean no fighting."

"Am I to command a thousand Heathens?" Roshay cried. "They'll murder me!"

"You can trust them. They're sworn. They've fought against King Thunder, so they know they can never go back to him."

"But what is the point of my marching your army up the mountain?"

"If those kids are wandering around up there," Helki said, "they might find the army before I can find them."

It was the best plan anyone could devise at the moment. Even this was wasting too much time, Helki thought. But he introduced Roshay to the chiefs among his following, and they all agreed to obey him.

"But why go up the mountain at all, Helki?" asked Tiliqua the Griff.

"Because it'll show everyone who's winning this war—and it's not the Thunder King." The chiefs liked that explanation! "But wait, just one more thing," said Helki. "What about that mardar that we captured? I think we ought to take him with us."

Santay, the Abnak, shrugged. "We can't—for the excellent reason that he's dead," he said. "After we won that last battle, he managed to get a hand loose from his bonds when no one was looking. He found a sharp stone and cut his throat."

"So no mardar magic out of him," Helki said. "And no information, either. So be it. Councilor, you and the army get on that road and march up the mountain. Show the world that the Thunder King is finished."

And at last, just as the sun was setting, Helki was able to plunge into the woods with Cavall sniffing out the children's trail and Angel perched on his shoulder, flapping her wings to keep her balance. Roshay Bault watched him vanish into a thicket.

"How did he do that?" Ellayne's father wondered. "He didn't make a sound—a big man like that!"

"He should have been an Abnak," Santay said.

CHAPTER 49

A Stranger on the Road

Over the Golden Pass it continued to snow steadily. The Thunder King had said it would stop soon, but it was still snowing. "So much for his commanding the weather!" Lord Reesh thought. "He can't stop the snow any more than one of those wooden idols in the banquet hall can."

Reesh had nothing to do but sit in his cabin all day until summoned to the nightly banquet. Two of Kyo's servants attended to his needs, but he couldn't speak their language. He missed Gallgoid; he even missed being annoyed by the man.

Supplies kept coming up the mountain from the East. Reesh couldn't imagine the labor needed to accomplish that. But they weren't sending troops or wagons down the mountain anymore into the West.

Something was wrong: Reesh was sure of it. The mardars' merriment around their banquet tables seemed forced. Kyo hardly spoke to him. The Thunder King still sat like a statue on his throne, silent behind his golden mask; but at the foot of the throne, the great cat fidgeted and lashed its stubby tail.

Fry Gallgoid's soul—he must have known something, Reesh thought: something he hadn't seen fit to tell his master, because this time his master couldn't help him. That was why he'd tried to escape: it must be. Gallgoid knew—"And he left me here all alone to face it, whatever it is!" Reesh thought. Always keeping things to himself, never letting you know what he was thinking—that was Gallgoid. And without revealing what had convinced him to risk his life, the cusset fool got himself killed. Reesh wouldn't be surprised if they'd fed Gallgoid to the cat.

If only the cuss't snow would stop! If only he could get back into his carriage and get down from this infernal mountain!

Such musings made the delicacies of King Thunder's table stick in Reesh's throat and rumble in his belly when they finally got there. And there was no one to talk to, no one he could trust; and the hollow gaiety of the mardars at their feast bred in him a lingering dread.

He didn't pray. "I won't, at least, be such a hypocrite as that!" he thought.

Martis hurried through the woods, making for the road. He would have gone faster alone, but he had Jack to slow him down. At least Jack seemed tireless and not overly troubled by the cold. It amazed him to see such endurance in a child.

"I feel like I've been walking back and forth across Obann all my life," Jack said. "I wonder if I'll ever be allowed to stop."

"I wonder how fast Chillith can go," Martis said.

"Well, he can't see, can he? We'll catch up."

It was useless trying to pick up the trail until they came to the road. Always assuming they're heading for the road,

Martis added to himself. But he couldn't think of any other way for them to get up the mountain—a child and a blind man.

They put their heads down and kept going, as fast as Jack could keep it up.

Ellayne was beginning to worry that they'd freeze to death, but Wytt found shelter for them. It was a big tree that had recently blown over, creating a large cavity in the ground. It was almost as good as a cave. Snow hadn't drifted into it, and it was dry inside. Ellayne was able to make a fire, although that took some doing. For supper they had some ranger-biscuit and a little bit of venison jerky.

"We're running short of water," Ellayne said.

"Fill the waterskin with snow and leave it lying near the fire," Chillith said.

After she did that, they cuddled up together under the blanket and the wolfskin, and Ellayne tried to tell the Griff one of the old tales of Abombalbap, from the book her father once gave her for a birthday present. She told Chillith about the single combat fought at the ford of the River Frewly, somewhere in Lintum Forest, between Abombalbap and the Green Knight who slew every man, woman, or child who crossed the river.

"They fought all day," Ellayne said, "and along toward evening they were so cut up and gored that their armor lay all in pieces in the river, and birds flew in and out of their wounds—and straight through some of them." But then she noticed Chillith was snoring, and his chin lay on his breast, so she stopped.

The silence of the woods came down on them like a blanket. They were only a stone's throw from the road, but for all the stillness of that night, they might have been a hundred miles from any human habitation. "And maybe we are, at that," Ellayne thought.

She flinched when Wytt hopped into their earth cave. He crept into her arms and chattered. As near as it can be rendered into human speech, this is what he said.

He'd been scouting, and caught a shrew and ate it. "Big people living in these woods, all over," he chirped softly. "Maybe bad, maybe good. Not see any, but they leave scent everywhere."

"Any sign of Jack and Martis?" she whispered, not wanting to wake Chillith.

"No Jack. No White-face," Wytt answered. "When they come close, I know."

Ellayne frowned. She hadn't meant to get too far ahead of them. "We'll have to slow down tomorrow," she thought. And then Wytt fell asleep, and she lay awake, listening to the silence of a winter night.

She saw to it that they got off to a later start than Chillith would have liked.

"We have to be careful," she said. "Wytt says there are outlaws in these woods, and it wouldn't do you any good to be captured by the likes of them. They wouldn't take you to the Thunder King. They'd only kill you."

"Too bad we don't have your friend Abombalbap to travel with us," said Chillith with a smile. So he had heard some of the story, at least—although he'd missed the most exciting part.

A little before noon they were on the road again, trudging through the snow, uphill, always uphill. The clouds drifted apart and let the sun peek out. The new snow glistened. Ellayne hoped she wouldn't go snow-blind. "We'd be in a fine fix then," she thought, "if neither one of us could see."

On and on they plodded. She stopped worrying about getting too far ahead of Jack and Martis: at this rate they wouldn't outmarch anyone. But Wytt ran along on top of the snow, finding the crusty parts and never breaking through. He was either far ahead of them or far behind, usually out of sight, scouting out trouble.

"It's warmer today," Chillith said.

"That's because the sun came out."

"I like the feel of this day. We Griffs don't mind the cold. Winter is much colder in our country than it ever gets here."

"It's cold enough for me," Ellayne said. Despite the boots she wore, her feet felt like two blocks of ice. What would she do if she got frostbite?

Just then Wytt came racing back to them from up ahead with news.

"One man comes, all alone. Very tired! Maybe sick, too. You like to see him, or you like to hide?"

"Maybe this man can tell us something useful," Chillith said, when Ellayne had translated Wytt's chirps and chitters. "You hide. I'll go on ahead and meet him."

Ellayne didn't like to leave him alone, but his idea made sense. "I'll be watching from the woods," she said, and Chillith nodded.

She followed Wytt into the trees and labored to keep up with Chillith. Somehow he managed to stay on the road; and before long, a man came into sight.

"He's just about had it," Ellayne thought. He came toiling along, barely able to lift his feet out of the snow, with a grey blanket wrapped around his head and shoulders. Chillith heard him panting and stopped to wait for him. The man almost blundered into him before he saw him. Deeming the stranger no threat at all, Ellayne came out of the woods to join them; but Wytt stayed out of sight.

"Who are you?" gasped the stranger.

"A blind man trying to get up the mountain," Chillith said. "I have business with the Thunder King."

The stranger's jaw dropped. If he'd had any strength at all, Ellayne thought, he'd run away. The poor devil was terrified. She felt sorry for him.

"It's all right!" she said. "We won't do you any harm. We won't tell anyone we saw you, so don't be afraid. Chillith, give this poor man a little something to eat. And I think we'd better try to build a fire somewhere."

A fire turned out not to be practicable: everything was too wet to burn. They sat together on a tree-trunk beside the road, and the stranger had a biscuit. The sun was strong now, thankfully.

"What's your name?" Ellayne asked. "Who are you, and what are you doing out here all alone?"

"I don't suppose a little girl can hurt me," he said, "and it's pleasant to hear someone speaking Obannese. As for me, my name is Gallgoid, and I was a servant of the Temple."

CHAPTER 50

What Gallgoid Discovered at the Golden Hall

North and south of the great river, and from the east to the west, bands of Heathen roamed Obann, remnants of the vast host that had been shattered before the city. As Ryons and his small army marched east, fragments of King Thunder's hordes came and made submission to him.

"I don't think this is what King Thunder had in mind when he challenged you to come to him," said Hennen to his king.

They came by pairs, by tens, by dozens: Abnaks and Griffs on foot, Wallekki riders, Fazzan in their wolf's-head caps, and even a few Zeph.

"Why do you come to us now?" Obst asked a Wallekki chief who'd brought thirty riders with him.

"The great beast destroyed us," said the chief, "and the winter, we know, will starve us. We can't go home because we failed the Thunder King, and he will not forgive us. Our gods have been taken away from us, and Obann's God is against us. What are we to do, and where are we to go?

"But a man came to us yesterday and told us that the King and Queen of Obann will spare us, and the God of

Obann will protect us, if only we submit to them of our own free will. What other deliverance can we hope for?"

Ryons exchanged a look with Gurun. She hated being called a queen, he knew that—but what man was this? Who could it be?

"What did the man look like, who spoke to you?" Gurun asked.

"An ordinary man—one of us, in fact. He never gave his name, nor told us his clan. He rode a beautiful white horse. He was old, and venerable, and I supposed he was a chieftain."

"Nobody we sent out!" thought Ryons.

"You have been told the truth, friends," Obst spoke up. "You and your men may march with us, Chieftain, under God's protection. Or else swear friendship to King Ryons and go your way, and do your best to return to your homes."

The chief and all his followers drew themselves up straighter.

"If he will have us," said the chief, "we will ride with the king!"

So these Wallekki were inducted into the army, and while Chief Shaffur was seeing to it, Gurun said to Ryons, "It must have been a servant of the Lord who spoke to those men, for it was no servant of yours. But I don't know why even these Heathen should call me a queen."

"If I'm to have a queen," said Ryons, "I'd like it to be you." He blushed violently as he said this. "I mean, who else should it be?"

"First we have to survive the malice of the Thunder King—and those mountains are still a long way off," Gurun answered. But Ryons noticed that she didn't say "no."

Helki would have liked to go faster, but all the snow on the ground made it hard for Cavall to hold on to Jack's scent. But Cavall was a keen tracker, and he never lost the scent for long.

Angel flew above the trees where Helki couldn't always see her. She understood that he was hunting some quarry. She couldn't help him do that, but she would give warning if anyone were hunting him.

The forest was his natural habitat, and he reveled in it. After the war, he thought, he would return to Lintum Forest and never again set foot outside of it. "But first find Jack and Ellayne!" This close to catching up to them, he'd never turn back until he did it.

Helki had no way of knowing it, but by now he'd made up most of the ground and was only a day behind Jack and Martis. And they had just struck the Thunder King's new road.

"I think those must be their tracks," Martis said, studying the snow. "Some of this has melted, so I can't be sure; but I am sure two people made these tracks."

"They just look like holes to me," Jack said.

Martis soon proved to be right. The tracks went off the road and led to an uprooted tree nearby, under which they found the ashes of a campfire.

"Here is where they must have spent the night," he said. "I hate to stop while there's still a bit of daylight left, but we'll never find better shelter than this."

"I don't want to spend another night out in the open,"

Jack said. The rangers had given them blankets, woolen socks, and caps, but the last night had been brutal. "Even my bed at Van's house would look mighty good to me right now."

He was wondering if he would ever see Ellayne again. She made him as mad as a flea sometimes, but he missed her. At their age, spending a year together was like knowing someone all your life. And he missed Wytt, too.

Would it ever be over? He supposed Ellayne's book never told you that adventures could be such cuss't hard work. A few more days of this and his legs would fall right off.

"Lord God," he prayed silently, after he and Martis had their supper, "will you ever be done with us?" And he imagined that he saw Obst's face smiling at him and heard Obst answer, "No, Jack, no—the Lord is never done with us. We belong to Him forever. Rejoice in it!"

But it was a little cold for rejoicing, Jack thought.

It was quite a story Gallgoid told: how the First Prester betrayed the city and let the enemy in through the Temple; how the Thunder King built a new Temple, way out East, and Lord Reesh was to be First Prester there; how they'd traveled up the mountain in a coach, Gallgoid and his master—and found the Thunder King himself waiting for them at the summit in a golden hall.

How could it possibly be true? Ellayne didn't want to believe it, even though Martis had often said what an evil man the First Prester was. But how could he be a wicked man and be First Prester? How could God allow it? Ellayne's mind reeled. Finally she could contain herself no longer.

"If the First Prester is such an evil man, and he did all those terrible things," she cried, "then why did you stay with him so long? How could you help him let the Heathen into your own city?"

Gallgoid answered with a bitter smile. "I was his servant, little maid," he said. "I was very good at what I did for him, and it was a good life for me. I was his assassin. If he ordered me to kill a man, I did it. Why not? He was First Prester, not I. He was the ruler of the Temple: the Temple served God, and I served Lord Reesh. Whatever he did was right. That's what I thought."

Chillith nodded. "So I served my master the Thunder King," he said. "But what happened at the top of the mountain at the golden hall? Let him tell his tale, Ellayne."

"Not much happens up there," Gallgoid said. "It's been snowing every day, and it's all the slaves can do to shovel it clear. Quite a few of King Thunder's mardars are up there, waiting for the spring when they can lead fresh armies down to Obann.

"Every night they gather in the hall and have a banquet. I was never allowed in, but my lord had to dine with the mardars every evening. The Thunder King granted my lord a private audience—trying to convince him that he really is a god. He sits on a throne above the banquet tables, and they all have to pray to him before they eat. I didn't think much of that, but Lord Reesh prayed with all the others.

"But all day long, unless you were a mardar, or a slave who had to shovel snow, there was nothing, not a cusset thing, to do. Lord Reesh sat in his cabin and stewed. So I decided to occupy my time with something else."

He paused. Telling the tale seemed to have given him

back some of his strength.

"What did you do?" asked Chillith.

"What I'm best at, aside from killing people—sneaking around and not being noticed and keeping my ears open.

"The mardars have many servants. They eat in another hall and tend the mardars' horses in the stables—and they talk. I never spoke to anyone except in Obannese, and they didn't know I could understand them when they spoke to each other. They use Tribe-talk for that, and I speak Tribe-talk. I also speak Abnak, Griffish, and two or three dialects of Wallekki.

"So I listened, and I learned. I found cracks in certain walls and put my ear to them. I spied on the mardars and their servants. There's nothing to do up there but talk, you see.

"And what I learned, I decided everybody ought to know. I now knew something that I had to bring back down the mountain. I waited for my best chance and escaped. It was snowing like mad that night. They chased me, but not very far. And I've been going and going ever since. I was beginning to think I wouldn't make it back down to Obann, until you two came along."

"Oh, stop shilly-shallying!" Ellayne cried out. "Tell us—what was this great thing you found out? What is it?"

Some moments dragged on before he answered. Ellayne jumped up and down where she stood, to get some feeling back into her feet.

"Well," he said, "it may be that if I don't tell you, I'll never get a chance to tell anyone." He looked Chillith in the eye, forgetting Chillith couldn't see him.

"There is no Thunder King," he said.

CHAPTER 51

How the Thunder King Prospered

"What! But Lord Reesh saw him—you said he saw him!" Ellayne's cry resounded up and down the deserted road.

"The whole East serves the Thunder King," said Chillith.

"They serve what they can see," Gallgoid said. "But what they see is a cheat. It's all lies. But people are so afraid of the Thunder King, they'll believe anything.

"There was a Thunder King, once upon a time. He conquered many nations and he claimed to be a god. People believed him. But it's all the mardars. All lies. The real King Thunder died some twenty years ago. The mardars put up another and said it was the same man. Why not? The Great Man lived behind a mask. His name alone was worth any number of armies. People believed he and his mardars worked evil miracles. They never saw the man behind the mask. So they never knew it was a different man, and the mardars kept on conquering."

Chillith shook his head. "The Thunder King sees and hears through his mardars. He sends his thoughts into their minds. His power flows through them."

"More lies," said Gallgoid. "The mardars do whatever they please, and they say it was a commandment from the Thunder King. They make their own plans and tell everyone that they received those plans from their god. Their servants put poison in the water, and the mardars say it was an evil spell. They're adept at poisoning whole herds of cattle without the owners knowing it. They tell no end of lies, and people believe them."

"But our gods—my people's gods are gone," said Chillith. "The Thunder King took them away."

Gallgoid sighed. "Your gods were never real, my friend."

Chillith sat in silence. His sightless eyes shone. He's going to cry, Ellayne thought: which meant that he believed this stranger. But was that wise? All those mighty armies that had poured out of the East—that was no cheat.

No one said anything. Somewhere off in the distance, a crow cawed. Ellayne studied Gallgoid's face, but all she saw there was a cold and tired man.

How much time passed, who could say? Ellayne couldn't understand how the mardars could get together and deceive the whole world. Who had ever heard of such a thing? What about the magic that the mardars did? She'd heard so much about it. They knew what their master was thinking, even if he was a thousand miles away. But Jack always said there was no such thing as magic. Could he be right?

Chillith stood up suddenly.

"I see!" His voice was like a thunderclap. "I see!" He spoke some words to Gallgoid in a foreign language: Griffish, probably. Before Ellayne could ask him what he'd said, Gallgoid seized her by the arms and held her tightly, held her close.

"What is this? Let me go! What are you doing?" She struggled, but there was no getting loose.

"Peace, peace, Ellayne—be quiet, and listen to me," Chillith said. Something in the way he said it compelled her to be still. "Dear friend, this is where we part. I shall go up alone to that golden hall and confront the Thunder King. I won't need a guide anymore. I see."

"I don't believe you! You're always saying that!" Ellayne shouted. "If you can really see, tell me what color Gallgoid's blanket is. Tell me what he looks like!"

Chillith smiled at her. "Not that kind of seeing," he said. "God took that kind of sight away from me because I wasn't using it properly. Now He has given me another kind of seeing, by which I know that this man's words are true and by which I shall be led to where I'm going. This man will go with you, back down the mountain. King Thunder's hall is no place for you."

"But they'll kill you!" Ellayne said. Now she was crying, and the tears froze on her cheek.

"Maybe," he said. "But through me the true God will destroy them." He kissed her forehead. "Good-bye—it was a good day for me when I met you. Help Gallgoid down the mountain with his news. All the world must hear it."

Words stuck in her throat; she couldn't answer. She watched in numb silence as Chillith picked his way back to the road, parting the brush with his staff. Once on the road, he headed into the East with long, strong strides—just as if he could really see. He steered a straight course right up the middle of the road.

"Griffs are great walkers. He'll be better going uphill than I am going down," Gallgoid said.

"Let me go!"

"I had to promise him I wouldn't. Besides, I'm nearly worn out. I need you to help me off this mountain." He squeezed her shoulders, but not hard enough to hurt. "Don't you think the people in Obann deserve to hear the truth? There's nobody but you and me to tell it."

Eventually Ellayne gave in, because she had to, and with Lord Reesh's servant holding her hand so that she couldn't get away, they turned back downhill.

Wytt was watching: she could be sure of that, he always watched. Sooner or later he'd do something about this. It might be dangerous for Gallgoid to go to sleep at night.

But before anything like that could happen, they met Jack and Martis coming up.

While Ellayne and Chillith were making their way up the mountain, Hlah was recovering from an illness. A few days before, a raging fever struck him down. The little community of refugees, dreading they might lose him, put him to bed in their newly finished log cabin. And first they had to build a bed.

When he came to his senses, he discovered that some surprising things had happened while he was sick.

"It's been quite wonderful," Sunfish, once Prester Orth, told him as he lay in bed. "The hunters you've trained did their best, but it wasn't good enough. But Ootoo heard about it and sent us three freshly killed deer—plenty for everybody. And a couple of his men came to see you, although you were too sick to know they were here."

More wonderful than that, Hlah thought, was the young

refugee woman who tended him night and day—mopping the sweat from his face, spooning broth into him whenever she could, and trying to calm him when he thrashed. Hers was the first face he saw when his eyes worked again. May, her name was.

"You'll be all right now," she said, smiling down at him. "Everyone's been praying for you." And her hand was over his.

Hlah smiled back. "I'm glad God granted those prayers," he said. It was funny, he thought: May had been around the camp all along, and he'd never noticed until now how beautiful she was.

In the spring they were married, Sunfish reciting the service over them. Nor was theirs the only such marriage in those hills. It was the beginning of a whole new people, half-Abnak, half-Obannese, who dwelt among the wooded hills on the west side of the mountains: hunters, trappers, settlers, and traders who believed in God and did their best to live in peace.

Wytt came running up first. He'd gone back and found them, and Jack and Martis hurried after him, huffing and puffing. Ellayne recognized them from a distance—who else, after all, could they be?—twisted her hand loose from Gallgoid's and ran to meet them. She threw her arms around Jack's neck: she really couldn't help it. Nor could he help hugging her, but not for long.

"That was some trick—sneaking off without us!" he said. "I ought to brain you."

"Just try it!" she answered. "Anyway, I knew you'd come,

so it wasn't really going without you."

They might have had an argument, only then Gallgoid trudged down to join them, and when he saw Martis, he stopped in his tracks.

"Martis!" he said. "For a moment there, I didn't know you."

"Gallgoid," Martis answered.

"We all thought you were dead."

"Disappointed?" Martis asked.

Something between the two men made the children forget their own quarrel. "You know this man?" Jack asked Martis. Ellayne remembered that she hadn't told Gallgoid anything about herself—including the fact that she'd been traveling all over Obann with another assassin from the Temple.

"What are you doing with Ellayne?" Martis said; and to Ellayne, "Has he hurt you?"

"I only just met him, Martis. Chillith sent me away with him. He's going up alone—and the Thunder King's up there!"

"Up where?" Jack said.

"Up on top of the mountain, stupid—up there!" Ellayne pointed up the road. "They'll kill him when he gets there. Can't we do something to save him?"

"Whoa!" Martis put up his hand. "First some explanations, please!" He pointed at Gallgoid. "You first."

It took some doing, to get the explanations out. Ellayne had already heard Gallgoid's story, but it was just as hard to believe the second time around. Martis admitted to being the children's protector, but Gallgoid wouldn't let it go at that.

"Lord Reesh sent you out to kill these children, didn't he?" he said. "He often spoke of it. He couldn't believe you failed. We all heard King Ozias' bell. That's how he knew you'd failed him.

"But never mind that! Obann must be told that there is no Thunder King—that it's all lies. That's why I have to get down from this mountain. Never mind your poor blind man. No one can save him."

"We can try!" Ellayne said.

Martis ignored her. "Your master, Lord Reesh, must think you've failed him, too, Gallgoid."

"Reesh is an old man who doesn't matter anymore."

"It may be that he matters to me," said Martis.

In the end he and the children and Wytt went up and Gallgoid went down, alone. They gave him some of their food to help him on his way. Gallgoid grinned at Martis.

"It'll be too bad if I don't make it," he said. "But maybe it's better if you and I don't travel very far together."

"He may not get there, Martis," Ellayne said, a few minutes after they'd lost sight of Gallgoid. She'd had her way, but now she didn't feel quite right about it.

"He's stronger than he looks," Martis answered.

"But didn't you believe him—about the Thunder King?" Jack said.

"No one in his right mind would ever believe Gallgoid. And Lord Reesh has a very subtle mind. He could invent a story like that. But it may be Reesh isn't up there, after all—and never was. But we'll see what we can do for Chillith."

Against the habit of a lifetime, Martis felt friendship

for the Griff. Maybe they could find some way to save him. With Wytt to scout for them, Martis had little fear of being taken by surprise by any enemy.

But also in his heart, despite his refusal to take anything said by Gallgoid as the truth, was a desire to see if Reesh was really there at the end of the road. And if he was … he left the thought unfinished.

"He didn't seem like such a bad man to me—Gallgoid," Ellayne said.

"He's an assassin. A creature of Lord Reesh. And a most artful and resourceful liar."

"So were you, Martis," Jack said.

To that he had no answer.

CHAPTER 52

The Last Stage of the Journey

As Gallgoid said, the Griffs are great walkers. You'd believe it if you could see Chillith striding along, straight up the road. He never stopped; he never slowed: just kept putting one foot after the other, over and over again. He barely felt the cold.

He didn't see as you see, with your eyes. He saw things he had done wrong in his life and things he'd done right, things he'd thought beautiful, or good, and other things he'd thought sad, ugly, or shameful. But most of all he saw himself, in his mind's eye, as proceeding down a wide and shining path with a great light at the end. That light drew him on his way and would not let him go. Nor did he want to be released from it. He wanted to come to the source of the light.

He went faster than Martis could go with two children to hold him back, but Wytt caught up to him before long.

Wytt understood that Ellayne and the others were following this man, trying to catch up to him. Maybe he understood more than they knew. Instead of trying to delay Chillith or distract him, Wytt ran far ahead of him and made sure the way was clear. He found nothing a lone man on foot ought to fear. The snow was deeper the higher up you went, but it wouldn't be too deep for a tall man like Chillith.

Wytt kept going until he saw a high wall stretched across the pass, at the top of the mountain. Some effort had been made to clear the snow so that the gates in the wall could be opened and shut freely; but the snow had defeated that effort, and now the gates had to stay open or no one would be able to get them open again.

This was not a nice place, Wytt decided. The mountains were heaped high with snow, and the grey sky promised more to come. Certain scents in the air, issuing from behind the wall, made Wytt's hackles rise. He wrinkled his face and bared his tiny fangs—at what, he didn't know.

This must be where the tall black-haired man was going. He wouldn't have any trouble getting there, and Wytt left him to it. Chillith never saw or heard him pass as he scampered back down the mountain.

"We'll have to stop soon and find a place to camp," Martis said. Most of the afternoon was gone, and they were tired. But they'd picked up Chillith's tracks, and it would now be very easy to follow him.

That was when Wytt came back and told them they were almost to the end of the road, where there was a wall across the pass.

"Bad things there," he reported.

"Can we catch up to Chillith before he gets there?" Martis said. "He must be nearly there already."

"Wytt says he'll be there very soon," Ellayne said. And

once Chillith went behind that wall, she thought, that was that: no one could help him then.

"We could keep going. It isn't far," Jack said. "I'm not tired. We could at least see what's what—and maybe we could do something to help Chillith."

"Are you crazy?" Ellayne said. "The Thunder King's up there. What do you think will happen if they catch us?"

"You're the one who wanted to follow Chillith in the first place!"

Martis interrupted. "We should make camp," he said, "and I'll go up alone at night, with Wytt."

"Why should they catch us?" Jack said. "Wytt says nobody comes out of that place because of all the snow. We won't get there till after dark. Who's going to see us?" He hated the idea of turning back after they'd come so far, without at least seeing if there was a chance to rescue Chillith. "Besides," he added, "it's too cold to camp. We'd only be awake all night, shivering."

It was lame reasoning, and Martis knew it; but he gave in. He felt a powerful urge to push on. Lord Reesh was there—Reesh, his master and his teacher: Lord Reesh, who'd taught him lies.

"We can go a bit farther," he said. "But tell Wytt to keep a sharp lookout. We may have to hide in a hurry."

Just before dark, Gallgoid met Helki coming up the mountain. Actually he met Cavall first, and being unarmed, and much too weary to do anything else, he stood perfectly still while the great hound paced back and forth in front of him, sniffing the air and showing his teeth. Moments later,

Helki came up—a daunting figure of a man, with his wild thatch of hair and a hawk perched on his shoulder.

Helki saw a man who'd just about used up all his strength and needed rest and a fire. He hadn't planned to stop until midnight, but now he would have to.

"Stranger, I'm looking for a man and a girl, and another man with a boy," he said. "They're friends of mine, and I wonder if you've seen them."

"I have," said Gallgoid, "all four of them, earlier today. You'll find them farther up the road." He might have said more, but just then his knees buckled. Helki had to help him up.

"Can't just leave you here, I reckon," he said. He led the man a few steps into the woods. Here many trees, chopped down to build the road, still lay where they'd been dragged out of the way; many more had been carted off for timber. Helki found a place where two large trunks lay at an angle to each other, creating a nook protected from the wind. He cleared the snow away, cleared off the topmost layer of wet leaves, and used all the skill he had to get a fire going. No one else in Obann could have done it.

He fed Gallgoid—just yesterday Angel caught two squirrels, and Cavall ran down a plump white hare—and revived him enough to get his story out of him. That took some time.

"I'd better hustle up this hill before my friends get into something that they can't get out of," Helki said. "You'll have to go on alone, tomorrow, my friend. But it won't be so bad. There's a small army coming up the road behind me. Just mention my name, and they'll take care of you."

"I'll be all right," Gallgoid said. "This fire and the fresh meat was all I needed."

"Keep feeding the fire, and you'll be fine." Helki suddenly stood up. "Let's go, Cavall!" he said.

CHAPTER 53

How Chillith Delivered a Message to the Thunder King

Lord Reesh sat alone in his cabin all day, with no one to talk to and nothing but his thoughts for company. They were not good company.

In the evening Kyo's servant escorted Reesh to the banquet hall. There as always sat King Thunder on his throne, immovable, with his face behind the golden mask. Below his throne, the monster cat tested its chain. The beast was restless. Its green eyes glared at the mardars assembled around their banquet tables. To Reesh it seemed the monster paid particular attention to him, as if marking him in its memory. He wondered if Gallgoid had been fed to the beast. Having dined on the servant, maybe the creature longed to thrust its butcher-knife fangs into the master.

When all were present, the mardars and Reesh stood and made their prayer to the Thunder King. The ritual no longer troubled Reesh quite as much as it had at first. "He's no less a god than any other god," the First Prester thought, "and certainly more than these silly wooden idols he displays around the hall."

The prayer being said, they all sat down; and slaves brought out steaming tureens of thick, dark soup.

"I hope you don't object to mule meat in your soup, First Prester," Kyo said. "It's been hard to get wagons up to the pass these last few days, so we've run a little short of provisions."

"Mule meat is fine," said Reesh, who had little appetite for anything these days.

"In the old days," said Kyo, "it used to be man's flesh that we ate, when there was nothing better. Our master has discontinued this custom, reserving it to himself alone. I cannot say I miss it. Mule is better."

Reesh only nodded. The Thunder King could do as he pleased—who could stop him? He was a law unto himself. The God of Obann caused His laws to be written down, long ago, so that all the world would know them. But King Thunder's law was whatever word came out of his mouth that day. No wonder all the people feared him, Reesh thought.

The soup cloyed in his mouth. The cat paced to and fro, as much as the chain would allow. Why was it so restless? Usually the filthy thing just crouched on the floor and glared.

But then a slave opened one of the doors that separated the banquet from the winter night outside; and the cat stopped pacing.

Chillith couldn't see that night had fallen, nor did he see the wall that rose in front of him with its gate stuck open in the snow. His face by now was numb, so he didn't feel that it was colder. But he smelled smoke, and the aroma of cooked flesh, and he knew he'd arrived at the hall.

A hoarse voice challenged him. "Halt! Who are you, out there?"

"Mardar Chillith. I've been blinded by the snow and cannot see," he answered. He raised his free hand and made the sign of the mardars. "Take me into the Thunder King's hall. I'm cold."

Someone took him by the arm and led him. He could not know that this was the only sentry at the gates. The guards had cast lots to see who would have to keep watch in the cold, and this man lost. He led Chillith over an expanse of hard-packed snow. Chillith sensed the unnatural stillness of that night. He sensed the presence of God.

Warmth flowed out to him when the guard let him into the hall. It seemed to him an unwholesome warmth; he preferred the cold. He heard the murmur of men's voices in many different languages; but silence fell when he came in. He heard his own staff thump against the floor. He took just a few steps, then stopped.

"Now what's this?" Reesh wondered. "A frozen wanderer!" Why should he wish to intrude on the feast? Who was he? But if what everyone said about him was true, the Thunder King already knew. Judging by the way they turned and stared, none of the mardars knew anything.

King Thunder only sat. Were those his eyes glittering through the eye-holes in the golden mask, or just a trick of lamplight?

"Hear the Word of God!" said Chillith. His voice boomed in the hall. "The true God knew that I was blind, so He took away the sight of my eyes and gave me understanding.

"He has seen the evil that you do, in the name of a god who is no god. He has heard your boasting against Him. So that all the nations of men shall know that He is God, you are delivered into judgment. His hand is stretched out over you: He will take you away, and none shall find you. No man in this place shall see tomorrow morning."

"Belabor my soul—the last of the mad prophets!" thought Reesh. "And this one a Heathen, by the look of him." In the city of Obann they had hanged such prophets. What would King Thunder do to this one?

But the mardars sat frozen in their seats, stunned into silence. Soup dribbled from Kyo's open mouth.

The Thunder King rose slowly from his throne. One by one he descended the stone steps of his dais. The prophet continued to proclaim.

"I was one of you, once. I would have been a party to the lies with which you deceive the nations. You who go clad in lies, God has torn off your robes and exposed your nakedness. The Lord has spoken."

Having delivered his mad message, the prophet lapsed into silence. King Thunder stood beside the monster cat, which dared not look up at him. When he answered, his voice was like silk.

"Now, what shall I do," he said, "to a man who blasphemes me to my face? It's not the sort of thing a god can pardon. Besides, you've ruined the banquet. But there is one guest here who hasn't feasted yet—and now he shall have his portion."

Chillith did not see the Thunder King, although he heard his voice. He didn't see him unsnap the chain from the great cat's collar.

What Chillith did see cannot be told here, or anywhere. There are some visions too wonderful, too overwhelming, for words. He still stood before the Thunder King, but in reality he was already somewhere else—somewhere he never dreamed existed.

But Reesh saw the Thunder King unleash the cat; and all the mardars saw it, too.

"What is he doing?" he muttered to Kyo. "He can't do that in here!"

But he did. He did release the cat, and with a terrific roar, it leaped forth to devour King Thunder's enemy.

The mardars were only human. When the cat roared, some of them tumbled out of their seats. A few got up without falling over, threw open the doors, and fled outside into the night.

The great cat charged right past Chillith without touching him and followed the fleeing mardars out the door.

And there stood the Thunder King, looking like a fool.

Following Chillith's tracks, Martis and the children pushed on, their way lighted by a reflection from a sliver of moon peeking through the clouds. Wytt kept telling them they had not far to go; but he also told them that Chillith had already passed through the gates.

"Then there's nothing we can do," Jack said. "Should we go on? We're almost there."

"Shh! Sound carries on a night like this," Martis said.

"That's that," Ellayne thought. "There's no point in going on. There's nothing we can do for Chillith." They hadn't been able to keep him from going where God had called him to go. Maybe they shouldn't have tried.

The snow was knee-deep on Martis, but Chillith had broken a trail for them: otherwise the children could have gone no farther. How they found the strength to keep going at all, Ellayne couldn't imagine. How they were going to get back down again was even harder to imagine.

They practically walked right up to the gates before Martis looked up and saw the wall. He held out a hand to halt the children. "If there are any watchmen up there, we're lost!" he thought.

But no sentry challenged them. Instead, at some undetermined distance, they heard a noise of men yelling, with a scream or two thrown in. It sounded like a riot.

Before they could decide what to do next, something like a mass of living darkness burst out through an open gate—straight at them. Jack had just time to realize it was an animal, a deadly beast with eyes of green fire, fangs like swords. Martis had just time to throw himself in front of the children: his life for theirs. And Ellayne had only time to scream.

No one can scream quite like a girl of Ellayne's age, and her whole soul poured out in this one. Piercing, shrill, and more than that—her scream filled the whole pass and caromed off the clouds above.

The charging beast veered and tore off into the woods.

And above the golden hall, the mountainside began to move.

For a moment they could only stare. It was as if the world itself had shrugged its shoulders. Weeks' and weeks' worth of heavy snow began to slide down from the mountains' slopes—slowly at first and with a low growl that you felt to the marrow of your bones.

The Golden Pass was the bottom of a funnel. The snow had nowhere to go but there. Martis suddenly snapped to life.

"Run!" He turned and pushed the children, almost knocking them down. "Run for your lives!"

The snow's growl turned into a roar, louder and louder—loud enough to burst your head right open.

And they ran, all three of them, as fast as they could run—which in the deep snow on the road, could be by no means fast enough.

At first Lord Reesh thought he was hearing the beginnings of a mighty thunderstorm. The whole hall vibrated. The panicked mardars suddenly stood still, amazed right out of their panic.

But no one saw the end except Helki's hawk, Angel. She hated traveling by night, and was sleeping in his arms when something woke her—she never knew what. She flapped her wings and went aloft.

She saw the snow on either side of the pass slide off the mountains and go pouring down into the space between, with a roar louder than the loudest thunder. In the twinkling of an eye, everything vanished—the golden hall, the outbuildings and barracks, cabins and stables, man and beast—all buried under snow. And Angel had heard Ellayne's scream, not knowing what it was, but knowing that it dislodged the snow piled on the mountains. Maybe the snow would have come down later, maybe not. But a girl's scream brought it down that night.

Not a trace could be seen of the Thunder King's works in the Golden Pass. The wall held the snow back from tumbling down the road; but it still broke under the snow's weight and was buried.

By then the force of the avalanche was spent, and the snow didn't follow Jack, Ellayne, and Martis down the road. It had done what God willed it to do, and now it rested.

Martis and the children didn't get far. Ellayne and Jack could pump their legs no farther. Martis sank into the snow beside them. Wytt urged them to get up, keep going. "Can't stop here—too cold!"

They would have died there, but they didn't. Helki, hurrying up behind them, found them before it was too late.

Many miles away, Jandra prophesied to King Ryons' army. It was encamped for the night, but the chiefs assembled quickly when Abgayle summoned them.

Once again the grown-up voice issued from the toddler's mouth:

"Hear the word of the Lord. Remember my servant

Chillith, the Griff, and write his name in your books: for tonight he is seated at my table with the saints."

That was all. Jandra fell back asleep in Abgayle's arms.

"Chillith the Griff?" Chief Shaffur wondered. "Who in the world is that, and why should we remember him?"

"We will surely know, in due time," Obst said.

CHAPTER 54

How Some Adventures Ended

Winter passed. Spring came, and most of that passed, too.

Jack lived at Ellayne's house now. Roshay Bault insisted on it. "But what about Van?" Jack said, when Roshay first proposed it.

"I'll give him back his job as municipal carter," the chief councilor said, "and he can owe that to you." So that satisfied Jack's stepfather, and neither of them missed each other.

Martis had a long rest in Ninneburky. He needed it.

Helki went back to Lintum Forest; but what with so many fugitives from the shattered Heathen host drifting into Lintum and setting up as outlaws, Helki didn't get much rest. But thanks to him, the settlers did.

King Ryons' army returned to Obann with him. Most of them doubted they would ever see their native lands again, so they made new homes there. Chief Spider died in Obann City and was buried with honors befitting a benefactor of the nation. Nanny died, too. The chiefs voted her a monument.

Gurun remained with the king, and everyone in Obann called her Queen. She couldn't stop them from doing it.

Obst took charge of copying the rediscovered books of Scripture and disseminating copies far and wide. There was an enormous amount of work to be done—enough to keep a hundred seminaries busy for a hundred years. He was amazed that he was still alive to do his share of it.

Toward the end of spring, the king and queen invited Jack and Ellayne to visit them in Obann, together with Ellayne's family and Martis. There Roshay Bault was dubbed a baron of the realm. He would never achieve his dream of becoming an oligarch because there was no oligarchy anymore; but being the first man to receive baronial honors more than made up for it.

Martis received a knighthood and a special title, Knight Protector. He was at first moved to decline the honor.

"Do they know the things I've done in the service of the Temple?" he wondered.

"No—and no one wants to know them, either," said old Uduqu, now a permanent adviser to the king. "Do you think God didn't know about those things? But He chose you to protect those children, and He chose well. After all, they're still alive."

As for Gallgoid: he went far enough to meet Helki's army coming up the mountain, and they saved his life. He told his story to Roshay, and later to King Ryons, Obst, and all the chieftains. His exposure of the Thunder King was proclaimed up and down the land by heralds; but his revelations of the treason of Lord Reesh and others in the Temple, Obst argued, would be better left unpublished.

"Many will refuse to believe it," he said, "and many in the Temple who are innocent will be unjustly thought to be guilty. Let the evil that Lord Reesh did, die with him."

Everyone knew that the Thunder King and many of his mardars—along with the First Prester, too—died in the avalanche at the Golden Pass. Jack, Ellayne, and Martis brought that news down the mountain with them. Chillith's name and deeds would be remembered; those of Reesh, Obst prayed, would be forgotten. But somehow the story got out among the people, and the clamor to rebuild the Temple died away.

At first Ellayne and Jack feared they would be dragged through any number of interminable ceremonies honoring them for this and that, with thousands of strange people gawking at them. They'd had to sit through Roshay's ceremony, and that had taken hours and hours. But Obst assured them they'd be spared.

"What you did will all be written down," he said. "It will be remembered forever. Still, you weren't brought here to be tormented! Your mother doesn't want you lionized, Ellayne: she says it would be bad for you. All the chiefs agree, especially those who've raised children of their own. And by the way," he added, "what's become of that little hairy man who used to travel with you? His deeds should be recorded, too."

"Oh, he's around," said Ellayne. She was being evasive. Wytt most emphatically did not want to be trotted out in front of a lot of Big People as if he were a calf with two heads. He lived now in the little piece of woods by Ninneburky where Jack and Ellayne first began their adventures. Most days, they went to see him there. And some nights he would creep into Ellayne's house and sleep in her arms.

Someday, he said, all the Omah in Obann would gather under the moon and dance at the same time. But that day had not yet come.

So Jack and Ellayne spent most of their time with King Ryons, who asked for them, and his dog, Cavall. The great hound romped with them. They admired Angel, the hawk that Helki had given him. One of the Ghols knew all about falconry and was teaching Ryons.

Sometimes they played with Jandra, who was just a little girl again. It had been months since she last prophesied. That horrible bird was still with her, and quite a few of the king's servants had been bitten. No one would have dreamed of taking the bird away from her.

Sometimes they played with Chagadai, the captain of the Ghols, who taught them to ride and gave them bows and arrows that he'd made for them with his own hands. They also played with Shingis of the Blays, who taught them how to sling stones. And they spent much of their time just sitting with King Ryons, swapping stories. He wanted to know all about their travels and adventures, and they wanted to know about his.

"Sometimes I think it must be all a dream," said Ryons, "and one of these days I'll wake up and be a slave again. But Obst and Gurun say that God wanted all these things to happen and decided on it ages and ages ago."

"Doesn't it bother you that all those Ghols call you their father?" Ellayne said, which made all three of them laugh.

They were still laughing when a servant came to summon the king to the council of the chiefs.

"They're asking for you, Sire," he said, "They're all waiting."

"What for?" Ryons asked.

The servant looked grave. "It's an emissary from the Thunder King, Your Majesty."

Once again the chieftains were assembled, this time in the old Hall of the Oligarchs. In their midst they had a throne for Ryons. Obst stood beside it on the right, and Gurun on the left. Ryons, having been hastily togged out in his royal headdress and sword, climbed onto the throne thinking how grand it would be if he were still sitting on the grass behind the palace with Ellayne and Jack.

He was amazed when he saw it was the same messenger who'd come to the city gate six months ago—Goryk Gillow, the renegade from Silvertown. He stood in his black cloak before the chiefs, who sat on ornate stools with weapons in their laps. How did he dare to come again? Ryons could hardly believe it.

"Have you come to deliver yourself to the hangman?" General Hennen asked. "What business can you possibly have here, sirrah? For your master the so-called Thunder King is dead, and his lies and impostures known to all the world."

"No, my lords, not so!" said Goryk, smiling wolfishly. "What—did you truly believe my master, the god, went in person to the Golden Pass, as an ordinary mortal man would do? No, not so, not so! That was but the least of his servants who perished on the mountain, along with a handful of the least useful of his mardars.

"No, my lords—my master and my god remains at Kara Karram, at the great Temple that's been built for him. Even now he musters fresh armies. You'll see them when the time comes.

"My master offers you one last chance to declare your submission to him and surrender your boy king to him. He won't make this offer a second time!"

"Then we won't have to hear it a second time," Uduqu said.

"Why do we give a hearing to this gallows bird?" Chief Shaffur said.

"I am a herald!" Goryk said. "It is not lawful to harm me. But what says your poor little king? Has he learned yet to speak for himself?"

Ryons felt like being sassy, but his teachers all said kings had to act a certain way. Too bad!

"You must think we're all jackasses," he said, "to be taken in by your master's tricks again. You'd better think of some new ones! We know there is no Thunder King, and hasn't been for years and years. We can't hang you, I guess. But it might be a good idea for you to hang yourself. Go away!"

Goryk showed his teeth. "Very foolish, my lords. You've seen but the merest fraction of my master's power. You have no idea what you face—no idea at all."

Obst laughed out loud, causing all heads to turn.

"We have no idea!" he said. "Poor fools! The living God has used your master as a tool in His hands to accomplish what He wished—the unfettering of His spirit. And yet the axe boasts itself against the woodsman! What could be sillier?

"The bell has been rung, the lost books recovered. You will see the hand of God stretched out all over the East, from sea to sea: for He desires all the nations of men to know Him. The more you vaunt yourselves against Him, the more you fight against Him, the more you do His bidding—in spite of yourselves!

"Go, Goryk, tell your masters that their weapons are turned against themselves; and that far from fearing them, we pity them. The spirit of the Lord is with us. Never again will it be far from us. Never again will God's word be kept from any ear who will hear it. And you, who would imprison pitiful Heathen gods who are only idols—you have only done what the true God raised you up to do."

The chiefs clashed their weapons on the legs of their stools. At a nod from Uduqu, two young Abnaks ushered Goryk from the hall.

"If he ever comes back," said Gurun, "hang him."

Obst shook his head. "Be sorry for them all," he said. "They have no understanding of what they've started and no thought of where it ends."

"Does it have an end?" King Ryons asked.

Obst smiled at him. "The work of the Lord have an end?" he said. "No, Sire—only one new beginning after another."

Follow the Entire Adventure with the First Three Books in this Exciting Series!

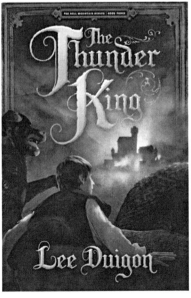

You won't want to miss a single moment of this thrilling adventure, so be sure to get *Bell Mountain*, *The Cellar Beneath the Cellar*, and *The Thunder King* to complete your collection. These engaging stories are a great way to discover powerful insights about the Kingdom of God through page-turning fantasy fiction.

Ordering is Easy!
Just visit
www.ChalcedonStore.com

CPSIA information can be obtained
at www.ICGtesting.com
Printed in the USA
FSOW02n0613010715
8397FS